HOLD MY HAND

Michael Barakiva

FARRAR STRAUS GIROUX
NEW YORK

Farrar Straus Giroux Books for Young Readers
An imprint of Macmillan Publishing Group, LLC
175 Fifth Avenue, New York, NY 10010

1 3 5 7 9 10 8 6 4 2

fiercereads.com

Library of Congress Cataloging-in-Publication Data

Names: Barakiva, Michael, author.
Title: Hold my hand / Michael Barakiva.
Description: First edition. | New York : Farrar Straus Giroux, 2019. | Sequel
to: One man guy. | Summary: As his relationship with boyfriend Ethan is
tested, high school sophomore Alek takes a stand to make his orthodox
Armenian church more progressive.
Identifiers: LCCN 2019007464 | ISBN 9780374304867 (hardcover)
Subjects: | CYAC: Gays—Fiction. | Dating (Social customs)—Fiction. |
Love—Fiction. | Armenian Church—Fiction. | Armenian Americans—
Fiction.
Classification: LCC PZ7.B229538 Ho 2019 | DDC [Fic]—dc23
LC record available at https://lccn.loc.gov/2019007464

Our books may be purchased in bulk for promotional, educational, or business use.
Please contact your local bookseller or the Macmillan Corporate and Premium Sales
Department at (800) 221-7945 ext. 5442 or by email at
MacmillanSpecialMarkets@macmillan.com.

To my exes:

Gail

Kim

Linsay

Ricky

Raymond

And, of course, Rafa

1

KISSING ETHAN.

Kissing Ethan rocked.

Kissing Ethan was like taking a rocket to outer space, floating in zero gravity, and marveling at the incomprehensible beauty of the creations of the universe. Kissing Ethan was sweet like the last piece of baklava, drenched in honey, snatched from the bottom of the box. Kissing Ethan was the answer to an unasked prayer.

And then there was being kissed by Ethan.

Being kissed by Ethan was not the same as kissing him.

Being kissed by Ethan was rapture, surrender. Being kissed was surfing a wave of joy, unpredictable and uncontrollable, that could break any moment and send you tumbling, an endless series of surprises.

Being kissed by Ethan was endorphins kicking in two hours into a tennis match, transforming pain into euphoria. It was being a ship in a violent storm, hoping you wouldn't be torn apart as the ocean churned beneath you. It was feeling like your skin, your very body, would explode because it couldn't possibly contain all the joy pulsing through it.

Alek brought Ethan's face back up to his own. He kissed Ethan back.

Kissing Ethan was safer than being kissed by him.

"Whoa." Alek pulled away, gasping for air, as if he'd just edged out a victory in the tiebreaker of a five-set tennis match, full of baseline strokes, cross-court slams, and net game saves.

"Come on," Ethan purred. "We're just getting started."

Hundreds of half-naked men stared at Alek from the images Ethan had plastered around his room, cut from magazine ads—a kaleidoscopic homage to homoeroticism. The effect was dizzying as wall and ceiling and floor merged, seemingly seamlessly, with sculpted torsos and abs and chests and calves.

"I promised my mom I'd help get ready for Thanksgiving." Alek retrieved his bright purple shirt with plaid-gray details from the chair by Ethan's desk, the only pieces of furniture in the room other than the bed, where Ethan remained.

"I hate to point out the obvious, but Thanksgiving isn't for another week." Ethan rolled over. "Or is this some weird Armenian thing, like Christmas, that you celebrate at a different time than everyone else in the whole freakin' world?"

"We Armenians celebrate Thanksgiving just like everyone else in this country, thank you very much. Although, did you know that Canadian Thanksgiving is celebrated on the second Monday in October?"

"No, I did not know that." Ethan sat up, surrendering to

Alek's departure. "You're going to your grandma's for Thanksgiving, right?"

"That was the plan." Alek finished the last buttons on his shirt and grabbed his leather book bag, groaning under its nearing-midterms weight. "But then Nana twisted her ankle, so she decided she wasn't up to hosting Thanksgiving. I will try to spare you the political saga that ensued as my dad and his two siblings negotiated who would assume the mantle, but suffice to say it involved three instances of blackmail, two of coercion, the reemergence of a fight from twenty years ago when my dad and his older sister were in college that had something to do with a cat, tears, apologies, more tears, and a complicated negotiation involving a credenza that both my dad and his younger brother would like once Nana finally passes to the next world. We're talking backroom deals that would almost put 45's presidential administration to shame."

"And this is sparing me the saga?"

Alek nodded. "The long and short of it is that we will be hosting Thanksgiving this year, so yes—seven days is barely enough time to prepare. My mom took the week off from the UN. THE ENTIRE WEEK. Because she knows that hosting her in-laws is a prime opportunity for Nana to judge my mom's cooking, housekeeping, and child-rearing. In fact, one of the Sunday-morning news shows theorized that Nana intentionally twisted her ankle just to have the opportunity to criticize whoever was fool enough to step up."

Ethan rolled over on his back, defeated. "Are all Armenian families this complicated?"

"From what I hear at church, we're on the simpler side. My

mom has six siblings who all live in the same town in Southern Cali. I'm amazed they haven't had a *Romeo and Juliet*–style feud spring up there." Alek finished tying his shoes. "I'll see you soon, okay?"

" 'Wilt thou leave me so unsatisfied?' " Ethan asked, eyes batting innocence from the bed.

" 'What satisfaction canst thou expect?' " Alek flirted back. "See, I can quote R and J, too, but I'm still outta here."

Ethan hopped out of bed and threw on a plaid flannel that hung open on his wiry frame. He kissed his boyfriend goodbye. "I'll see you soon, okay?"

As Alek pedaled his way home, he tried to imagine what his life would be like if he hadn't met Ethan last summer. They had lived in the same township for the entirety of their lives, but Ethan was a badass skater boy who hung out with other badass skater boys, and Alek was a geek/nerd combo with honor roll aspirations. They hadn't met until they found themselves in summer school last June: Ethan because he'd failed Standard Geometry as a junior, and Alek to raise his C in Freshman Algebra to an honors grade.

Alek jumped the curb, landing lightly, his body hovering in midair, before lowering back down on the frame of his bike. Soon, it would be too cold to ride and he'd exile his bike to the shed until spring rolled around to liberate it. He adjusted the secondhand leather backpack that Ethan had found for him during one of their clandestine trips into NYC, early in their relationship.

It was easy to imagine what life would be like without the external stuff that had come from Ethan, like the backpack and the haircut and the clothes infinitely hipper than the suburban fare to which his mother had restricted him. He wouldn't have any of those things if Ethan hadn't strutted into his life. But those weren't important.

It was the emotional stuff that had wrapped itself around his very being, like ivy around a building, that was impossible to untangle from his imagination. For one thing, he probably wouldn't have come out if not for the super-chill pixie skater boy who made his insides yearn every time they were within arm's reach. And if Ethan hadn't taken Alek into New York City, Alek would've never discovered the one place where he truly felt himself, unlike the suburbs where he'd spent all 14 and 11/12 years of his life. It wasn't that Ethan had changed Alek: rather, he'd helped Alek discover who he was. The alternate-universe Alek who'd never cut summer school to go with Ethan into New York on that first fateful trip would have no way of knowing how unrealized he was. But luckily, Alek wasn't that Alek anymore.

He pulled up to his house, depositing his hybrid bike in front of the three stairs leading to the front door. The sun was setting earlier and earlier now, and within a week or two, it would be dark even at five o'clock. Normally, his mom would still be at the United Nations, having rejoined the workforce last year, deeming her teenage sons old enough to grow up without her full attention. She usually caught the 5:37 p.m. train that would have her walking through the Khederian front door approximately one hour later. But her red Toyota was docked in the garage today, as it would be for most of the following seven days leading up to Thanksgiving. Alek didn't bother locking his bike up, just as his family didn't bother locking the front door to their house. South Windsor, New Jersey, might've only been fifty miles from New York City, but it may as well have been another universe.

Even from outside, Alek could smell the odors of deliciousness wafting from the kitchen. Although his dad had assumed most of the domestic responsibilities since he got laid off last year, when it came to the major cooking events, he served as sous chef to his wife.

Alek made his way through his parents' old-world living room: doilies hand-knit by both grandmothers adorned Queen Anne–legged furniture, proudly standing on authentic Persian rugs, with coasters aplenty to protect every surface from possible water stains. He dropped his leather backpack on the banister leading upstairs, took a deep breath, and braved the kitchen.

"There you are, Alek." His dad was furiously scrubbing the black onyx kitchen counters they'd installed a few years ago. Every detail in the kitchen renovation, from counter material and color to cabinet hardware, had been selected with more agony and care than most parents spend on selecting their children's names. The entire room sparkled.

His mother was taping recipes to the cupboards along with the master schedule for the next week, which she had created as a three-page Excel document with color-coded timetables. She applied the final piece of tape and appraised the room with a combination of determination and satisfaction. "Let's get to work."

* * *

The next seven days were a blur of cooking, interrupted by school, homework, and explaining to Ethan why Alek was too busy to see him. The battalion of Armenians who would descend on the house to celebrate the most American of holidays included Nana (paternal grandmother) and both of his dad's siblings: (older) Aunt Elen and (younger) Uncle Samvel. Elen's husband, Hayk, was coming, of course, with their children Mariam, Ani, and Tigran. Uncle Samvel was on his second wife, who (luckily) was even more Armenian than his first, and he was bringing the kids from his first marriage (Nare and Milena), along with her kids from her first two marriages (Davit, Anahit, Erik, and Mary). It would be, in other words, a full house.

No room in the house was safe from the whirlwind of activity. In the dining room, the table was extended to accommodate both leaves, the good china was removed from its boxes, and the silverware still needing polishing was laid out like soldiers awaiting marching orders. In the bathroom, every surface had been sterilized. The furniture in the living room underwent deep cleaning, which felt perhaps like overkill to Alek since it was kept enshrined in plastic when it wasn't in use (on average, 361 days of the year). But this was the first time the Khederians would be hosting this holiday, and his mother wasn't taking any chances.

Charts, schedules, and recipes were added over the next few days, taped to every available cabinet, transforming the perfectly coordinated, granite-countered, oak-cabinet-lined kitchen into the headquarters of a complex military campaign.

And then there was the cooking, which resumed the moment

Alek and his older brother Nik returned home from school and went late into the night. Even with the entire week of preparation, however, not a single dish was ready to be served an hour before the guests were scheduled to arrive.

Which was why Alek was so perplexed when his mother took a break from cooking and started making calls from her landline, hanging up a moment later.

"What's she doing?" Alek asked Nik.

"Have you ever wondered why we get prank-called every time we have to go to a family function?" Nik was showing no signs of halting his growth spurt. The effect, in Alek's humble opinion, was that Nik resembled a wannabe hipster beanpole, all legs and arms and trying-too-hard accessories, like the chunky glasses he was sporting today.

"Now that you mention it, it does seem weird." Alek removed the soaking carrots from the bowl in the sink and began peeling them. "And they always just hang up the second we answer."

"This is the time-honored tradition of our family: call the homes of your guests, and if they pick up, you know they haven't left yet."

"Wouldn't it just be easier to text?" Alek asked.

"These Armenians . . ." Nik trailed off.

"These Armenians indeed," Alek agreed.

When Alek's mother finished her phone reconnaissance, she gathered her family and addressed them like a general might her platoon. "I have good news, everyone! I'm estimating that our first guests won't arrive for at least two hours, maybe even three, which gives us just enough time to get everything done.

I've already removed the turkey from the malt/beer brine and put it in the oven to roast, but we'll need to flip it in ninety minutes. The apples for the dressing are peeled but still need to be cored. The sweet potatoes have been boiled but not peeled. The chestnuts have been roasted and peeled but not chopped, and the cranberries have been soaked but not boiled." Alek's mom paced back and forth in the kitchen as she recited the litany of work remaining. "Nik, have you trimmed the Brussels sprouts and chopped the parsley?"

"Yup." Alek's older brother, like all the members of the family, wore a crisp, clean apron whose daily stains had disappeared into the washing machine every night for the last week. "But I still haven't peeled the pearl onions because Dad said he was going to show me a trick."

"Cut a small 'X' on the root side with a paring knife, then drop them into boiling water for thirty seconds. They'll pop right out." Alek's father chopped the winter-squash varietals as he talked, never taking his eyes off the task at hand.

"Got it, Dad."

"We could just use frozen pearl onions, you know." Alek was only being half serious. The other half wanted to see how his mom would respond.

She didn't disappoint, inhaling sharply and clutching her imaginary pearls. "You know that there is only one vegetable we use frozen."

"Peas," Alek and Nik intoned in unison.

"And why is that?"

"Because frozen peas actually taste better than fresh peas."

"Only when fresh peas are out of season," Mrs. Khederian amended. Then, to make sure that aliens hadn't abducted her children and replaced them with changelings, she asked, "And when are peas in season?"

"Spring," her sons replied in unison.

Satisfied that Alek and Nik were her own flesh and blood, Mrs. Khederian continued. "Now, Alek, have you finished the mushrooms for the gravy?"

A heap of soiled paper towels smeared with dirt from the mushrooms Alek had wiped clean surrounded the pile of quarter-inch-sliced creminis on his cutting board. "I still think it would be easier to rinse them out."

"The water content in mushrooms is already high, which is why they take so long to cook down. It makes rinsing them simply impractical." Alek's mom relished the opportunity to educate her sons on anything, and especially on all items culinary. "Okay—Nik, I'm going to have you peel the sweet potatoes for the gratin, and the parsnips and carrots that I'm going to throw in with the turkey. Alek, you're going to get started on the kale, then I'll need you to stir the farro as it cooks." Mrs. Khederian issued the orders with the effortless confidence of a master. "And all we need to do for the pies is whip the cream. Although I do wish we had made another one yesterday." Mrs. Khederian wrung her hands, tormented by the most frightening of all Armenian bugbears: running out of food. "Are we sure that six pies are enough? We could still bake one more before the guests arrive. Two, actually, if we put them in together and increase the cooking temperature, of course. We could even use the convection setting!"

"Six is plenty, mom," Alek reassured his mother. "That's forty-eight slices."

"Watch out, PSATs," Nik mumbled just loud enough for Alek to hear.

"I'm just saying, we're expecting fourteen people, right?" Alek continued, ignoring his older brother. "Plus the four of us—that means everyone could have two slices and we'd still have a pie and a half leftover."

"Yes, but what if all your cousins decide they want a second slice of the chocolate pecan and all we have left is pumpkin?" This doomsday scenario tipped Alek's mom over the edge. "Boghos, would you roll out another two crusts, just to be safe?"

Alek's father nodded wordlessly. He rose from behind his pile of now-peeled winter squash and fished out two fists of dough from the fridge, replacing them with two from the cache in the freezer. Alek was impressed that he'd been able to find them so quickly. Between the terror of running out of food and the refusal to throw out anything even possibly edible, Armenians' relationships with their freezers was the stuff of which reality TV hoarder shows were made. Alek theorized that since the genocide over a hundred years ago, all Armenians were programmed to have enough food on hand at any given moment to survive six months of unexpected calamity.

For another family, the seven classic Thanksgiving dishes (three-day-brined roast turkey with root vegetables, corn bread dressing, mashed sweet potato gratin, Brussels sprouts with pearl onions and chestnuts, cranberry relish, braised kale with sautéed bacon, maple-roasted squash) and eight pies (four chocolate pecan, two pumpkin, two apple) might've sufficed.

But not for the Khederians, who believed that any holiday meal should be prepared as if twenty uninvited guests might show up unannounced. This must've happened plenty in ye olde times, Alek decided, since it had never happened once during his own life.

In addition, lest they be accused of assimilation, every traditional American dish needed to be matched with its Armenian counterpart. Alek removed the kale from the fridge, eyeing all the other dishes his family had prepared over the course of the last week.

"I don't think there are any accounts of the pilgrims and the Native Americans sharing a fifteen-pound turkey *and* two legs of lamb."

"Still, it's nice to have options," Alek's father answered happily, sprinkling flour on the counter. "Hand me the rolling pin?"

Alek dug it out from under the counter. It was a classic French tapered cylinder, not the rotating contraption with handles that his parents scoffed at "these Americans" for using.

"Sure, options are nice, but did we need to make six kinds of buregs? And stuff all those peppers *and* roll all those grape leaves *and* bake the kufteh?" Alek rinsed the kale, stripping the leaves from the stems.

"That reminds me . . ." Alek's father expertly rolled out the dough, picking it up and rotating it forty-five degrees after every stroke so it wouldn't stick to the counter. "Do you think you'll have time to make some hummus? I want to make sure that there's something to snack on when the guests arrive."

"Good thinking, Dad," Alek said. "With only three hors

d'oeuvres and four appetizers, our guests might die of hunger before the four entrees and eighteen side dishes hit the table."

"I'm glad you agree!" Mr. Khederian was apparently deaf to sarcasm.

"I'll do it, Dad." Nik had just popped out the last flash-boiled, X-sliced pearl onion. He retrieved chickpeas and tahini from the pantry, then opened the latter and began the laborious process of stirring it with a long cocktail spoon to reincorporate the liquids and the solids.

Somehow, in a repeating miracle that Alek still couldn't fathom regardless of how many times he'd witnessed it, every dish transformed from impossibly-far-from-done to perfectly garnished by the time the first guest rang the doorbell two-and-a-half hours later, at 3:30 on the dot.

"Tell them I'll be down in a minute," Alek's mom yelled, untangling curlers from her hair as she disappeared upstairs.

2

FIVE HOURS AND TWICE AS MANY COURSES LATER,
after serving the soup (Armenian lentil, of course), almost
burning his fingers making sure the buregs were hot enough,
toasting the marshmallows for the sweet potato casserole,
watching his father and uncle fight about how to carve
the leg of lamb and then repeat the fight exactly ten minutes later about the turkey, hoping his mother didn't notice
the lumps in the gravy that resulted from his failure to
whisk the thickening agent thoroughly enough, enduring
his grandmother's criticism about the lack of dessert options,
saying goodbye to his aunts, his uncles, five real cousins,
four step-cousins, doing the dishes, putting away the silver,
and packaging up the leftovers, Alek mustered the courage
to ask to be excused.

"Ask your grandmother," his father responded.

Alek made his way to the living room, where his nana sat by herself, sipping cognac. "Nana, may I be excused?"

"Ask me in Armenian," she instructed him.

"Gnerek, paytz bedke ganouch tsehem aysor?"

"Close enough, although I wonder what they're teaching you in Saturday school if you don't know how to conjugate a simple verb." Nana crossed her legs and placed the cognac down on a coaster. "And where are you going this late on Thanksgiving?"

For a moment, Alek considered dodging the question, since he hadn't actually come out to his grandmother yet. But instead, he took a breath, then another, and said as evenly as he could, "To my boyfriend's."

"And why didn't you invite Ethan over? Isn't it time I met him already?" his nana asked without missing a beat. "You guys have been together—what—almost six months?"

Alek regarded his grandmother anew. "And how do you know that, Nana?"

"You think I don't have Instagram? How adorable the two of you are! I set it up so that I get a notice every time he posts. Like that one from Asbury Park last month, on the abandoned carousel?" Nana leaned and whispered conspiratorially. "I wish my other grandchildren were doing as well in this department. Thank goodness things didn't work out between your brother, Nik, and that Nanar girl. And have you met Ani's boyfriend? He looks like a gangster." His grandmother continued to criticize every one of Alek's cousins' significant others, revealing a familiarity with social media and their personal lives that left Alek amazed.

But not as amazed as he was by how unconcerned she appeared to be about Alek having a boyfriend. It wasn't like he had any reason to believe that his grandmother was homophobic. At the same time, he didn't have any reason to believe that she wasn't, either. And perhaps, if she didn't have a grandson who came out by age fourteen, her thoughts on the issue would be different. But she did. And between that and a familiarity with Instagram that would put most people Alek's own age to shame, his grandmother had apparently joined the twenty-first century.

Finally, Alek was excused to go to Ethan's house. He flew out of the house, onto his bike, pedaling so quickly past piles of corn bread, pumpkin, and cranberry-colored leaves, that he almost missed the turnoff for Taylor Street. He took the turn sharp, the back wheel of the bike skidding behind him. The slight slope allowed him to coast on momentum until he arrived at Ethan's house. He knocked on the door, a formality he'd been told repeatedly that he could forgo, and let himself in.

"Hey, Mr. Novick," Alek called out from the foyer. He held out the bag of Tupperwares he'd carried over. "I brought you guys some leftovers."

"Thanks, Alek—how considerate of you." Mr. Novick took the bag from Alek and placed it on the side table next to the front door. Earlier, this kind of behavior would've caused Alek great anxiety. Mr. Novick was a professor at NYU—surely he understood that the leftovers would spoil unless refrigerated. Why wasn't he putting them in the fridge immediately? Who leaves a perfectly good container of food out at room temperature?

But now, more than five months into the relationship, Alek knew what to do. He plucked the bag from the side table and navigated his way through the piles of books, records, newspapers, and magazines that surrounded the Novick furniture, heading into the kitchen. "Did you guys have a nice Thanksgiving?" he called over his shoulder, opening the sparsely populated fridge. He placed the Khederian leftovers on the same shelf as three takeout boxes and a plastic takeout soup container that had been repurposed as a condiment receptacle, teeming with mini soy sauces, duck sauce, hot sauces, spicy mustards, and ketchups. For good measure, Alek threw away a carton of milk that had expired around Halloween but left the half-and-half after a quick whiff. He knew the chances of it being used before it went bad were slim, and he was tempted to salvage it by pouring the cream into an ice-cube tray and then, on his next visit, emptying the frozen cream cubes into a ziplock bag, as he would've done in his own house, but he ultimately decided against it.

"We went to the Prestige again." Ethan's dad had already resettled into his reading corner, adjusting the lamp and then his glasses. "I guess it's really becoming something of a Thanksgiving tradition for us."

Alek could already imagine his mother's horror at the idea of celebrating the holiday with canned cranberry sauce, mashed potato mix, and a possibly previously frozen, most certainly not-organic turkey that someone else had made.

"Ethan's up in his room," Mr. Novick called from inside. "It's good to see you, Alek. Happy Thanksgiving."

"You too, Mr. Novick." Alek climbed up the stairs. He

entered Ethan's room and was greeted by the sight of his boy-friend, shirtless, sitting at his desk with his back to the door, feet propped up, slowly grooving to whatever music pumped out of his chunky headphones, oblivious to Alek and everything else in the world. Alek waited, watching, taking in the wiry frame, almost entirely smooth body, and wavy, sandy hair, all of which pointed to Ethan's Western European mutt ancestry.

Alek admired Ethan's absolute ease. Even alone, Alek didn't believe he achieved a fraction of his boyfriend's effortlessness, his absolute lack of self-consciousness. Ethan carried it around like a force field, making him impervious to the anxieties of the world. And when they were together, that force field envel-oped Alek, too.

Slowly, Alek closed the door, approached Ethan, and laid his hand on his bare shoulder. Alek would've startled at the sur-prise of an unexpected presence, but Ethan didn't even flinch, as if he had been expecting Alek to do exactly that exactly then.

When the song ended, or when Ethan deemed that enough time had passed, he slid the headphones off. "You're what I'm thankful for, boyfriend." He arched his neck up and kissed Alek long and deep.

"I feel like this is the first time we've been together in, like, forever." Ethan caressed Alek's face. He kissed his lips, his face, his ears.

"I know," Alek whispered back.

Kissing Ethan.

Kissing Ethan rocked.

Alek shifted, pulling Ethan up, away from the desk, and

down onto the bed. They lay next to each other, legs intertwined, punctuating words with kisses.

"I love it when you're like this," Ethan purred.

"Like what?" Alek asked innocently.

"Frisky." Ethan's mouth traveled down Alek's neck. Alek squirmed under the onslaught of pleasure.

"Well, it's been a whole week since . . ." Alek trailed off.

". . . since we've been alone?" Ethan finished for him, between kisses.

"Uh-huh," Alek managed.

Alek thought, all the time, about what he and Ethan did when they were alone together. Whenever he zoned out, in class or in church or in the back of his parents' car, that's where his mind would inevitably wander. He'd recover from those daydreams abruptly, returning to reality aroused, terrified that technology had been invented that could project thoughts into image and that everyone around him had been witnessing his carnal meanderings.

But during these daydreams, Alek didn't just reminisce: he also tried to make sense of it. Where did the urge come from? Was it as primal and necessary as eating, drinking, or sleeping? What happened to priests or other celibates who abstained? Did a part of them shrivel up and die? Or did they get some special insight, some wisdom from their abstinence, like martyrs' hallucinations while fasting in the desert? And most importantly, what triggered the chemical reaction that made it impossible for him and Ethan to keep their hands off each other when they were this close? What was the nature of that kind of basic, carnal, human, undeniable attraction? And how did it compare for Ethan with the other guys he'd been with, like his ex-boyfriend, Remi? Was it more, or less, or just different?

Sometimes, when Alek and Ethan hadn't seen each other for a while, like when Alek visited Nana over Labor Day weekend, their making out was urgent, hungry, and desperate. Their bodies communicated on an atomic level infinitely more efficient and direct than words could ever be, drawn to each other like metal to a magnet.

Other times, it would be leisurely, like on a Sunday after church, when neither one of them had anywhere to be. They'd kiss, then they'd listen to music, then they'd kiss some more. But regardless of its nature, their making out was always effortless, the antidote to reality.

Until it wasn't.

"You wanna do it?" Ethan asked suddenly.

"Do what?" Alek asked, even though he already knew the answer.

"Have sex."

And there it was, the question, hovering between them like an enemy drone, threatening to destroy everything beautiful they had built.

"I think—" Alek stammered, pulling away abruptly, groping for words that weren't there. "Not yet," he finally managed to get out.

"That's cool." Ethan kissed Alek again, quickly, lovingly. But underneath it, Alek could feel Ethan's disappointment lingering the rest of the night, tainting their time, like an otherwise perfect dish spoiled by a single rotten ingredient.

3

ALEK WANTED TO TELL BECKY. HE WANTED TO TELL his best friend about Ethan's proposition when he saw her the next day, on that funny Friday after Thanksgiving that wasn't actually a holiday but that everyone treated as one. But he didn't know where to start.

"You haven't been paying attention to a single word I've been saying, have you?" Becky asked him at the end of a long story about the Thanksgiving she'd had to spent at her crazy grandparents' house, with intricate detail of the process her grandfather underwent to remove his dentures after eating and impressions of other family members that would normally have Alek howling with laughter.

Alek examined his options. Lying to Becky was a dangerous business—her BS-ometer was finely attuned, especially to him. As options went, however, telling her that he had spaced out was only slightly more promising.

"Sorry, I'm distracted," he admitted, trying to split the difference. Alek adjusted himself on the long, brown fold-out sofa that had been banished to the basement after the Boyces got a new furniture set for the living room a few months earlier.

Becky scrunched up her nose, as if she could tell he was holding something back. But she didn't pursue it.

Every time Alek came over to Becky's, her parents claimed they were finally going to finish the basement, where he and Becky spent most of their hanging-out time. But with the exception of the corner where an entertainment unit had been set up, the rest of the basement remained rough and raw, bare concrete with a hodgepodge of unpacked and often unlabeled boxes and discarded furniture, separated by sheets of exposed drywall. Only the near corner, defined by a bright green square of cut carpet just large enough to house the sofa and entertainment system, was inhabitable.

"And what could possibly be distracting you?" Becky removed an Honest Tea from the mini-fridge next to the sofa, which had previously been stocked with Diet Dr Peppers until Alek's mom began forwarding Becky articles about carcinogens in artificial sweeteners.

Alek almost blurted out the truth. Maybe, if Becky had been a guy, he would've. Or maybe his best friend's gender didn't play a factor in his decision to chicken out. Maybe he just couldn't find the words.

"Are you going to say anything or just sit there like a fish with your mouth hanging open?" Becky asked.

"I have to finish my 'What Being Armenian Means to Me' essay for Saturday school."

"I still can't believe you have to attend Saturday school on top of Sunday school. Isn't that, like, a bit overkill?"

"We Armenians, we can't help ourselves. We have to do more. And that more, in this case, means Saturday school, at eight a.m., which my parents have decreed that every young Khederian must attend beginning their sophomore year. So even though everyone else, including the Jews and Muslims and atheists and other non-Armenian Christians all over the world, get to sleep in, the Armenians have devised a whole new way to torture the next generation: a school to teach teens about the language, culture, and heritage of being Armenian."

"I wanna tell you something, Alek." Becky sipped her Honest Tea thoughtfully. "If my people had been genocided over a hundred years ago, the last thing I would make them do is wake up early on a Saturday. Haven't you all been through enough? It's like rubbing lemon juice into the wound."

"You know you're supposed to roll a lemon before you juice it?" Alek asked. "It increases yield."

"You increase yield."

Becky was the kind of girl who tended to blend into her surroundings: Caucasian, light-brown hair and eyes, average build that had just broken the five-foot threshold, and dressed like most of the other Gap/Old Navy girls in their tenth-grade class. Everything about her appearance was normal. But to assume her average appearance belied an average personality would be a tragic mistake. "Well, I guess you get to list Saturday school as an extracurricular when you're applying to colleges. Isn't that exactly the kind of thing Ms. Schmidt is telling

23

us admissions officers are looking for? That's why I've been hitting those competitions every weekend."

"Really? I thought it was so that you could exact your revenge on Dustin."

She tried to play it cool. "Oh, please. I don't even think about that guy." But then, as Alek had anticipated, she couldn't help herself. "But if I did, I'd probably think about how I outscored him in the last three competitions in a row!"

"So you're totally over what happened in September?" Alek enjoyed getting Becky riled up about Dustin Chinn, a Chinese-American junior who was one of Ethan's skateboarding buddies and the only person who had outscored Becky at the meets she'd begun entering since returning from rollerblading camp in August.

"September was a total fluke! And the judges must've been blind—everybody said so. You were there! You saw that my plasma spin was perfection, while his nollie was painfully basic. And don't even get me started on how superior my switch-ups were. Why do you think I outscored him at Plainsboro, Cherry Hill, *and* New Hope? I'll tell you why. Because my alley-oop into makio combos were like *boom*! That's why I haven't given him a single thought since!"

"I'm going to pretend that I understood even a fraction of what you just said so that you don't repeat it." Alek leaned back against the overstuffed arm of the sofa, catching a patch of sunlight from the small landscape windows at ground level. "I'd much rather be at those competitions, cheering you on, than at stupid Saturday school. And as if having to get up that early isn't bad enough, they're giving us homework, too."

"Seriously, I would picket." Becky produced a bag of Haribo Fruit Salad candy seemingly from midair and began munching. "Can't you just repurpose one of your English essays?" She offered the bag to Alek.

"I wish," Alek said, although they both knew that even if he could, he'd never do that. He picked out a grapefruit wedge, speaking while chewing that disgusting and delicious Haribo sweet-and-sourness. "I've got to finish my essay so I can email it tonight."

"And you don't have anything else going on?" Becky squinted in the way she did when she felt like she wasn't getting the full story.

Alek considered, again, telling her all about Ethan. But something stopped him. "I think you're underestimating the magnitude of the assignment. And I know I could just write about the famous story of Armenia's conversion to Christianity, or the genocide, but I just don't want to."

"The famous what?"

"You know." Alek got up and began pacing, the way he did when he talked on the phone. Not a cell phone, of course, since his parents still insisted that he didn't need his own and could just borrow theirs when he needed to. "The Armenians were the first nation to convert to Christianity."

"I did not know that."

"Seriously?"

"Seriously."

"Everybody knows about that," Alek scoffed. "The famous story of how King Trdat III converted the nation, back in the third century of 'our lord.'"

"Never heard of it." Becky propped her legs over the side of the sofa and stretched.

"I'm sure that when I start telling you, you'll recognize it."

"Oh my God, Alek Khederian, I'm sure I won't!" She rotated her ankles, making small circles in the air. "I'm sure that it's one of those weird things that only Armenians know, like the recipe for stuffed grapevine leaves. Which I can't help but point out you haven't made for me in weeks."

But Alek remained unconvinced. "You're telling me you don't know the story of how King Trdat III became obsessed with this nun, Hripsime, and when she rejected him he killed her and everyone else in the abbey where she was hiding? And then, as divine punishment for his crime, God started turning him into a boar, but his sister Khosrovidukht had this dream that their old friend Gregory the Christian, who the king had banished into a pit twelve years earlier, could save him from the curse of lycanthropy? So they save Gregory from the pit and he's, like, miraculously still alive, and he and the boar-king kneel in prayer and then the king's humanity is restored and he converts the entire Armenian people to Christianity? You're sure you never heard that one?"

"I'm sure I would've remembered a story of obsession, rage, murder, of turning into a boar, for God's sake—"

"Lycanthropy."

"What?"

"It's called lycanthropy." Alek resumed his position on the sofa. "When a human turns into an animal. Sometimes they can turn back, as is the case with werewolves. Other times, the transformation is permanent, like in *Elder Scrolls*. Unless you're Dragonborn, of course, in which case . . ."

Becky regarded Alek for a solid moment. "I've often wondered how you've ended up the way you are, Alek Khederian." She popped a Haribo sour cherry into her mouth. "Were you exposed to cosmic rays as a youth, and instead of developing superpowers you just developed super weirdness? Or was it being brought up in your foreign house where your parents still don't own a microwave because they're convinced the rays make food radioactive and you're not allowed to watch more than thirty minutes of television a day—"

"—when I turn fifteen next month, my parents said they'd consider increasing it to forty minutes."

"Has anyone told them that THERE ARE NO SHOWS THAT ARE FORTY MINUTES LONG?" Becky almost-screamed before regaining her composure. "But now I think I understand. And in some small way, it's almost a wonder you aren't more messed up. So can we watch a movie? Or is there something else you need to tell me?"

There was, of course, something Alek was dying to tell Becky. About last night and Ethan and the proposition. But he couldn't. At least not yet.

4

ROUTE 95, WHICH DOUBLED AS THE NEW JERSEY
Turnpike in certain sections and was its own entity at others
in a mysterious anastomosis that even most New Jerseyans
didn't understand, was a real highway running north-south—
the spine that held the state together.

The secondary highways ran more or less east-west, parallel
to each other. Route 95 more or less bisected them all, making
the state's road map look like a vintage tie rack. Route 33,
smack in the middle of those east-west parallel secondary highways, was what the Khederians used to get to church: a mere
four lanes, divided by a strip of land that would've been green
in a different season, framed by wires strung high above either
side of the road, connecting the part of New Jersey that bor-
dered Pennsylvania with the part known for its boardwalks
and funnel cakes and unfortunate MTV shows.

Classical music played as Alek's dad sat behind the wheel,

driving his family to St. Stephen's Armenian Orthodox Church. The Khederians were a reliable twenty minutes late to Saturday school, just as they always were to Sunday services. Their reason for tardiness changed weekly, like the specials at a diner. But for the last few trips, one topic had been so charged, so contentious, that it and it alone reigned supreme: the heated debate Nik always lost about whether or not he'd be allowed to drive.

"I got my license two months ago, but you *never* let me behind the wheel."

"That's not true." Mr. and Mrs. Khederian stood next to each other, presenting a united front. "You drove just last Tuesday."

"To the 7-Eleven. Which is three blocks from our house. And both of you came with me," Nik responded.

Alek suppressed a chortle as his father responded. "But you have so little experience. How are we supposed to trust you behind the wheel?"

"But if you don't let me drive, how'm I going to get any actual experience?" Nik tightened the loop on his skinny plaid tie. "It's the ultimate catch-22!"

Popcorn was the only thing missing from making the spectacle even more enjoyable to Alek. Now Nik sat in sullen silence next to him in the back seat as they made their leisurely way to St. Stephen's Armenian Orthodox Church.

South Windsor and its surrounding townships had plenty of places to worship: a plethora of churches, the largest of which was the Catholic brick and glass St. Anthony of Padua; a handful of synagogues, such as Beth El, with its Hebrew letters proudly marching across the facade; the Islamic mosque, adorned with its perfectly polished gold dome; and even a Baha'i House of Worship. But every weekend, the Khederians passed these local holy places and drove ninety minutes east on Route 33 to the nearest Armenian church.

With all of the spots in the adjoining parking lot claimed by the less-tardy Armenians, the Khederians had to settle for the secondary overspill lot, a solid five-minute walkaway, Alek believed, intentionally to punish latecomers. Alek stuck his thumb out when they began the trek, parodying a hitchhiker's plea, but no one in his family seemed amused.

When they finally arrived, he and Nik bid goodbye to their parents, leaving them upstairs in a sea of pale-white skin and dark hair and eyes to drink coffee and catch up with the other Armenian parents who made the pilgrimage from all over New Jersey. Downstairs they went, to the basement of the church, where Saturday school classes were taught in rooms created by partitions that everybody claimed were movable, although Alek had never actually witnessed the gray monoliths reconfigured.

The Khederian brothers passed the elementary and then middle Saturday school classrooms before settling into their high school section.

In eager anticipation of her favorite season of the year, their teacher, Mrs. Stepanian, had decked out the classroom with Christmas paraphernalia. Trees and wreaths made out of green construction paper decorated the walls, the doors, the windows, even the ceiling of the otherwise drab basement classroom.

Even though they were late, class hadn't started yet, which

felt to Alek a perfect metaphor for the entire Armenian existence. He sat on the far side of the room, behind Nik, who made a point of taking a front-row seat to illustrate his maximum nerdiness. Around a dozen other high school students, ranging from awkward freshmen to near-adult upperclassmen, checked their phones or chatted with one another while Mrs. Stepanian organized papers at the front desk. She always wore dark jackets over white blouses and even darker skirts that came down to her ankles, like she was auditioning to be an extra in *The Sound of Music*. A few minutes later, just after Arno, a freshman with deep, sad eyes, ran into the classroom, mumbling an apology for his tardiness, Mrs. Stepanian decided that now would be a good time to start.

"I know you're all very excited to get back your 'What Being Armenian Means to Me' papers that I graded this morning, especially because the student with the highest score will be awarded the privilege of reading their paper at our Christmas Eve service!" Mrs. Stepanian was clearly more excited than the rest of the class combined. "But I'm going to save that for the end of class. Now, for the language section of class, we're going to read a Christmas pageant out loud. In Armenian!"

Mrs. Stepanian handed out photocopies that appeared older than even she. Once the roles were assigned, the students fumbled their way through the text. Alek could almost hear the groans of their Armenian ancestors with every butchered sound and syntax.

The major impediment to completing the exercise was Shushan, a senior from Red Bank, who proved her inanity in new and exciting ways in every class. Last week, for example, she consumed thirty minutes of class with a presentation about why Kim Kardashian should be the next Catholicos of the Armenian church. This week, the seventeen-year-old from two school districts away, who was reading the Virgin Mary in a bold casting against type, stopped every two lines to ask a question.

"Um, Mrs. Stepanian?" Shushan interrupted the reading again, for the seventh time in five minutes.

"Yes, Shushan," Mrs. Stepanian replied wearily.

"How come some kinds of incense are more honest than others?"

Mrs. Stepanian sucked in her breath, eager to return to the reading of the pageant but knowing that as an educator, she had an obligation to engage her inquisitive pupil. "I'm afraid I don't understand."

"Well, the second wise man brings *frank* incense?" Somehow, Shushan's gift for upward inflection made every sentence sound like a question.

"It's one word—*frankincense*." Alek tried, to the best of his ability, to keep the judginess out of his voice. "It just describes the incense's odor. Not its moral quality."

"Oh." Alek saw Shushan's brain trying to process the information. Whether or not it succeeded was up for debate. "Can I ask another question?"

"Myrrh is a kind of perfume," Alek responded in anticipation.

"Wow—everyone must've smelled horrible in biblical times if two of the three gifts to the baby Jesus were about BO." Shushan shuddered as she conjured her worst nightmare:

ancient personal hygiene. "Thank God we have, like, toilets and things today? And breath fresheners?"

In the moment before Alek could perform his signature exhale and eye roll, he heard a chortle from the corner of the classroom. He and Arno locked eyes, sharing a quiet moment of existential absurdity at the phenomenon that was Shushan Keshishian.

"Is there something the matter, Alek? Arno?" The teacher's question shattered their little spell.

"No, Mrs. Stepanian," the boys said at the same time.

"Very well, then." She managed to arch an eyebrow at each of them, even though they were sitting at opposite ends of the room. "Let's continue, then."

For the rest of class, every time Shushan or one of the members of her gaggle butchered the Armenian language, Alek and Arno shared a secret smile across the classroom. The surprise at finding an ally in Saturday school almost trumped Alek's confusion about how Shushan could have survived in the world this long being so challenged. Almost.

Alek and Arno had only been in the same Saturday school since the start of the school year; Arno had just graduated into the high school section. He had thick, dark Armenian hair like Alek's, but not as curly, and eyes like bottomless pools that made him look older than his thirteen years. The only thing Alek could remember about Arno was that he was the youngest of a large family—maybe five or six siblings who'd passed through St. Stephen's.

Alek wasn't sure who was happier that the class finally reached the end of the play: the teenagers themselves or Mrs.

Stepanian, who felt it necessary to correct every mispronunciation, leaving her to interrupt just about every student on every line. She collected the ancient photocopies after they had reached the end then stored them in the file cabinet as if they were precious artifacts. Then she returned to her desk and produced a stack of papers, like a magician finishing a trick with a dramatic flourish. "I wonder who will be chosen to read their 'What Being Armenian Means to Me' paper at the Christmas Eve service?" she said, as if she didn't already know.

Traditionally, the nerdiest senior won this great honor, and in Alek's mind, his brother, Nik, was a shoo-in. He'd even heard Nik telling his mom how honored he'd be if he were chosen, in that humblebrag way that made Alek want to gag.

Mrs. Stepanian deposited Nik's paper on his desk. He held it up so that Alek could see the big fat A on top, written in a thick green marker. Alek only hoped his own paper wouldn't be graded much lower, since his parents' passive-aggressive disappointment would be annoying at best and maddening at worst.

"The student reading is my favorite part of the service," Mrs. Stepanian confided as she continued handing papers back—to Shushan, to Arno, to Voki, a jockish boy from Neptune, one town south. "Hearing you young people talk about being Armenian on Christmas Eve—it's just the perfect way to start the year!"

Nik positively beamed as he flipped through his paper, pretending to care about the comments that had been written in the margins.

"I'm sure that Mr. and Mrs. Khederian are going to be

especially proud this Christmas." Mrs. Stepanian handed Alek's paper back to him, finally, facedown.

He handled the paper carefully, like it might be booby-trapped, bargaining with a God whose existence he doubted. *I'll learn all my Armenian verb conjugations if you just give me a B-. And if we can get into the B+ range, I'll even memorize my vocabulary list.*

"Congratulations, Mr. Khederian," Mrs. Stepanian announced to the entire class, as if it were some big surprise.

Nik cleared his throat to deliver the speech he no doubt had prepared to appear incredibly spontaneous.

But Mrs. Stepanian cut him off. "Alek, you will be speaking at this year's Christmas Eve service!"

Alek flipped his paper over, blinking away disbelief at the A+ that indicated his perfect score.

Nik refused to speak to Alek after class. And after Alek brokenly told his parents that his essay had been chosen, he felt Nik's simmering fury turn to a full boil as their parents heaped praise upon Alek. They trekked back to the car, which was buried in the inch of snow that had fallen since they entered their house of prayer.

"We'll read Alek's essay while you boys tend to the car." Mr. Khederian popped open the trunk, handing his sons the ice scraper and brush.

"I left it inside," Alek admitted, relieved.

"Then go back and get it!" Mrs. Khederian put her purse in the trunk and opened the passenger door.

"I'll just print it out again when we're home," Alek said.

"But then we won't be able to read Mrs. Stepanian's comments," Alek's father said.

And see your A+ with our own eyes, Alek added mentally.

"Hurry on up, Alek." Mrs. Khederian stepped into the car, cranking the heat up to high. "I'm sure Nik won't mind scraping the car."

His brother was radiating so much anger, Alek suspected he could just melt the snow and ice entrapping their mom's red Toyota with pure fury. He turned, half walking, half jogging back to the church.

The side door that was only open on Saturdays was still unlocked, thankfully, and Alek took two steps of the yellow linoleum stairs at a time, hurling himself down to the basement, turning at the kitchen, and sprinting past the bathrooms to the little room where Mrs. Stepanian tortured them weekly.

He swung the door open and found Arno, sitting alone, in the far corner. A memory of Arno singing in the children's choir last year popped into Alek's consciousness. He'd never heard Arno speak because he was painfully shy. But in the choir, his tenor solo had soared through the sanctuary.

"Hey, Arno." Alek swiped his essay from the bin underneath the chair where he suffered every Saturday. "What're you still doing here?"

Arno's silence was the first sign that something was wrong. Even though making his family wait would annoy them, or maybe because it would, Alek waded through the desks to the boy sitting in the corner by himself. That's when he saw the word, written on the inside cover of Arno's textbook in the thick, black streaks of a Sharpie.

Gyot.

Alek froze.

He couldn't remember the first time he'd encountered that word. It must've been in church, or maybe during a family function where his cousins were present. Alek had been called many things in his life: nerd, geek, dweeb, douche, pussy, choad, tool. In the same way that he couldn't remember when he learned what those nastier words meant, he couldn't remember when he first learned that *gyot* was the Armenian slang for "faggot."

Of course, Alek had been called a faggot, too, although, ironically, less since he came out last summer. And no one dared to whisper it under their breath when Alek and Ethan walked hand in hand down the hall together, because of Ethan's school-wide reputation as a badass, solidified during the infamous food fight he instigated last year. But when Alek was by himself, he'd still heard it muttered as an upperclassman "accidentally" clipped his shoulder during the hurried five minutes between periods.

And yes, it hurt. And yes, life would be better if he didn't have to deal with that shit. But also, he didn't really care. To worry about what people like that thought would be like engaging the people who denied that the Armenian Genocide happened. He didn't need or even want the approval of people who chose to live in a close-minded world.

Alek closed the book so they wouldn't have to stare at the

offending letters. "You have to remember that when someone does something like this, it's because they hate themselves, and hating on someone else makes them feel better, you know?"

"It's such an ugly word." Arno tried to keep a brave face, but Alek could tell what it was costing him.

"Totally."

Arno's voice dropped down to a whisper. "Tell me that it gets better," he pleaded.

"What does?"

"You know. This."

And then Alek understood that Arno was coming out to him.

Although Alek had come out to various people over the last six months, this was the first time someone had come out to him. He knew firsthand how much this moment meant to Arno and how important his response would be.

None of the people Alek had come out to responded in a way that would qualify as horrible: no disowning, no Bible-fearing "You're damned to hell," none of that after-school-special, old-fashioned bullshit. But certain responses, nonetheless, had been better than others.

The worst was probably from his former friend Matthew, who lived around the corner.

"I always suspected." The condescension dripped off his voice, like ever-wise Matthew had been just waiting for Alek to figure out what was so obvious to everyone else. Well, Alek was happy to find an excuse to unfriend Matthew and his bad breath.

The totally unfazed responses weren't much better. The people who were just like, "Okay—is that all?" felt like they were working too hard to show how little it mattered to them. And besides, Alek hated having to wonder if they hadn't actually heard his coming out or had mistaken it for something else. *Are they trying to show how cool and accepting they are?* Alek would have to wonder for the rest of the conversation. *Or are they just hard of hearing?*

On the other side of the spectrum, and equally irksome, were the people who made a huge deal about it and how accepting they were, like his guidance counselor, Ms. Schmidt. "I guess except for discovering that I'm a homosexual, nothing else really interesting happened over the summer," he had blurted out.

Ms. Schmidt responded with a clearly prepared multi-minute monologue about how accepting she was of queer identity, and how she would support him in all his school endeavors, curricular and extracurricular, before adding a discreet "Be safe" in that disturbingly ominous way, as if being queer was, in and of itself, a way of becoming HIV positive. The whole time Alek was in Ms. Schmidt's office, he felt like all he was, in her eyes, was queer. And yes, sure, Alek was queer. But he was more than that, too.

Alek tried to give Arno the kind of response he appreciated most: chill, supportive, interested, and not too precious. "Of course it gets better. We can, like, start a gay Armenian club." Alek assumed a radio broadcaster's voice. "Genocided and homosexual? We know your plight!"

Arno chuckled his wry, dry laugh. "Does it even count? It's not like I've even—you know—done anything."

"That's so cool, Arno. I didn't know until, well—my lips were actually planted on my boyfriend's."

"Ethan?" Arno asked.

"Yeah—how'd you know?"

"I follow him on Instagram. Everyone follows him on Instagram."

"Including my grandmother, apparently."

"He's got, like, four thousand followers. You two are, like, celebrities in the Central NJ queer teens scene."

Alek laughed. "(A) That can't possibly be a thing. And two, I think it's awesome that you know yourself enough to be out. And don't let the ass-wipe who did this change that."

Arno fingered the pages of his script. "You know, it's not even an Armenian word."

"No?"

"It's Turkish."

"Big surprise." Alek went for the cheap laugh and got it—nothing like two Armenians sharing a racist joke about the country that continued to deny the genocide it had committed over a hundred years ago. Alek undid his scarf and tossed it on the desk. "I had no idea. Just like when I first met Ethan, I had no idea he was gay."

Arno laughed. "You didn't know Ethan was gay?"

"I can be sort of blind sometimes, okay?"

"Sort of?"

"Okay, mega-blind. Ethan was this supercool badass skater boy who'd convinced me to cut summer school and go into the city with him. But when we were together I just felt—I don't know—free. Free to be myself. And then we were alone in his room and before I knew it . . ." Alek trailed off rather than risk TMI. "The first mini-fight we got into was when he used the word *faggot* before I knew he was gay and I got all kinds of offended. But he showed me how we can control the power that words have over us. Just like now you and I can make *gyot* into whatever we want it to be." Alek stumbled over the word, his tongue resisting those letters in that combination. "It's just a word."

"But it's a bad word."

"And saying it can take its power away. Watch and listen, young one." Alek interlaced his fingers and cracked his knuckles, then gave himself a moment to stretch, as if he were preparing to perform a challenging physical feat. "Okay: you can be such a . . . *gyot* sometimes." Alek tripped over the word, just a little, before playfully punching Arno on the arm. "Now you try."

Arno cleared his throat. *"You—"*

"You have to warm up," Alek instructed him.

The younger boy stood up and played along, stretching his hands up above, over his head. *"You* are a total *gyot*." Arno punched Alek back on his arm, equally playfully.

"See—screw whoever did that. I'm going to make sure that that never happens again, to you or me or any other *gyot* who has the unique misfortune of having to attend this Saturday school."

Arno's eyes widened. "How're you going to do that?"

"I'm going to talk to Mrs. Stepanian about it, obvi."

"Seriously?"

Alek nodded.

"I don't know, Alek. Maybe it's just easier to let it slide, you know? Who cares?"

"It might be easier, but that doesn't mean it's right. How old are you, Arno?"

"Thirteen. And a half."

"Well, I'm about to turn fifteen, and let me tell you what wisdom I've amassed in those eighteen months. If we don't do anything, then, in some ways, we're just as bad as the people who did this. Think of all the future up-and-coming *gyots* who're going to have to sit through endless boring hours in this Saturday school. That's torture enough. It's our duty to make sure they don't have to deal with even more agony. Evil is what happens when good people do nothing."

Alek got up to leave the classroom.

"Hey, Alek."

"Yeah?"

Arno stood up and handed Alek his now-twice-forgotten essay, their fingers brushing for the briefest of moments. "Congratulations, by the way. What a great honor."

5

FOR MOST OF THEIR RELATIONSHIP, ALEK AND ETHAN
had made sure that every few days, they'd find alone time.
Usually, that meant they were at Ethan's house. More specifically, in his room, where they'd first kissed and where they'd
kissed infinitely more since. The sexiest hours of Alek's life had
been spent there, cocooned in the images of half-naked men
covering every inch of the walls and ceiling. Ethan's room was
infinitely more conducive than Alek's, which had simple, clean
lines.

Besides, Ethan's dad wasn't home most of the time. This was
especially true now that he'd started dating Lesley, a sociology
professor at NYU with whom he'd spend one or two nights a
week in New York City. And even when he was home, Ethan's
dad afforded the boys a degree of privacy that never occurred
to the Khederians. Although Alek's parents always welcomed
Ethan when he came over and even let the boys hang out in

Alek's room with the door closed, they did so in the exact same way they had whenever Nik had a girlfriend over. That meant that fifteen minutes couldn't pass without them knocking on the door and asking Alek and Ethan if they wanted something to eat or for help with the computer in the downstairs office or a question about how to set the DVR. Alek didn't know if this was a brilliant ploy or not, but either way, it guaranteed the two of them would never get to an intimate place.

Every time he and Ethan had been alone together since Thanksgiving, however, *he* was there, too. He would arrive imperceptibly, this demon of anxiety and expectation, watching, distracting, so it became impossible for Alek to lose himself the way he had before.

Alek even started fabricating excuses to avoid situations where they would be alone. He'd make Ethan come over to his house, or when he went over to Ethan's, he'd make Becky accompany him. Like today, after school, halfway through the first week of December.

"Come on, Becky, we're going to be late." Alek paced up and down Becky's bedroom as she pulled on woolen socks and rooted through her closet for a pair of shoes.

"Let's see—you follow me home after school like a total stalker, insist that I go with you to your boyfriend's house pronto, even though I've told you plenty of times I'm tired of having to play third wheel while the two of you coo at each other like rabid doves, and then you give me grief when it takes me more than five seconds to change."

"Why do you even need to change? You look fine." Alek stayed standing, hoping it would motivate her to move faster.

"Forgive me, your highness." Becky affected a British accent and took an outrageously low bow. "Next time, I shall hop to follow your orders more promptly." She finally dug out a pair of boots from the pile inside her closet and yanked them on. "Now out. I'm changing my sweater." Becky gestured to the door to her room.

"Seriously?"

"I know all about your deviant tendencies." Her eyes narrowed. "How do I know you're not going to steal a glimpse of me when I'm just in my bra?"

"Becky, I know it's difficult to forget this because of the kind of raw masculine energy that just pours out of me effortlessly . . ."

"As your best friend, is it my obligation to shatter your delusions or to let you keep them?"

". . . but as a homosexual, I'm not attracted to members of the fairer sex. Besides, I know what's going to happen—if I'm not here reminding you that we're working on a schedule, you're going to take FOREVER figuring out which sweater you want to wear, and that whole time, I'm going to be stuck in the hallway outside of your bedroom, like I'm in exile. So how about this?" Alek tossed her a Christmas sweater, designed with white snowflakes against a red-and-green background.

"That makes me look like an ornament."

"You're impossible." Alek scooted over to the corner of Becky's bed, covered with the gray-and-pink quilt her mother had stitched for her birthday three years ago, and turned to face the corner of the room. "Satisfied?"

"Okay—but no turning around till I say so."

" 'The lady doth protest too much, methinks.' "

"The dork doth quote Shakespeare too much, methinks."

Every time the two of them had gotten together since Thanksgiving, he had wanted to talk to her about Ethan and sex. But now, weeks later, the words still wouldn't come out, like they were shackled to the back of his throat.

"It's good that you came over, because I've been wanting to tell you something anyway." Alek heard Becky's drawers being opened and closed as she searched for just the perfect top.

"Is this about Mahira and John? Because seriously, I couldn't care less if they got back together or not. Gossip about your band-nerd friends is almost as boring as Saturday school."

"It has nothing to do with them," Becky insisted. "Although I'm surprised you're not more shocked by a flutist dating a clarinetist. It is quite scandalous."

"So . . ." Alek prompted.

"Well . . ."

"What already?"

"I'm building up to it, okay? Sheesh." Becky took another pause. "At my competition last weekend—"

"What happened? Did Dustin beat you out? Again?"

"Of course not! I scored three points higher than him, thank you very much."

Alek continued to scrutinize the corner of Becky's room during her extended silence. She kept all of her rollerblading paraphernalia in this corner—wheels and pads and gears and tools Alek couldn't identify. "Just spill it, okay? And while you're at it, can you speed up this sweater-selection process?"

"I'm taking care to change my outfit, you see, because after Ethan's, I'm going to see Dustin."

"Is there a competition tonight?"

"They don't have competitions on weeknights, duh."

"So?"

"Oh my God, you can be so thick sometimes." Becky wasn't even trying to hide the exasperation in her voice. "I have plans *to hang out with* Dustin. How much more obvious can I be?"

"Rebecca Amy Boyce—do you have a boyfriend?" Alek turned around, finding Becky wearing only a bra above the striped skirt she'd changed into. "Sorry! Sorry! Sorry!" Alek turned back around quickly, almost giving himself whiplash.

"I didn't say he was my boyfriend. I just said we're hanging out."

"*Hanging out* hanging out, or just hanging out?"

"I don't think it's appropriate to say any more. Ladies don't kiss and tell."

"I don't care what ladies do! Remember what you said when I told you I kissed Ethan the first time?" Alek plowed on, not waiting for an answer. "Well, I do. You said, 'I'm your best friend. I have a right to know these things *before* they happen.' So spill it, Becky." The words rushed out of his mouth like a river. "Have you already kissed, or do you just think it's going to happen? Have you done more already? If he's tried to get to second base with you, I'll beat the shit out of him. Unless, of course, that's what you wanted. Did you want to get to second base with him? I'm not judging, I just want to know, you know?"

"Oh my God, Alek, calm down, okay? We just started hanging out. And I'd love to tell you more, but I'd hate to make us any later to Ethan's. Now turn around—I'm done."

Becky had changed skirts again, ending up in a dark-blue woolen one, with a turtleneck sweater on top.

"And, Alek—and this is the most important thing." Becky cleared her throat.

"Yes, Becky?"

"No one says 'second base' anymore. We just call it groping."

Alek didn't think Ethan had minded when he and Becky showed up together, but when Alek left with her just an hour later, he could feel his boyfriend's disappointment. And he felt it again when he told Ethan, during lunch two days later, that he couldn't come over that night for their study date.

"No prob, man." Ethan, ever chill, didn't even ask Alek why he'd changed his mind. "How about tomorrow afternoon, then, after Saturday school?"

Without an answer prepared, Alek nodded meekly. Afternoon, at least, felt safer than night.

Sitting in Saturday school the next morning, thoughts of how he was disappointing Ethan were trumped by his own disappointment that Mrs. Stepanian hadn't responded to the e-mail Alek had sent her earlier that week, detailing what had happened with Arno. He was beginning to think that she would ignore the issue altogether, until her husband, the reverend father, appeared a few minutes before the end of class.

Alek scanned his Saturday school class, trying to guess the identity of the guilty party. Voki looked bored, the way he always did. Shushan looked puzzled, the way she always did. And the rest of the class all looked innocent enough, making it even harder to figure out who in that room would be capable of something so hateful.

"My wife has told me about a deeply troubling incident that occurred in this classroom. It was so troubling, I insisted on coming to speak to you directly." Reverend Father Stepanian stood motionless, like he was delivering a sermon. His deep baritone echoed in the classroom, too small to contain its rich vibrato.

Shushan made eye contact with the gaggle of girls in class. Alek reconsidered his assessment of their collective vapidity as they wordlessly communicated like a flock of birds through furtive eyes and head tilts, if any of them knew what was going on and none of them did.

Or at least, they all pretended not to know. But could one of them be the guilty party? Nik slipped down in his chair, trying to look too jaded to care about the reverend father's presence.

"There is never a situation that justifies the use of hate language. Just so that there is no confusion, I repeat: there is *never* a situation that justifies the use of hate language. I will not repeat the word that caused the incident, but words of hate, be they about race, class, ethnicity, sexuality, or religion, are never acceptable in a house of worship. Or anywhere else, for that matter, if you want to be a good Christian."

Arno stared straight ahead, doing his best to make it look like he was equally surprised by what the reverend father was saying. Alek didn't feel the need to feign ignorance. He was proud of having gone to Mrs. Stepanian. He was proud of his church and of being Armenian and of having such a powerful, reasonable man at the head of his institution.

"I trust this is the last I will have to say to you all about this matter." The reverend father ran his hand over his perfectly trimmed beard. "It is our duty as Christians to love everybody and to welcome them back to the fold, regardless of how far from the Lord's path some of them may have wandered or how confused they may be. So I hope, in the future, rather than resorting to the language of hate, or to bullying, you will find a more Christian approach."

An awkward silence followed, broken by the equally awkward sound of the students' muttered yeses and profound confusion about what the hell the reverend father was actually talking about.

Alek, however, didn't feel confused. He felt betrayed, as if he'd learned that he'd been lied to by someone he trusted. He replayed the words in his mind, trying to convince himself that he had misheard, that somehow, reconfigured, the words coming out of the reverend father's mouth meant something different. But any way he looked at them, any way that he used his cognitive functions to understand what had just happened, he arrived at the same conclusion: in trying to condemn what had just happened, Reverend Father had inadvertently condoned it.

Alek's nice Saturday school clothes were strewn about Ethan's room. His dark slacks hung lopsided on Ethan's orange plastic rolling desk chair. His formerly crisp white button-down shirt lay on the floor, and his serious navy-blue tie, improbably, had found its way to the ceiling fan, a passenger hanging on to a lazy carousel.

"Do you think . . ." Ethan asked between heavy breaths. ". . . Do you think you might be ready now?"

The question had become inevitable, like lightning after a clap of thunder. Knowing he was going to disappoint Ethan sucked, but not nearly as much as how knowing the question was coming made it impossible to enjoy their time together.

It would've been so easy, Alek thought, to have just said yes. To get it over with. To give his boyfriend, the guy who'd given him so much, what he wanted. But it wouldn't have been honest. Alek didn't compromise on small things, let alone things of this magnitude.

Alek didn't verbalize his no. He just gave his head the slightest of shakes, and Ethan rolled off him and onto his back, next to Alek on his bed.

Even though it was just before four p.m., the sun had almost set on this December Saturday, a few hours after the reverend's epic fail. Ethan flipped on the overhead light, revealing the half-naked men that plastered his walls. Alek felt exposed, suddenly. He wrapped himself in Ethan's comforter.

"I'm—I'm sorry," he stuttered.

Alek missed the days of simple groping. He missed the innocence of the beginning of his relationship with Ethan, before the sex thing had entered the world of possibilities.

Ethan was never pushy. Ethan never guilted. Ethan always accepted Alek's decision. But he had asked more times than not since Thanksgiving. And even if he didn't say the words, Alek didn't need him to. Alek could hear Ethan's thoughts. And his hunger.

"Hey, man, it's cool." Although Alek suspected it was a cover, Ethan acted as if he were totally unfazed by Alek's repeated rejections. "There's lots of other stuff we can do." Ethan smiled his positively feline smile, leaping out of bed and onto his desk chair in one fluid gesture, not bothering to get dressed. He sat in his boxers, clicking the mouse wheel. "Come check this out. I thought we could hit it before your birthday dinner next weekend."

Keeping the comforter bundled around him, Alek lumbered over to Ethan's computer. "Oh my God! They're doing a Star Trek Academy simulation at the Intrepid museum!"

"Do I know my nerdy boyfriend or what?" Ethan beamed.

"You know your nerdy boyfriend," Alek conceded. He leaped out of the down comforter and embraced Ethan.

"Whoa! We should nerd out more often."

"Ethan, seriously, you're the best." Alek pulled back, but his mind was already speeding with the possibilities. "Do you think your dad might be able to take us?"

"I already asked, and the forecast is doubtful. He's got plans with Lesley during the day, and then he's seeing Remi right before your b-day dinner."

Alek stopped. "Remi? Like, *your* Remi?"

"He's not *my* Remi." Ethan's shoulders and neck tensed up. "He's not my anything. Except my ex, I guess. But yeah, apparently he's back in town, and apparently he reached out to my dad."

"They're like, what—getting together?"

"Sure—you remember, my dad used to be his prof. That's how Remi ended up living here when he lost his scholarship."

"And he didn't reach out to you?"

"Nopers."

Alek gathered his clothes, using the activity as an excuse to buy himself a few moments to think. When he'd met Ethan last summer, Ethan was still grieving the Australian college student who had become his first boyfriend, then abruptly moved back to Brisbane, severing all contact with Ethan. But since Alek and Ethan had gotten together almost six months ago, all traces of Remi had disappeared from Ethan's life, from the picture he used to have of the two of them on his nightstand to even mentioning his name. "So what do you think you'll do when he does reach out to you?"

"'If,' you mean?"

"No, I mean 'when.'"

"I don't know that he will, and I don't know what I'd do," Ethan admitted. He kicked his feet up on his desk, reclining into the chair.

"Ethan, you know I trust you. Do whatever you think is right."

"So you'd be okay if I hit him back?"

"Sure."

"What if I got together with him?"

"What do you mean, 'got together'?"

Ethan laughed. "Just, like, saw him, dude."

Alek squirmed. "Also sure."

"Seriously?"

"I am not my boyfriend's keeper, Ethan."

"There's no point in even talking about it, because apparently that a-hole thinks it's okay to hit up my dad without even like PMing me or whatever, so who cares, you know?"

Alek broke the awkward silence a few moments later. "As much as I love the Intrepid idea, if your dad can't do it, it's pretty much dead. You know how my folks are." Alek could already hear the complaints about traffic, the price of parking, and every other possible detail.

"Maybe they'll let us do it by ourselves," Ethan, ever hopeful, said.

"Totally," Alek played along. "And you know who I suspect will deliver to us that news? A flying pig that escaped from a frozen hell."

"Point made."

He surrendered himself to the pleasure of Ethan's hands running over his body, like he was clay being sculpted by a master artist, confident of every stroke.

But before things got carried away, Alek pulled back. "Come on—I have to get going."

"You do?"

"Yeah—don't you remember—movie night at Becky's."

"You can be late, you know."

"To Becky's?" Alek stepped on the desk chair, retrieving his tie from the ceiling fan. "Have you met her?"

Ethan leaped out of bed. "Then I'm coming with."

"Seriously?

"Sure! It's just you I want to be with. I don't really care what we're doing." Ethan threw on whatever clothes he could find from the piles littering his bedroom.

Alek stopped and look at Ethan. "It's Remi's loss, you know."

"What is?"

"You are. Because I'm sure you're the best thing that ever happened to him. Just like you're the best thing that ever happened to me."

6

"SO WHAT'RE WE WATCHING?" ALEK KICKED OFF HIS shoes and leaped up onto the brown monolith of a sofa in Becky's basement, cuddling up against Ethan, their fingers intertwined.

"*María Candelaria*," Becky gushed with joy.

"Maria who?" Ethan asked.

"Becky and I have been working our way through the classics of the Mexican Golden Age," Alek explained.

"Subtitles?" Ethan groaned. "You two are getting to be so pretentious in your old age."

"*Moi?*" Becky said, splaying her hand against her chest.

"House rules, Ethan." Alek reached back and wrapped his hand around his boyfriend's neck. "Besides, we're lucky Becky let you stay."

"Seriously, Ethan, my basement is harder to get into than *Hamilton*."

Ethan had propped his skateboard against the wall behind the stacks of old DVDs that looked like fingers, emerging from the earth below.

"I'll take your word for it." Ethan raised an eyebrow. "You're just about the only people I know who still watch movies. TV is the present, people. Television is the culture of our time. Look at all the good shows now—it's impossible to keep up. Television is our mythology."

"And I'm the pretentious one?" Becky snorted.

"I don't care if it's TV or movie—as long as it has super-heroes in it, I'm in." Alek looked at his boyfriend and best friend. "If you could choose any superpower, what would it be?"

"I hate this game." Becky rolled her eyes.

"On that, we can agree," Ethan said.

Alek chose to ignore them both. "You want me to go first? All right, but only if you insist." Becky and Ethan groaned. "I'd choose reality manipulation."

Becky sat on the floor, flipping through DVDs. "Okay—I'll bite, in spite of how my instincts are telling me that even asking you about this is a huge mistake. What is reality manipulation?"

"Duh—you can control reality. Like, if I wanted a slice of pie, I would just . . ." Alek waved his arms around, demonstrating how he would activate his power. ". . . and then a slice of pie would appear."

"Any kind of pie?" Ethan asked suspiciously.

"Any kind! That's the whole point. You can *manipulate reality*."

Becky put the DVDs down. "Alek Khederian, that is the dumbest thing I've ever heard."

"What better use for your superpower than to get pie?" Alek demanded.

"No—I mean—that is just a superpower that would let you do anything." Becky smacked two DVDs against each other for emphasis. "That's not being a superhero. That's being a god."

Ethan tried a different approach. "Does any superhero actually have that power?"

"Um, of course they do—Legion, for one. And the Beyonder, of course."

But Becky had lost interest. "Whatever. Reality manipulation is too powerful. It's a cheat."

"Okay, well, which superpower would you pick?" Alek asked.

Becky finished sorting the piles of DVDs into new piles that, to Alek's perception, were equally random. "Superspeed."

"How come?" Ethan leaned forward.

"That way, I could finish up all my chores and homework, like, superfast and be done with the boring parts of life. So I would have more time to enjoy the fun ones. Like watching movies." Becky underscored herself, singing a made-up sentimental Hallmark instrumental. "With friends like you."

"You know, we could be at Mercer Mall in twenty minutes." Alek started speaking like a country bumpkin. "You should see what they've got in these movie the-a-ters, Ma! Real popcorn with butter! And an arcade and everything!"

"Give it up. Dustin made me go see one of those last night, and I've had my fill for this year."

"I'd heard that you and D-Dawg were hanging out," Ethan said, trying hard to sound as casual as possible.

"D-Dawg, my ass." Becky began fiddling with the DVD player controls. "Why do you and your friends have such stupid names for one another?"

"Maybe the four of us could—you know—double-date sometime. It'd be fun!" Ethan said.

"I'm glad you think so. Because he should be coming over any second now," Becky informed them.

Alek stood up. "He is?"

"Yeah. Why?"

"Just that—I always tell you in advance if I'm inviting Ethan when we hang out."

"Except for today."

"Okay, except for today."

"What's the big deal, Alek?" Ethan shifted. "Dustin's the bomb."

"No big deal. I'm just saying . . ."

"Besides, Dustin's into all that sci-fi stuff you like. The two of you can go to the movies together and see as many explosions and things going kablooey as you want, and neither Ethan nor I will ever have to sit through two hours of trying to make sense of how radioactive material in outer space and genetic mutations cause superpowers."

"You're conflating three totally different origin stories!" Alek protested. "And besides, I'm not going on a movie date with Dustin. He's your boyfriend. You deal with him."

Becky turned quickly. "I didn't say he was my boyfriend."

"But you didn't say he wasn't, either," Ethan pointed out.

"Why don't you just ask him out?" Alek nuzzled into his boyfriend's parka.

"That's not how it works," Ethan responded. "In the hetero world, boys have to do the asking."

"Really? I guess this is one of the many superior things about being gay," Alek said. "We don't have the luxury of those heteronormative expectations."

"Oh my God—I didn't realize there could be such a thing as a pink soapbox until you just stood up on one. Are you guys done mansplaining, or do you have any more prefeminist propaganda to spout?"

"You've got to admit we have a point." Ethan adjusted himself, putting his arm around his boyfriend.

"Who has a point?" Dustin appeared at the top of the basement staircase. He strolled down, his bright green skateboard almost matching the bright green carpet. He unzipped his white hoodie, revealing a red Flash T-shirt.

"What's up, D-Dawg?" Ethan leaped from the coach, finger-snapping Dustin a greeting infinitely more complex than any feat of agility Alek could perform.

"They think I should stop waiting for you to ask me to be your girlfriend." Becky didn't even look up from her DVDs. "So what do you say, *D-Dawg*? You want to do this?"

Dustin propped his skateboard next to Ethan's. "I thought you would never ask." He plopped down next to Alek and put his hand around Alek's shoulder. "This is so lit, right? Becky's bestie, his bf, and her bf all hanging together?"

For Becky's sake, Alek swallowed all the snarky responses that presented themselves and simply grunted his consent.

"I'm glad we have that settled." Becky began munching on a bag of Haribo sour grapefruit candies that Alek would've sworn she did not have a moment ago. "Are we ready to start?"

The next morning, Alek curled up in the back of the car on the way to church, watching his brother's ability to drive diminish with every piece of criticism their mother offered. Although it would be exactly two years and one week before Alek could get his driving license, he made a mental note to begin strategizing now how to avoid his brother's fate.

"Okay, now there's a stop sign coming up, so slow down." Mrs. Khederian clutched the inside car door handle, bracing herself for the accident that she clearly regarded as inevitable as the rising sun.

"That stop sign is a full mile away." Nik clenched his jaw.

"Do what your mother says," Mr. Khederian chimed in from the back, next to Alek. When Nik finally won the weekly debate about driving to church today, Alek had just pitied his older brother. There was no such thing as victory with their parents. Just different kinds of defeat.

Nik stepped on the brake as lightly as possible, aiming for the impossibly slim passage between the Charybdis of his parents' hyper-cautiousness and the Scylla of the irate drivers behind him.

"Now, at a four-way intersection, you come to a full stop and look all ways," his mother instructed him. "I said 'full stop'!" she yelped when the vehicle began moving again.

"That was a full stop!"

"I don't think it was. Boghos, what do you think?" Mrs.

Khederian didn't wait for her husband to respond. "What if a car had been lurking on Maple, where they'd have the right-of-way? Or even worse, what if another car had flown through their stop sign altogether? It would've come barreling down the intersection and—WHAM!" She smacked her hands together to illustrate. "That's why it's important to always practice defensive driving."

Nik's jaw clenched tighter, like a vise being cranked. "I am trying to drive this car."

"Don't think of it as a car." Their mother clutched her seat belt. "Think of it as a two-ton death machine!"

"What's wrong with you?" Nik abandoned the calm he had so desperately been holding on to. "It's like you're trying to get inside my head!"

"Don't speak that way to your mother!" Mr. Khederian leaned forward to make sure his admonishment had sufficient emphasis.

"Forget this!" Nik pulled into a stranger's driveway. "This is impossible!"

"You should put your signal on at least five seconds before you make a turn." Their mother looked around anxiously to see if any police officers had witnessed the unforgivable traffic violation.

The Khederians had traveled only a fraction of the distance between their house and the entrance ramp to Route 33: approximately three miles. Alek was impressed; he didn't think Nik would've made it half that distance with a Cassandra of vehicular doom sitting in the passenger seat, predicting death and destruction at every possible turn.

"Nik, we want to trust you with the car." Mr. Khederian again leaned forward from the back seat. "But every time we give you the chance to drive, you don't want to. Now let's try again."

"I do! I do want to!" Nik began maneuvering the car in a K-turn. "But now my PTSD kicks in whenever I sit behind the wheel!"

"You're getting too close to the curb," Mr. Khederian warned.

"It's fine!"

"At least slow down!" Mrs. Khederian yelled.

"Would you calm down?!"

"But you're going to hit the . . ." Mrs. Khederian reached over and grabbed the steering wheel, sending the car lurching.
Thump.

"I told you," Mrs. Khederian stated simply. Her husband hopped out of the car to investigate.

Alek turned and saw his father holding up a broken post with a breadbox-size mailbox on top.

Nik dropped his head on the steering wheel. The horn blared out aggressively, obnoxiously, existentially.

Fifteen people to go.

The more Alek had thought about what the reverend father said when he addressed the Saturday school class just yesterday, the more indignant he had become.

Eleven.

But actually engaging the head of his church required more

courage than he had anticipated. Now that the service had ended and he was a mere eleven (make that seven!) people away from confronting the reverend father, Alek began second-guessing himself.

Five.

He had told his family that he'd meet up with them afterward, ignoring their quizzical looks and questions, and gone to the end of the line of congregants, whom Reverend Father Stepanian greeted by name after the service as they left the sanctuary.

Two.

"How's your mother's holding up, Pertag?"

"Did you enjoy your time in the Caribbean, Zanazan?"

Finally, Alek and the reverend father were face-to-face.

"You have any exciting birthday plans coming up, Alek?" He smiled.

"Yes, thanks for asking." He spent a precious minute telling the reverend father about his birthday plans in the city. But he forced himself to get to the point. "I was wondering if I can talk to you about something else for a moment?"

"Of course." Reverend Father Stepanian put one of his strong, solid hands on Alek's shoulder and led him to a pew inside the sanctuary. "What can I help you with?"

"It's about when you came and spoke to our Saturday school class yesterday, Reverend Father."

"Ah, yes. I want to thank you for telling the Yeretzgin about that incident. I'm so glad she brought it to my attention."

It would've been easy to leave it at that, to have accepted a compliment from this figure he'd admired his entire life.

But as Reverend Father Stepanian turned to go, his robes rustling with the movement, Alek found his voice. "I really appreciate you coming and talking to the class about what happened, but I'm not sure you actually helped."

The reverend father turned back, regarding Alek. "Is that so?" He sat back down. "What would you have done differently?"

"When you use phrases like 'people who've lost their path from God,' you're actually encouraging bullying. You're telling people it's all right to treat them differently."

"But, Alek, you must know the church's view on homosexuality."

"Come on, Reverend Father. We live in the twenty-first century. Gay marriage is legal in every state in this country, as well as Canada, Brazil, New Zealand, Ireland, Chile, Germany, and Mexico! You don't really believe that nonsense, do you?" Alek immediately wondered if he'd taken things too far. But the reverend didn't seem upset—just reflective. It was something that Alek had always admired about him—the amount of time he took before speaking.

After a few more moments of deliberation, the reverend father said, "As a pastor in this church and the reverend father of this congregation, it is my duty to shepherd the spiritual lives of my flock."

"So you're saying that you agree with the church's position?"

"Alek, you want a simple answer here, but sometimes the truth lies in the space between more complex things."

"And sometimes it doesn't!" Alek's exasperation found its

way into his voice. "Have you, or anyone in the whole church for that matter, ever thought about what it might be like for someone who doesn't subscribe to these heteronormative standards to be part of this congregation?" Alek hadn't meant to out himself to the reverend father. But as the words came tumbling out of his mouth, they both realized that he had done so.

"Oh! I see." Reverend Father Stepanian exhaled gently as he realized what Alek was telling him. "I see," he repeated, without judgment.

"So what—now you think I'm a bad Armenian?" Alek pressed.

"How long has your family been coming to St. Stephen's?"

"I'm not sure; since before my brother was born?"

"So almost twenty years."

"At least."

"I remember baptizing you. You were a very good baby—no crying at all. Unlike your older brother, Andranik. He made such a fuss, you should've heard him. Screaming at the top of his lungs. I've known you your whole life, and I know you are a good boy, Alek. And a good Armenian. Learning this isn't going to change any of that."

"Thank you, Father." Alek leaned back in the pew and released the breath he hadn't been aware he was holding.

"The world has changed in many ways since you were born—mostly for the good, I'm happy to say. But the church takes a long time to catch up. That's why I ask you to understand my position. I adore your family, even though I know that I can count on you to be at least twenty minutes late."

The reverend and Alek shared a smile at his own joke. "After service, your mother's dolma is always the best at the buffet."

"My father's dolma, you mean," Alek corrected him.

"Excuse me?"

"My father makes the dolma."

The reverend father smiled, sheepishly running his hand over his immaculately trimmed beard, which showed the slightest signs of graying. "My apologies—I suppose it was foolish of me to make that assumption. We learn so much about ourselves by the things we take for granted, don't we?" He started again. "Your *family's* dolma is always the best. But the church is very clear about its doctrine. Homosexuality is a sin."

"Do you have any gay friends, Reverend Father?"

He regarded Alek. "Of course I do . . ."

"And do you believe, in your heart of hearts, that your gay friends can lead upstanding lives, but when they get to heaven's gates, they will be denied entrance for being gay? If I died right now in some freaky alien invasion, would I go to hell?"

"What I believe is not relevant here, Alek. The belief of the church is what's important."

"So your beliefs are different than the church's?"

The reverend father smiled. "You're not going to trick me into an admission, Alek. We pastors wrestle with this all the time. But the church's position is that love and sex are special gifts from God to be enjoyed within the sacrament of marriage. I say therefore to the unmarried and widows, it is good for them if they abide even as I: But if they cannot contain, let them arry: for it is better to marry than to burn. 1 Corinthians, 7:8-9. All sex outside of marriage is considered the sin of fornication."

"So if Ethan and I got married, everything would be all right?"

Sadness crept over the reverend father's face. "I'm afraid not. Romans chapter one, verses twenty-one, twenty-two, twenty-six, and twenty-seven make it very clear that the special gift of love is reserved for a man and woman. So does Leviticus."

"Leviticus also says not to eat shellfish or the fat from a goat, lamb, or sheep. And I'm sure I don't have to remind you about good ol' Leviticus's stand on mixed seeds or fabrics. Who gets to decide which passages in the Bible you have to take at face value and which ones you get to interpret? And how?"

"That's the whole point of the church, at least the Armenian Church. We priests have spent our lives studying the Bible, Alek—its writing, its interpretation, its meaning. That's our job."

"From where I'm sitting, mixing fabrics is much more shocking than me having a boyfriend. Why, just last week, I saw your wife sporting a cashmere pashmina over a wool jacket. And I think her blouse was made of cotton. I prayed extra hard for her that night, Reverend Father."

Father Stepanian laughed heartily. "It's nice to talk to you like this—and see how passionately you feel about it." The reverend father leaned in, confiding. "To be honest, between you and me, I think the church's view on some things could use updating. But it takes time, Alek, for a ship this size to change direction. You have to remember, the Armenians were the first people to convert to Christianity, and it is my job to uphold the church's beliefs. You know, a heretic is not someone who doesn't believe. He's someone who picks and chooses which doctrines he follows and which ones he doesn't. But true faith doesn't work that way. It's not a buffet that you can sample at will. You have to sign up for the whole deal."

"So single-fabric outfits for everyone from now on?" Alek asked.

The reverend father laughed again. "From now on, for simplicity's sake, let's make it easy, okay? Just keep your personal life personal. I will think about this conversation, Alek, and I hope you do, too." The reverend father got up to leave. "And happy birthday, Alek."

"The big one-five."

"I consider our congregation very lucky to have such an intelligent young man speaking at our service on Christmas Eve. Mrs. Stepanian shared your winning essay with me, and I can't wait for you to share it with the whole congregation."

The very germ of an idea began sprouting in Alek's mind. "Neither can I, Reverend Father. Neither can I."

7

"HELLO, AND WELCOME TO GREEN HILL. MY NAME IS
Beckett, and I'll be tending to your needs tonight." A mustache
so bushy it looked fake sprouted from the waiter's nose. The
disdain with which he looked at the empty chair at the table,
which the Khederians were saving for Ethan's dad, made it
clear what he thought of seating incomplete parties. "Can I
start you off with something to drink while you're waiting?"

Mr. Khederian, Nik, Alek, and even Ethan turned to Alek's
mom expectantly. "Just water for me, please," Mrs. Khederian
said, the first step in an elaborate dance that everyone at her
table knew well.

"Flat or bubbly?" the waiter asked, inadvertently playing
along.

"What bottled waters do you have?" she asked on cue.

"Actually, we stopped ordering bottled waters years ago."
Beckett's tone hovered between bored and droll. "Plastic bottles

are full of polyvinyl chlorides and bisphenol A—entirely defeats the purpose."

"That's why I only order glass." Mrs. Khederian gently adjusted the folded napkin on her lap.

"Glass is even worse!" Beckett spoke with the superiority of the environmentally conscious. "Do you know how much fossil fuel is burned to transport those heavy bottles? It's like a giant stomping around a forest, leaving carbon footprints everywhere! That's why Green Hill triple-filters our own water. We use a state-of-the-art Natura system that removes all the metallic impurities, like lead and zinc, as well as the chemical impurities, like chlorine. All of the water here, even what we use in cooking, goes through the same process." Beckett sat down across from Alek, in the red upholstered seat being saved for Ethan's dad, and crossed his legs, oblivious that it might not be appropriate to leisurely lounge with the party he was serving. "So, flat or bubbly?"

"We'll take one of each," Alek's dad answered, putting his hand around his wife's shoulders to make sure she was okay. Mrs. Khederian just looked away, like a true believer recently discovering her god was false.

Beckett nodded, uncrossed his legs, rose, and slowly drifted back to the kitchen.

The dining room at Green Hill smelled exactly the way Alek had imagined when he chose it as the location for his birthday meal: sophisticated, earthy, fragrant, and exotic, the odors wafting from the open kitchen in the back of the restaurant.

Nik wore the scowl that had been permanently imprinted on his face ever since Alek's essay had beaten his. And the fact that the Khederians had celebrated Nik's birthday a few months ago at their grandmother's house didn't help, Alek surmised.

Alek's hand nestled into Ethan's under the restaurant table, always the perfect fit.

"This is as good a time as any for gifts, right?" Mrs. Khederian smiled, reaching into her purse and removing a small, wrapped box the size of a candy bar.

"We know we said you'd have to be sixteen to get one, but we've been so proud of you in school this semester, we decided to get you . . ." Mr. Khederian trailed off.

Alek attacked the box as if unearthing its contents was a life-or-death scenario. He didn't dare dream. He didn't dare wish. But could his parents have finally relented and gotten him . . .

". . . a cell phone!"

"Oh my God, you guys are the best!" Alek exclaimed. He yanked the box open. It didn't have to be the latest iPhone or Galaxy or even LG. He just wanted to join the ranks of everyone else his age. And now he'd finally be able to do it. His hand reached into the box and pulled out his brand-new . . .

"Is that . . ." Wonder and curiosity inflected Ethan's voice. "Is that a flip phone?"

Nik chortled.

"Wow!" Alek did his best to muster enthusiasm. "Gosh, I didn't even know they made these anymore."

"We had to search extra hard to find it!" his father said proudly.

"We didn't want you distracted by Internet access or apps. I'm sure you've read all the articles I sent you about how cell phones are destroying attention spans. And you know that ligament reconstruction and tendon interposition surgery for thumbs has increased by over four hundred percent in the last decade, right?" Alek's mother tentatively took a sip of the water that had just been poured.

"Thanks, guys." Alek flipped his phone open, wondering if the artifact was even capable of getting a signal. It was so perfectly like his parents to get him exactly what he wanted and yet still miss the point entirely.

"And we've got one more gift for you, Alek," his father said.

"We've thought about this long and hard, and . . ."

His mother paused dramatically as Alek steeled himself. The entirety of the car ride into the city that Saturday to celebrate his birthday had been full of the kind of signs that had taught him to be suspicious: He'd caught his parents making nervous eye contact on multiple occasions without saying anything. His mother hadn't complained about the traffic, the pollution, or even the noise.

The chatter of the sophisticated New Yorkers dining nearby swelled for a moment. When his mother didn't continue after it dipped back down, Alek prompted her. "Yes?"

But she couldn't finish the sentiment, so his father stepped in. "We've decided that now that you are fifteen, you can go into the city without adult supervision."

Alek waited for his parents to tell him they were just kidding. He didn't even dare to make eye contact with Ethan, who was trembling with excitement. And before he let himself hope, he asked his father to repeat what he'd just said, to make sure he'd heard the actual words uttered and not his fantasy of them.

"With a few caveats, of course." Alek's mother jumped in just after his dad had confirmed Alek's wildest dream. "You'll have to come home before sunset and call us every hour to make sure you're okay. And we'll need to approve your itinerary a week in advance . . ." She continued to recite rules and regulations more arcane than the US electoral system. Alek nodded through them all.

"So, like, if Alek and I wanted to go into the city next Saturday," Ethan mused when Mrs. Khederian finished speaking, "to celebrate our six-month, we could?" Ethan's hand squeezed Alek's hopefully.

Mrs. Khederian closed her eyes, as if the horror of actually having to implement the gift was too much. "Yes," she whispered.

"Rockin'." Ethan beamed.

"This totally sucks." Nik glowered. "You only let me go into the city without you after I turned *seventeen.*"

"But, Nik, you are forgetting all the other liberties we permit you," his father chimed in. "Like allowing you to join the National Honor Society and the debate team, even though we were worried that those extracurricular activities would interfere with your schoolwork."

"Whatever." Nik slouched in his chair even farther. "You guys are totally heterophobic."

Alek, a dumb smile plastered to his face, was too happy to even gloat in Nik's general direction. It was inconceivable that anything would stop this from being the best birthday to date.

Until Ethan's dad walked into the restaurant a moment later. "Hey, everyone, sorry I'm late. I was just catching up with a former student." He stepped aside and revealed the tall, strapping young man whom Alek immediately recognized as Ethan's ex, Remi. Alek had first seen a picture of Remi almost six months ago, and neither that one nor the ones he'd seen since conveyed how movie-star handsome the young Australian was.

"Hope you guys don't mind I popped by." Remi stood by the head of the table, smiling sheepishly. "When Rupert told me where he was going, I insisted on walking him over so that I could wish you a happy birthday."

"You don't mind, do you?" The cluelessness surrounding Mr. Novick like a cumulonimbus cloud dispersed for a moment, and Alek saw him consider the potential bad taste in showing up to your son's boyfriend's birthday party with your son's ex. But it reformed a moment later.

"What up, Remi?" Ethan seemed as unaffected as always, as if running into the ex who ghosted you over a year ago happened every day.

"How's it going, Eth?"

Alek knew Remi was not going to stay. His parents had also taught him to be a good host, and especially since there wasn't room for an extra chair and moving to a larger table wasn't an option in the packed Manhattan dining room, he didn't think he was actually risking anything when he stood up, shook Remi's hand, and said, "Pleased to meet you, Remi. Would you care to join us?"

"Thanks, mate." And just like that, Ethan's ex crashed Alek's birthday party.

"Here, you can take my chair." Nik stood before Remi even had a chance to respond, stumbling over himself like he was trying to impress a girl he was crushing on. It would take Nik five minutes to hail a waiter, convince him to find another chair, and figure out how to fit it around the table. The whole time, Remi appeared unimpressed by Nik's sacrifice, as if he were doing Nik the favor.

"So you were hanging out with Ethan's dad?" Alek asked, wondering what horrible karmic thing he had done to deserve this, especially on his birthday.

"Rupert took me in when I lost my scholarship," Remi said between mouthfuls of sprouted bread dunked in organic olive oil. "Now that I'm back, I looked him up so that I could thank him properly."

Ethan smiled blankly, opaque and indecipherable.

"So tell us about yourself." Mrs. Khederian looked over her menu, which she was mentally dissecting, the way a macabre scientist might a frog, in preparation for round two with the waiter.

"I'm not from around here, in case you couldn't tell." Remi leaned into his vowel sounds, elongating his vowels to emphasize his Australian accent, as he launched into the story of his life.

Alek watched in horror as everyone else at the table fell under the spell of the tan young man with perfect rows of ivory teeth and blond ringlets cherubically framing his head.

Like an accent makes you interesting, Alek thought to himself. *Like, all I'd have to do is move to another country and then—wow—I'd be incredibly interesting, too.*

"Then we moved to Brisbane, but I was only there for a few

76

years, because I graduated from high school in three years and then came to the States to go to uni. But after the first year, things took a turn in Oz, so I went back to help my mum out."

"Is she okay now?" Mr. Khederian poured Remi a glass of sparkling water from the decanter on the table.

"Thank God, yes. She had a real scare, but she pulled through." Remi took a sip of the purified water before continuing. "I just got back to the States a few weeks ago. If I pick up an extra class every semester and do a few summer courses, I'll be able to graduate on sched."

Alek knew there were details that Remi was omitting: that while living with the Novicks in South Windsor, Remi and Ethan had started dating. But it wasn't Alek's story to tell.

Remi stood up and removed the three-button jacket he was wearing over the tight T-shirt that clung to his broad shoulders like a jealous lover. "By the way, happy birthday!" He reached behind Ethan's chair and punched Alek playfully. "Sorry I didn't bring you anything. But I promise I will next year, okay?" He swung his jacket onto the back of the chair and sat back down, propping one arm on the table. His bicep bulged obligingly.

Alek had never been this close to someone who looked like he'd walked out of the pages of a magazine, like one of the images from Ethan's room had stepped out of the glossy photograph and assumed three dimensions. In spite of the season, Remi was tanned bronze, and the maroon T-shirt accentuated the V-shaped torso that every guy aspired to. He looked airbrushed, down to the sculpted eyebrows and perfectly groomed stubble. Remi looked too perfect, Alek decided. Like if anyone actually touched him, he'd dissolve into a pool of red, blue, and green computer pixels.

"You guys are so cool to take your son and his boyfriend out to a posh New York meal." Remi turned his eyes, like spotlights, on Alek. "I hope you know how lucky you are to have folks like these."

Alek almost gagged while his parents basked in the compliment.

"Your parents, are they not . . . as open-minded?" Mrs. Khederian gently put her hand on Remi's.

"That's one way of putting it. My dad's basically the most close-minded guy Down Under. Why do you think I went to uni on the other side of the world?"

Mr. and Mrs. Khederian shared a look, half sympathy, half self-satisfaction for being the kind of modern, liberal parents who accepted their gay son without question. As long as he kept up his GPA, of course.

"Sorry that took so long." Nik finally returned carrying a folding chair far shabbier than the red-velvet chairs that populated the rest of the dining room. "This was all they had."

Alek waited for Remi to offer to take the flimsy chair. But he didn't. And Nik's joy at his own sacrifice was all the proof Alek needed that this man crush was blossoming at a dangerous speed and intensity. At this rate, Alek was pretty sure Nik was going to ask Remi to "watch the game" or "play some pickup" or any of those other things that straight guys did when they wanted to initiate a bromance.

"Are you sure you don't mind if I stay?" Remi asked Alek's

parents, who almost fell over themselves assuring him that his presence was welcome. And if that wasn't bad enough, what happened when the waiter arrived a few moments later disturbed Alek even more.

"Can you recommend a full red with body, but not too sweet?" Remi picked up the wine list, which had previously been lying ignored on the table.

Alek expected the waiter to laugh, or at least have the decency to card Remi, who couldn't possibly be twenty-one.

"I like the Oregon cab." The waiter opened the leather-bound binder and pointed to a selection. "The cab franc is also great."

Remi looked at Alek's parents in the perfect act of a deferential young man.

"Whichever you like," Mr. Khederian responded offhandedly, as though he and his wife didn't have a policy of not drinking in front of their children and of not providing alcohol for minors. As if this was a totally natural occurrence. AS IF IT WASN'T ILLEGAL FOR REMI TO BE DRINKING.

Remi's presence, like the music of Orpheus, apparently soothed even the wildest beasts, as the Khederians didn't complain about a single thing for the rest of the meal. Alek's mom didn't send her pork tenderloin back. Not even once. And Alek's dad didn't tell the waiter which items he thought should be on the menu, the way he usually did. Nik didn't even try to eat food off Alek's plate.

But Alek would've happily upset the karmic universe and sacrificed the waiter's happiness if it meant removing Remi from his birthday dinner. It just didn't seem fair that the event that was supposed to celebrate Alek had become all about his boyfriend's ex.

"Remember that chew and screw we did at Westville?" Remi asked Ethan between bites of rack of lamb.

"Totes." Ethan laughed.

"What's a 'chew and screw'?" Alek hated having to ask but hated being excluded even more.

Remi pitched his voice down so that it would be inaudible to Alek's parents, who were currently engaged in a heated debate with Ethan's father about why Republicans repeatedly voted against their own interests. "You know: dine and dash, eat and run."

"People actually do that?" Alek asked. "Isn't that a violation of, like, the most fundamental Lockean principles?"

"I didn't realize you'd landed yourself such a smarty, Eth." Remi wiped his mouth with his napkin. "Bet he's a good influence on you." He winked. "Unlike me."

While the words were ostensibly complimentary, Alek somehow felt insulted nonetheless. Alek put his hand on Ethan's, intertwining their fingers on the table.

One of his favorite things about being with Ethan was that they held hands everywhere and anywhere—in suburban malls, New York City subways, at family or school functions. He knew there were places in the country, and certainly the world, where it was still dangerous to be gay, let alone show it publicly. And although they'd certainly gotten their share of obnoxious looks and even comments, Alek treasured living in a place where he didn't have to pretend to be someone else and having a boyfriend who was never scared to show the world who he was.

But for the first time, Ethan's hand recoiled from Alek's. And not just a few inches away. Under the table. Out of view. Alek felt its absence even more acutely than he would've its presence.

By the time that Beckett, the bushy-mustached waiter, came to ask about dessert, Alek didn't even have to feign queasiness to bring the meal to an end. "I think we'll just get the check," he responded, more curtly than he meant to. "I don't feel so great."

"Is it something from the restaurant?" Alek's mom asked conspiratorially, begging for the evidence she needed to prove her theories that no restaurant could be trusted under any circumstances.

"I think I just wanna get home, okay?" Alek replied miserably.

"That's too bad." Remi T-shirt lifted as he slipped his jacket back on, his ripped abs revealing themselves for a blinding moment. "I was going to invite you guys out to this kickin' party in Greenpoint."

"Really?" The curiosity dripped off Ethan's voice.

"Yeah—it's off the G, so you know it's legit. House party called Church. Heard about it from some great peeps I met at Metropolitan a few nights ago. You know what . . ." Alek could see the wheels turning, and he didn't like the direction they were going. "You wanna come solo, E?"

Ethan deliberated for a single torturous moment before making the only acceptable decision. "Thanks, man, I'm good."

Alek knew that Ethan would leave the restaurant right now and never mention Remi or the party in Greenpoint again. But he really didn't see the point of making Ethan suffer pointlessly. Besides, Alek was so tired of disappointing Ethan that being able to give him what he wanted for once was its own reward. "You should go," he said.

"Really?" Ethan asked, hope blossoming in his puppy eyes.

Alek nodded with what he hoped was a modicum of cool.

"You. Are. The. Best. B. F. Ever!" Ethan exclaimed, slipping on his waist-length, puffy, neon-blue down coat. "Feel better, okay? And happy birthday!"

"I'll leave the keys with the doorman," Ethan's dad called over his shoulder as he put on his very professorial jacket with elbow patches.

"Roger that."

"You're letting Ethan go out by himself this late? In the city?" Mrs. Khederian tried her best to make it sound like she wasn't judging Ethan's dad's parenting.

But Ethan's dad, protected by his perpetual cluelessness, didn't even notice. "Of course. He'll be seventeen soon. He can just take an early train in tomorrow."

The Khederians exchanged the kind of judgy look that Armenians had mastered, that somehow attributed the ills of all the world to New World parenting.

Nik looked on enviously, like a prisoner watching his cell mate go free. "You have no idea how lucky you are," he whispered to Ethan. "Even when I'm in college, I'm going to have to ask for permission to stay out past ten."

"Feel better." Remi popped a mint from the maître d's desk into his mouth. "And happy birthday, Alex."

"It's Alek," he corrected his boyfriend's ex. "Alek. With a *k*."

Remi smiled. "Isn't that what I said?"

8

ALEK SUFFERED THROUGH CHURCH THE NEXT DAY, waiting a few respectable hours before calling Ethan on his new cell phone. He left a second message that evening, hoping it didn't sound half as pathetic to Ethan as it did to himself. He snuck glimpses at his cell phone during all of his morning periods the next day, the final Monday before winter break, but the only thing that changed on the analog device's display was the time, mocking him with its apathy. He burst into the cafeteria, searching for Ethan so that he could interrogate him about everything that had happened after they'd parted two nights ago. Even if Ethan hadn't gone to some cool hipster NYC party, Alek was sure that Ethan's night had been better than his, which consisted of listening to his parents giddily extolling the virtues of Remi like he was a god who had taken the form of a human mortal and deigned to visit them.

"What excellent manners—you can tell he's been brought up right!"

"And did you see how kind he was to the waiter?"

"So few young people these days really understand the art of conversation."

But Ethan was nowhere to be seen during lunch. "Been MIA all day," Dustin informed Alek. He called Ethan on his new old-fashioned cell phone, again, to make sure he was all right, but the phone went straight to voice mail. Again. He texted him, investing a full minute on the barbaric contraption that he'd received for his birthday to write *U OK?* Alek spent lunch with Becky, the two of them crammed at the end of the skaters' table, catching her up on his birthday the night before.

"I hope everything's okay," Alek told Becky as they walked down the locker-lined halls of South Windsor High to Health class. "With Ethan, I mean."

"Of course it's okay." Becky popped a bubble with the gum she was chewing. "I mean, what could possibly go wrong with Ethan hanging out with his ex unchaperoned at some super-cool house party in a hipster neighborhood in Brooklyn?"

A pit of dread formed in Alek's stomach. "I am going to revoke your best friend license."

"Oh, chill out, dude," Becky said. They filed into the class-room, sitting next to each other in the second row, close to the door and opposite the windows.

"I hope you do egg-cellent in your final assignment this marking period." Mrs. Sturgeon giggled at her own joke, adjusting the cat's-eye glasses she always wore. They had a long chain that looped down to her shoulders. "But as we've been learning all month, being a parent is an enormous responsibility, which is what you'll learn in this egg-cercise!"

Mrs. Sturgeon called out each student's name, who then went up to her desk and received a hard-boiled egg that Mrs. Sturgeon had specially marked. After she handed out the last one, she detailed the parameters of the assignment, explaining how the egg had to be carried at all times, just as if it were a real baby. "If you return your child to me after break in the same condition that you are receiving him, her, or them, you will receive an A. A few cracks: B. Missing shell: C." Mrs. Sturgeon slipped off her glasses, getting serious. "And if you lose your child, you will fail. Please don't lose your child."

Alek had spent the previous night painstakingly gluing cotton balls to the sides of a tin tea box that he had deemed just the right size. He spent the rest of class drawing eyes, a nose, a small mouth, and an impressive curved mustache on his egg. "Becky, meet Señor Huevo."

"*Hola*, Señor Huevo." Becky had stuck her egg unceremoniously in a cardboard box.

Alek finally heard from Ethan right after school, when he got a text message back. It said Ethan had woken up feeling sick and that his dad had let him stay in the city with Lesley until he was better. Alek called him twice that night, getting his voice mail both times. He woke up the next morning to a text from Ethan saying that he was back in South Windsor but still not well enough for school. They spoke for a few minutes that Tuesday night, just long enough for Alek to hear about the details of Lesley's beautiful apartment and the stomach flu that descended on Ethan out of the blue. But before he could get the details about Remi and the party, Ethan excused himself to get back to sleep.

When Ethan returned to school on Wednesday, Alek finally had the opportunity to question him properly during lunch.

But Ethan was even less responsive than the mystery meat loaf being served that day. "The party was okay."

"And what about Remi?"

"You know—Remi's still Remi."

"What does that mean?" Alek pressed.

"It means all he thinks about is himself. Just like he always did."

Ethan's curt tone made it clear that he didn't want to talk about it more. And Alek didn't make him.

"You know what I can't wait for?" Ethan changed the subject.

Alek shook his head.

Ethan flashed two Intrepid museum tickets with passes to the Starship *Enterprise* Simulation. "This weekend!"

"You got them!"

"Natch!"

"Our first authorized trip into the city!" Alek beamed. "And guess who I'll be bringing with us?"

"Someone's going to crash our date?"

Alek opened his tin tea box and revealed the hard-boiled egg inside, cushioned with cotton balls on all sides. "Meet Señor Huevo!"

"I just chucked mine in my locker the day Mrs. Sturgeon gave us the assignment and brought it out the day it was due." Ethan picked up Señor Huevo and inspected the facial features and twirly mustache Alek had Sharpied on. "*Hola*, Señor Huevo."

"*Hola*, Señor Novick," Alek offered in his best approximation of a Spanish accent.

Thursday and Friday, obstacles to his first authorized unchaperoned trip to NYC and the beginning of winter break, could barely pass quickly enough.

Wind whipped through the train station on the surprisingly sunny Saturday, the first day of winter break and, more importantly, Alek and Ethan's six-month anniversary.

"Hey, Mr. and Mrs. Khederian!" Ethan strutted up to the Khederians, zipping up his electric blue puffy jacket. Alek didn't know a single other person who could make that jacket work with thick corduroys the color of radioactive oranges, but somehow, Ethan did. A faux-fur trapper hat with the flaps pinned up sat on his head, completing the ensemble. "Hello, six-month boyfriend." Ethan enveloped Alek in a glorious hug and kissed him solidly on his lips, as if Alek's parents weren't standing two feet away from them.

The entire car ride after Saturday school, Alek had waited for his parents to rescind his new freedom. He had spent the class imagining them, upstairs, agonizing to the other waiting parents over coffee and Armenian breakfast pastries. Now, waiting with Ethan on the platform for the train, he still didn't truly believe that they were going to let him journey into the city without them.

"Call us the moment you arrive!" His mother had spotted

the train in the distance. "Boghos, maybe we should go into New York today as well. Nik can drive himself home, and I've never been to the Intrepid, and . . ."

"Kadarine, you hate being on ships, remember?" Her husband gently put his hand on her shoulder. "It'll be fine, okay?"

Alek's mom nodded, then turned back to Alek. "Don't talk to strangers!" she continued desperately.

"But what if they offer me candy?" Alek couldn't resist asking.

"With high-fructose corn syrup? That stuff is poison!" his mother responded quickly over the sound of the train as it pulled into the station. She pulled him into a tight embrace. "I love you, honey. Don't forget I love you."

"Jesus, Mom, it's not like I'm going to war. You'll see me in a few hours. I'll be home by six. Just like I promised." He unwrapped himself from his mother's embrace and followed Ethan through the train's open doors. Alek prayed to the gods that this train wouldn't stall in the station, allowing his parents precious seconds to change their minds. Luckily, the doors beep-beeped closed shortly after Ethan and Alek stepped on board.

South Windsor faded in the distance, like a memory, as the train whisked them to New York.

They quickly found a pair of empty seats on the top level.

Alek opened his leather backpack and showed Ethan everything he'd brought along for the trip. "This is not just our six-month anniversary—it's also Señor Huevo's first trip into the Big Apple!"

Ethan popped the lid to the tea box open and addressed the

egg. "Now, Señor Huevo, I want you to look both ways before crossing the street and stay close to us at all times, okay?"

Alek opened the backpack and slid Señor Huevo's tea box into the interior pocket.

Ethan peered inside. "You brought bicycle helmets?" Ethan unzipped and took off his blue puffy jacket.

"Yup. We're Citi Biking it today." Alek tossed Ethan the helmet he'd "borrowed" from his brother's closet.

"But it's the middle of winter!"

"Yes, Ethan, it's the middle of winter. But it's sunny, and I've been wanting to Citi Bike around the city with my boyfriend, so that's what we're going to do."

"Anything you want." Ethan pulled Alek into a train-seat embrace. "I want you to have the best six-month anniversary ever."

"Don't you think it's funny that we use that day in the cafeteria as our start date?" Alek turned over, leaning back into Ethan's wiry frame.

"No, I do not," Ethan responded.

"I mean, we could use the first time we went into the city, or the first time we kissed." The train slowly accelerated, the images of highways and houses blurring faster and faster in the windows across the aisle.

"But that time in the cafeteria was the first time we ever really spoke, and I saw what a cool guy you were. Of course that's the date we should be using."

The limping conductor slowly lumbered up the aisle. Ethan handed him his phone, displaying the tickets he'd insisted on purchasing for the both of them. The conductor examined the phone suspiciously, as if this was the first time he'd encountered the ticket-purchasing app that had been out for years. He absentmindedly ran his hand along his white, patchy beard, nodding curtly (and begrudgingly) before hole-punching and tearing two white seat checks that he slipped underneath the tabs in front of their seats.

"I've always wondered how these work." Alek made sure that the grumpy conductor had left their train car before removing his seat check to examine it. Both sides were identical, white with a grid of boxes, some containing multiple letters that were clearly abbreviations for cities, others with only single letters. The rest of the boxes were numbered from one to twenty-three. "I mean, how hard do you think it would be to get a bunch of these printed up and decipher the hole-punching/tearing system so we can ride the train gratis?"

"When did you become such a degenerate?" Ethan asked, feigning offense.

"I learned from the best," Alek shot back.

"My dad and I figured out some of the notations during all the trips we've made into the city together." Ethan removed his own seat check. "Like, a rip down the middle usually means a split fare. And if they don't do anything or give you a blank one, it usually means you're getting off quickly. But each conductor mixes it up to prevent miscreants like you from hacking the system."

"I didn't say I was going to do it. I just said that's how I would do it if I were going to."

"And why would you even consider such a thing?"

"As nice as it is to do a legit day in New York, I understand why people don't come in more. It's freakin' expensive!"

Ethan laughed. "I know, right? My dad is going to kill me when he sees his credit card bill."

"I mean—let's see." Alek started mentally tabulating. "If we didn't get the kid rate, the round-trip tickets alone would be sixty-four dollars."

"And the Intrepid was another fifty-six," Ethan added.

"Seriously?"

"Yeah, that's also the youth rate. And the simulator was extra. And ice-skating's another ninety bucks."

"We're going ice-skating?" Alek exclaimed.

"Damn, that was supposed to be a surprise." Ethan slid his trapper hat over his eyes and crumpled into the corner of the seat.

"I can still pretend I don't know if you want," Alek offered, snuggling into his boyfriend. Their hands found each other and their fingers familiarly folded intertwined.

"I would very much appreciate that." Ethan lifted his hat so that his eyes peeked out.

"Ice-skating! My God! How unexpected!" Alek rehearsed, hands on face in mock surprise.

Ethan shook his head. "Thank God you're not in Drama Club."

"It's a good thing that I can't pretend. That way, you'll always know I'm telling you the truth."

"So we've already spent, like, two hundred bucks!" Ethan exclaimed. "And that's before food."

Alek and Ethan sat on the top level of the double-decker, the white ripped-and-hole-punched seat checks inserted into the tabs in front of their chairs proof that they were lawful, ticket-carrying passengers.

"It's nice, isn't it, sitting in an actual seat?" Ethan had rolled his jacket into a makeshift pillow placed behind his head.

"I guess."

The white-gray train car with blue seats was a little less than a third full. A middle-aged man wearing a business suit spoke animatedly to his mother on his cell phone two rows behind. A small swarm of girls had taken over the front of the car, gossiping and texting and chewing bubble gum in tandem.

"You prefer the way we used to do it, illegally hiding in the bathroom with that very romantic smell of piss and shit?" Ethan asked.

"I prefer being close to you."

Ethan put his arm around Alek, and they snuggled into each other. "How's that?"

"Worth the price of admission." Alek wiggled out of his winter coat and wrapped his arm around Ethan's waist. He must've dozed off, because the next thing he remembered was the train pulling into Penn Station.

"This was an actual battleship?" Ethan stared up at the *Intrepid*, docked in the Hudson River at 46th Street, the skyline of New Jersey like a postcard in the background. The massive ship tapered into the most elegant of lines at its base.

"Yup. In World War II. Then it was decommissioned and

made into a museum." Alek walked up and took his spot in the line of people waiting for admission. "I remember the first time we drove by this, a few years ago—we'd come in to see a show, and on the way out we got lost and ended up driving north on the West Side Highway, and suddenly, I saw this battleship in the river! I just thought, 'Could New York be any cooler?' And now I finally get to go inside!"

"Without waiting in this line!" Ethan dragged Alek toward the front. "Since there's no need to join these brave souls facing the winter elements when you have purchased your tickets online."

"You are so lucky that you have a smartphone. Since, you know, my walkie-talkie is basically useless." Alek offered his flip phone as evidence.

"At least your folks got you a phone. Maybe when you turn sixteen, they'll even let you get a Facebook account!"

Alek groaned.

They journeyed up to the front, hand in hand, where a guard scanned Ethan's phone, then made the boys walk through a metal detector before letting them into the actual structure.

"I've been coming into New York for years now, you know." Ethan had forgotten to unloop a chain from his baggy jeans, accidentally setting off the metal detector. The guard made him walk through again. "And I think I know so much about it, but still, there are thousands—no, probably hundreds of thousands—of things I still don't. Like this one city is really a million cities laid on top of one another, and even if you spend your entire life here, you can only get to know a handful of them."

They walked past the small aircrafts housed inside the

hangar deck of the battleship, up to the flight deck. Next to the aircrafts, helicopters awaited the museum guests, lined up neatly on the port side. It was colder up here as the wind whipped off the Hudson, but it was warm enough in the sun.

"Aren't people the same way?" Alek looked south, at all the piers extending into the Hudson like piano keys. He made out two men, holding hands, sitting on a bench next to a dog park. "You meet someone, and you see one version of them, then you get to know them better, and you get to know more of them. And the person they really are is the compilation of all those identities, stacked on top and around and into one another, just like this city is really a million cities coexisting in the same space."

"But what if you decide, when you get to know all the versions, that you don't like the person as much as you did when you first met them?"

"Then I guess you break up."

Ethan looked away. "That's so dark."

"But it's true. I mean, I don't mean to be unsentimental, but the truth is, most people don't end up with their high school sweethearts, you know?" Alek leaned into Ethan as he spoke.

"That's so cold that you just made December feel warm, man." Ethan shuddered.

"But it's true, Ethan. Just like it's true that I can't imagine what would break us apart."

A mischievous flicker entered Ethan's eyes. "Me neither. But I can imagine what would turn our world upside down."

"Is it time?"

"It's time."

Hand in hand, they half walked, half ran down the stairs, back inside the ship, to the G-Force Encounter simulator.

They got inside the booth, listening to the instructions as they were being strapped in. "This is around a thousand percent better than any video game," Alek whispered. The simulation began, and soon, Alek and Ethan were rotating 360 degrees, holding on for what felt like dear life and screaming with joy and fear as they twisted and turned in every possible direction.

Ethan slipped on his bright yellow gloves. They had black tips on the thumbs and index fingers for smartphone usage.

"The ice-skating rink is at Rockefeller Plaza." Ethan punched his code into the Citi Bike dock. He adjusted a seat on the bicycle that had just been released for him. "We can take 46th Street over."

"We could, if we were tourists who wanted to stay in line for forever." Alek was already sitting on his Citi Bike, strapping his backpack into the front basket. "We might not be real New Yorkers yet. But we're not tourists coming in for the first time, either."

"Truth. It's like you know more about New York than I do these days."

"So we don't go ice-skating at the touristy places. We go ice-skating at the Sky Rink in Chelsea Piers, with the real New Yorkers."

Alek kicked off, riding his bike down the West Side Highway. Ethan followed.

* * *

Ankles throbbing from their time on the ice, Alek and Ethan hobbled out of Chelsea Piers.

"So now hot chocolate at the City Bakery." Alek referenced the itinerary his parents had insisted on. "A quick hop to the Picture Collection, then back home, right?"

"Sure . . ." Ethan trailed off.

"Sure, or what?"

"Or we can go to Lesley's apartment." Ethan's eyes twinkled as he jingled a set of keys.

"Seriously? I've never been in, like, an actual New York apartment before! Won't she mind us just dropping in on her?"

"She's out of town for the holidays. And my dad's back in South Windsor. And we've still got a few hours before you turn into a pumpkin. So . . ."

Alek let all the information settle. Although the idea of being alone with Ethan had filled him with anxiety since Thanksgiving, being inside an actual New York apartment won out.

"Lead the way!"

9

THE BUILDING WAS A PREWAR MONOLITH STANDING at the very bottom of Fifth Avenue, guarding the entrance to Washington Square Park like a sentinel.

"Pleasure to see you, Mr. Novick." The doorman nodded them up, as if Ethan actually lived there and wasn't just the son of the guy who was dating its actual owner.

The apartment itself was a four-bedroom with hardwood floors and arched doorways between rooms, wrapping around the top floor of the building, offering panoramic views of New York that made Alek understand why that function had been added to smartphone cameras.

These are the kind of views of New York most people will never see, Alek thought to himself as he scanned the skyline from the south to the east. In spite of the weather, and the cold, he had to force himself to leave the wraparound terrace and go back inside. "Ethan?"

"I'm in the guest room."

Snow fell slowly outside the apartment window, a flurry that felt like an afterthought, completing the perfect picturesqueness. This was the first time Alek and Ethan had been alone together inside an apartment in the city. This was the first time they'd been alone in two weeks. Alek sat next to Ethan on the bed in one of the guest rooms, so sparsely furnished it could've been the sleeping quarters of a devout religious order.

Ethan leaned over and gently kissed Alek.

The pattern, both predictable and awful, commenced. Things would start getting intimate, as they were right now. At first, it was bliss. Achingly rapturous, curious and fun. But then, when enough clothes had come off, Alek would anticipate the question. He could see it in the distance, like a billboard proclaiming doom far in the horizon, looming in the future, growing larger every second. And then he'd pull away, leaving them both unsatisfied.

Like now. On their six-month anniversary.

The demon of anxiety knock-knock-knocked until the bubble that usually protected them from the world finally burst.

"That's—I think that's . . ." Alek pulled away from Ethan abruptly. "I think that's enough."

"Okay." Ethan's voice betrayed no feeling as he rolled over onto his back.

"Are you angry?"

Ethan didn't respond.

Alek tried again. "I said, are you angry?"

"Of course not."

Ethan jumped off the full-size bed. With snow still falling slowly outside, the only thing that would make the apartment look more like idyllic would be a fire roaring in the marble fireplace.

"You sound angry for someone who says they're not angry."

"Alek, seriously, it ain't no thing."

"But it *is* a thing. It is!"

"Only because you're making it one!" Ethan snapped.

"I told you you were angry." Alek sat up, wrapping the sheet around himself.

"I'm only angry because you insisted I am!" Ethan grabbed his faded T-shirt from the floor and yanked it on. "Here's the sitch, Alek. This is a real damned-if-I-do-damned-if-I-don't. I want to do it. With you. My boyfriend. And I can't change how I feel or what I want." Ethan climbed back into bed. "And I want you. I always have. Every time I see you, whether you're freaking out over a grade or ice-skating or just doing your stupid homework, I want you. But you, my boyfriend, don't want me."

"It's not that. I just . . ." Alek shifted in his sheet. Why did being shirtless feel so natural when they were making out but so uncomfortable now?

Ethan spoke softly. "See! This is exactly what I mean. When I go hermit, you press. You push. You make me talk. But when I talk, you clam up, like there's some kind of big dark secret you're not telling me."

"I guess it's my fault, really." Alek stared at the flat paint of the bedroom wall.

"Why do you say that?"

"Let's see, you invite me to NYC and into this apartment on our six-month anniversary. I knew no one else would be here. I mean, what did I think was going to happen? Movies and popcorn?"

Ethan nudged his way a little closer to Alek on the bed. "That's really messed up. Can you imagine if you were a chick saying that? It's around one step away from 'I was asking for it.'"

"You know that's not what I mean."

"So what do you mean?"

"I don't know, Ethan. Back off, okay?" Alek shifted uncomfortably, trying to wrap himself up against the cold breeze cheating in through the ancient windows.

"What's going on, Alek? It's like every time we get here, you put up some wall and you lock me out, and that hurts more than anything."

"Okay." Alek looked away, at the paisley-green comforter cover, at the ceiling, anywhere but at Ethan. "There is one thing."

"I knew it!" Ethan exclaimed, smiling for the first time since they'd stopped kissing. He made a *swoosh* sound. "Two points for Novick!"

"But if I tell you."

". . . *when* you tell me . . ."

". . . *if* I tell you, you have to promise not to laugh."

Ethan assumed the most somber expression he could. "When someone says that, you know, it's impossible not to crack up."

"Do you want to know or not?"

"I do! I do! And I promise"—Ethan raised a few fingers in

his approximation of the Boy Scouts sign—"not to chuckle. Not to giggle. Not even to smile."

"All right." Alek cleared his throat. He swallowed. "The thing is I'm not sure—I don't exactly—know—what it is."

"What *what* is?" Ethan asked neutrally, guarding against any potential amusement.

"Okay . . ." Alek tried again. "I took Health class, so, like, I know what it is when a guy and a girl, you know, well . . ." His voice cracked, the awkwardness he was feeling wrapping itself around his vocal cords like a strangling vine. "But I'm not a hundred percent sure I know exactly what it is when . . ."

"When what . . . ?" Ethan encouraged him.

"When two guys, you know . . ."

"Uh-huh?"

"You know, when two guys actually . . ."

"Uh-huh . . ."

". . . do it." Alek said, too embarrassed to make any more words, hating his ignorance, hating how stupid it made him feel, hating everyone who knew and kept it from him, perpetuating the conspiracy, hating his parents especially for never having talked to him about it, and hating even more how awkward it would've been if they had tried.

"I know your folks are bringing you up old-world and whatnot but, I mean, you have Internet access, right?" Ethan asked, slowly, making sure not to do anything that could be vaguely construed or misconstrued as a laugh. "Why didn't you just Xtube this shit?"

"I tried," Alek confessed miserably. "But they put parental controls on all the computers in the house."

"And you couldn't get around them?"

"I don't know what to tell you. My parents can't format a résumé in Word or download a song on iTunes, but they have figured out how to make sure that neither of their sons ever downloads anything even vaguely salacious. And this useless piece of junk"—Alek held up his flip phone—"can't even access the Internet, let alone the adult sites."

"And what about the school library?"

"Those Internet controls are even stricter than my parents'!" Alek exclaimed. "And the screens are positioned so that everyone can see what you're surfing!"

Ethan didn't laugh. Not even a little. "No, I mean, couldn't you find a book?

"Oh, yeah, I can just see how that would go. 'Excuse me, Ms. Thompson, my name is Alek Khederian, and I'm a recently out student, but I only sort of think I know what it is when two guys engage in the act of intercourse. Is there a section that has tomes I might reference to illuminate myself? Ideally with highly detailed pictures? Maybe a flip book?'"

"Okay—that's not fair—now you're *trying* to make me laugh!" The corners of Ethan's mouth cheated up as he struggled to keep a straight face.

"I just don't understand how we're supposed to learn these things. I thought about ordering something online, but my dad opens everything the moment it arrives," Alek continued. "It's like we're expected to download information from the etheric wild straight into our brains. 'Happy birthday, here are the .zip files about sex. And don't forget to download the attachments about STDs and protection. And, of course, the embedded videos will answer any other questions you may have.'"

"Yeah, I know, it's all kinds of messed up." Ethan gathered Alek up in his arms and hugged him close.

"The truth is, I'm sure I could've found a computer in an Internet café without those restrictions and googled 'adult male homosexual intercourse'." Alek leaned into Ethan's embrace. "But both times the opportunity presented itself, I chickened out. I don't know why. Maybe because that's not really the way I wanted to learn what it was, you know? And it's not like I'm totally clueless. I mean—I have some theories."

"Which are?" Ethan asked.

"Why don't you tell me what it actually is, oh wise one," Alek negotiated. "And then I'll tell you how close I was."

Now it was Ethan's turn to shift uncomfortably. "It's hard to talk about it, you know?"

"I do know! I do know! But if you're not going to tell me, who the hell in the world will?"

"Okay, dude, okay. It's all good. Let me try it like this." Ethan cleared his throat. "Every guy has . . . let's call it a hot dog, okay?"

"A what?" Alek asked.

"A hot dog."

"A hot dog?"

"A hot dog. A *hot dog*. Every guy has a hot dog!" Ethan repeated until Alek understood.

"Oh. Oh!" The blush rose into Alek's face as the metaphor dawned on him. "Can we call it something else? My parents don't approve of hot dogs. Too much processed meat."

Ethan shook his head. "It doesn't matter what we call it."

"So let's say kebab, okay? That's like an Armenian hot dog, but it uses real meat and actual spices."

"Okay. Kebab. Every guy has a kebab," Ethan continued. "Some guys even name theirs."

Alek's head jutted forward as he did his best to keep his eyes from jumping out of his head. "Some guys *name* their kebabs?"

"Sure," Ethan replied nonchalantly. "A bunch of my buddies did. 'Smacker's not getting any play this week 'cause Justine's not talking to me anymore.' Or 'Baloney Pony's been out riding all night.' Or 'Thomas the Tank Engine likes to go choo-choo but . . .'"

"I don't think I'll ever be able to forgive your so-called friends for how traumatized I will be every time I see a Thomas the Tank Engine from now on." Alek shuddered. "Can we please go on in the hope that I'll only need years and not decades of therapy after this conversation?"

"Hey, you're the one who asked. And you're the one who, let me add, is lucky enough to have an older boyfriend who actually knows this stuff."

"Okay, Mr. Kebab."

"You're Mr. Kebab. I'm Mr. Hot Dog."

"Whatever!"

"So every guy has a kebab, right?" Ethan searched for the right words. "And every guy has buns also, right?"

"Buns?" Alek asked.

"Come on! How much more obvious can we get? Buns! Like those jeans that we got at Housing Works before Thanksgiving.

You know, the really tight ones that you spent like ten minutes admiring how they made your *buns* look?"

"Relax, Ethan." Alek shifted, stretching out his legs. "That's what I thought you meant. I just wanted to make sure. Why don't we call that the pita?"

"Are you going to Armenianize every one of my euphemisms?"

"I'm the innocent virgin here, okay? Is it such a crime to use words that make me feel more comfortable?"

"Anything you want, innocent virgin." Ethan, to his credit, was able to deliver the last two words with something resembling sincerity. "How are your theories holding up so far?"

"They're in good shape, thank you for asking," Alek responded. "So every guy has a *kebab* and every guy has a *pita* . . ."

"And when, you know . . ." Ethan stalled.

"Yes . . . ?" Alek encouraged him.

". . . when two guys, well . . ."

"Uh-huh . . . ?"

"When they do it . . ."

"Yes?"

". . . one puts his *kebab* in the other's *pita*!"

Alek exhaled. "See—that's what I thought!"

"Great!" Ethan responded, equally relieved.

"So now tell me—what's the big deal? You just put your *kebab* on the other guy's *pita*—and that's sex?"

"Not on," Ethan corrected him. "In."

A puzzled silence descended as Alek tried to understand.

"You mean—like—vertically?" Alek used his fingers to illustrate.

"No no no. Not vertically," Ethan answered. "Horizontally." Alek tried, and failed, to imagine that. "I don't get it."

"In. All the way in." Ethan placed a hand on Alek's, making a loop with the index finger and thumb. He inserted the index finger of the other hand in and out of the circle, withdrawing and reinserting it a few times, to make sure he was being clear. "Over and over and over again."

"ARE YOU KIDDING ME?" Alek screamed.

"What is wrong with you?"

"Inside! Inside the hole where . . ."

"I don't see what you're freakin' out about. It's not so different than the straights, when a guy puts his kebab in a girl's—"

"I get it! I get it!" Alek cut him off. "Please, let's not add another item of food that I'll never be able to look at again, let alone eat, okay?"

"What's the big deal, Alek?" Ethan asked. "Sex is the most natural thing in the world."

"Sure, that's what they say, but . . ."

"But what . . . ?"

"I assumed that when people said sex was the most natural thing in the world, they were talking about a guy and a girl having sex. You know. Because that's how the human race procreates. So it has to be natural."

"But you think it's not when two guys do it? Or two girls, for that matter?"

"I don't know . . ."

"I *do* know." Ethan's eyes narrowed, the way they always did

106

when he got really serious. "Lots of people have sex all the time for different reasons. But what makes sex natural is not the possibility of pregnancy."

"Then what is it?"

A radiator in the corner of the room hissed to life, and Ethan adjusted the sheet covering him. "It's one of the few things that everybody can do. Like breathing or eating or shitting. And it's the purest expression of love between two people."

"Wow." Alek paused to take that in. "That's really beautiful, Ethan."

"It's true. That's the reason it's important to do it with someone you lo—" Ethan stumbled for a moment before continuing. "You know."

Alek did know. Alek had thought about using the L-word and almost had a few times with Ethan. But he had always backed away, the way Ethan did now.

"Is there anything . . ." Ethan changed the subject. ". . . I don't know—is there anything I can do to help you? To make you feel ready?"

Alek blushed.

"Come on, man," Ethan urged. "I'm not pressuring you. I'm asking you as a guy who knows more and wants to share his experience."

"Okay, well, if we're just chatting like two guys . . ."

"Exactly! Two normal guy buddies, just hanging out, shooting the shit . . ."

"Okay, bro . . ." Alek played along. "So what was your first time like?"

Ethan looked away. "I don't want to talk about Remi now."

107

"Oh, come on!" It was Alek's turn to be exasperated. "You just said that we're two bros hanging out. And since Remi's the only guy you've been with . . ."

Ethan tensed up for a moment, like he was going to say something, but then he didn't.

"He's the only guy you've been with, *right*? Or is there something else you want to tell me? Because this would be a good time."

Ethan barely paused before responding. "He's the only guy, Alek. I promise."

Alek exhaled. "All right, then I think hearing about your first time might help me. With mine. So . . ." Alek trailed off.

"Okay, so . . ." Ethan began begrudgingly. "We'd been together for like a month . . ."

"A month!" Alek exclaimed. "Just one month!"

"And how old were you?"

"Fifteen."

"Like me," Alek said miserably. "Why is this making me feel even worse?"

"We don't have to talk about it."

"No no no. Go on."

Ethan continued, slowly. "So we'd been together for like a month, and things were getting rather . . ."

". . . steamy?" Alek offered.

"Yes! Steamy! Exactly! And then he pulled out some condoms and lube . . ."

"What's the lube for?"

"It's for . . ." Ethan trailed off, looking for the right words. "You know how hot dogs taste better with ketchup?"

"Lube makes you taste better?" Alek asked, confused. "I thought you put the kebab in . . ."

"No no no—let's see, um . . . lube makes it easier to put the kebab into the pita," Ethan explained before resuming his story. "So Remi pulled out some condoms and lube, and, well . . . He didn't even know that it was my first time until I told him later. And that was that."

Alek looked at Ethan in disbelief. "That was that?"

"Yuppers." Ethan smiled in an unquestionable display of self-satisfaction.

"And did you know what sex was before you had it?"

"More than like you," Ethan said. "I had an idea about what went where. But that's about all I knew—if I'd had to take a test and write an essay about it, I'm pretty sure I would've failed, too. And then maybe I'd have to go to summer school, where maybe I'd meet the most handsome if oddly dressed Armenian boy who'd change my life."

Alek snuggled into Ethan, savoring the warmth of his body. Alek had spent so much time marveling at how much Ethan had changed his own life—helping him come out, improving his wardrobe, introducing him to New York City—that it hadn't occurred to him that he'd changed Ethan's as well.

"Sex is funny like that, isn't it?" Alek mused. "Nothing else lives in this weird nebulous world of knowing and not knowing. It's the opposite of school. Like, take the quadratic formula. You're in geometry, you learn that there's a way to discover the variable in a quadratic equation and the mystery is both introduced and solved in one day. But with sex it's like this thing that you know exists in the world, but it's clouded in your brain, sort of taking form but mostly obscured behind clouds. I wonder how many people don't even know what sex is before they have it."

"Plenty, I'm sure, because plenty of people don't have sexy older boyfriends like you do to help show them the path."

Alek pulled away from Ethan and started getting dressed. "Ethan, I would give anything to be like you."

"Wise beyond my years?"

"No—I just mean—to be able to make huge life-altering decisions in the spur of the moment. Not to torture myself by examining everything from every angle, obsessing about all the possible repercussions." Alek had to stop himself from punching something—anything—in frustration. "Doesn't it make you crazy, being with someone like me?"

Ethan laughed. "In some ways, sure. Like I'd love for you just to say what the hell, let's do it, and we'd be making the beast with two backs all winter."

A pit of misery formed in Alek's stomach.

"But at the same time, the thing that's made us work is that we're different, you know?" Ethan said just the right thing, the way he always did.

"You really believe that?" Alek asked hopefully.

"I'd never say it otherwise." Ethan scooted closer to Alek. "Can I ask you something?"

"Anything."

"All right, then—does knowing what sex is make you feel any readier to have it?"

"The thing is, I think it sounds . . ."

"Yes?"

". . . pretty gross," Alek admitted.

"That's because it is pretty gross! Sex is sticky and messy."

"It is?"

"Sure!" Ethan exclaimed.

"So what if I don't like it?"

"That's okay, too—there are lots of ways to get off."

"Okay, Ethan, I do have another question. About—you know—about it."

"Shoot."

Alek summoned his courage. "Does it hurt?"

Ethan gently laid his hand on Alek's. "If you don't take your time and do it right. Also, honestly, it depends which side you're on."

"What do you mean?

"Okay . . ." Ethan searched for the words. "Being the kebab is different than being the pita."

"And I guess most couples switch back and forth, right? To be fair?"

Ethan laughed. "Some do, I'm sure. But some figure out which one each likes and they do that."

"Which kind would we be?"

"You try both and see which one you like more. Remi said people usually have preferences. But for starters you can be the kebab. It's easier."

"Really?"

"Of course! All you have to do is thrust!" Ethan demonstrated, laughing.

"But some people prefer to be the pita to the kebab?"

"Sure. And some people prefer to be the kebab."

"And do some people like being the pita *and* the kebab?"

"They do," Ethan confirmed. "Just like some people like both guys and girls."

"And does it feel very different?"

"Like night and day. This is one of the reasons that gays are the most fabulous creatures in the universe."

"How do you mean?"

"In straight sex, the guy is the kebab and the girl is the pita, right? Each one of them only participates in half of the experience. But we can do both! We get to be both the yin and the yang. To be both sides of the coin!"

"The head and the tail, if you will?" Alek's eyes twinkled.

"Oh, I most certainly will," Ethan flirted back.

"Okay, so if it's gross and messy and often painful, what's the big deal about sex, anyway? Why for the history of the world have people risked pregnancy and disease and nations and God knows what else to have it?"

Ethan didn't say anything, but his mind was clearly working in the silence. Alek had come to love these pauses in their conversations, when Ethan searched for the right words, gears turning in his head. Alek knew they meant that whatever came next would be extraordinary.

"Something happens during sex," Ethan finally said. "An amazing thing."

"And what is that?" Alek demanded to know.

"A unity. Like that Armenian word you taught me last summer, right after we got together."

"Miasnut'yun."

"For a moment, you stop being two individuals and you're

112

so close, so connected—literally inside each other—that the boundary between you disappears and you're one cosmic creature. It's holy."

"Wow, Ethan." Alek swallowed, surprised by how dry his mouth had suddenly become. "Is that what it was like with Remi?"

"Come on, Alek, do we have to talk about him now?"

"It's just, he's the only point of reference. Unless . . ."

"There's no unless—I told you he's the only guy I've ever been with."

"So—was it like that with him every time?"

"No. Sometimes it was hot and heavy and sometimes it was fast and furious. And sometimes it was just okay. And sometimes it wasn't even okay. But when it was great—yeah, that's what it was like."

"What if it's not great with us?" Alek asked miserably. "What if I mess it up, or if it messes up our already-great relationship?"

"I guess that is within the realm of the possible. But relationships are like all living things—they need to evolve to survive. And if we try it and it's not great the first time, well . . ." Ethan smiled. "We'll just try and try again until we get it right."

Alek swallowed again. "You know—I show great persistence and discipline when I put my mind to something."

"And is this a cause you'd be willing to invest in?" Ethan asked hopefully.

"Wholeheartedly." Alek exhaled, not realizing he'd been holding in his breath.

"Whenever you're ready, of course, at your own pace, and without any pressure." Ethan gently ran his fingers through

Alek's hair. "Because really, who wants to be that dick boyfriend pressuring someone into having sex before they're ready? So I want you to know—I'm here. Whenever you want."

"I love you, Ethan." Alek had known, for a while, that he was going to say those words. He had rehearsed them, in his mind and out loud, wanting to make sure that he got them just right the first time. He'd pondered over which word to emphasize, how much to pause between them. But now, they just came flying out. "I love you."

"I wanted to say it first!" Ethan blurted. "I can't believe you beat me to it!"

"That's what you have to say? I tell you that I love you and that's your response?"

"It is, because we will always know that you had the balls to say it before me. And I hope that you don't hold it against me too much. Because I love you, too, Aleksander Khederian."

Alek hadn't expected to hear those words back any more than he'd known he was going to say them in the first place. And he certainly hadn't expected his heart to burst into a thousand tiny glittering pieces.

"I love you, too," Ethan repeated, gently stroking his hands through Alek's hair. It would be frizzy now, Alek knew. That's what having an Armenian 'fro meant. But for Ethan's touch, it was worth it.

"Let's do it!" Alek said.

"Do what?" Ethan asked.

"You know. Sex. Let's do sex!"

"Really?!"

"It's our six-month anniversary, I'm here with my boyfriend

who I love, who loves me, in New York City, which we both love. Snow is falling, we're alone, my parents have no idea where the hell I am, and if losing my virginity means I may break curfew, so be it! Is there ever going to be a more perfect time?"

"You don't have to ask me twice." Ethan jumped off the bed, stripping his clothes off as he went.

"What about condoms?" Alek asked.

"I'm on it." Ethan rifled through his bag and extracted a box that he tossed to Alek. "Now let me see what Lesley has in the way of lube."

Alek inspected the light-blue paper box of Trojans.

"We're in luck!" Ethan reentered the room with a bottle of K-Y Jelly.

Alek removed one of the condoms from the already-opened box. "How old are these? Mrs. Sturgeon said you should throw condoms away after a year to be safe."

Ethan smiled. "All good, man, I just got them."

"Really?" Alek examined the condom in his hand and then looked at the remaining one in the three-pack box. "When?"

"Just—" Ethan stumbled. "Just last week."

And then it all dawned on Alek, so clearly he couldn't believe he hadn't seen it before. "Oh my God. You cheated on me."

10

HE CHEATED.

Ethan cheated.

Ethan cheated on me.

There was no fight. There was only flight.

Even if he'd wanted to, Alek couldn't physically have made himself stay in the apartment. Ignoring Ethan's protests, he grabbed his jacket and ran, cursing the front door as he fumbled with its latches and locks. He finally got the damn thing open and burst into the hallway.

He knew better than to wait for the elevator: "In case of emergency" didn't just mean fire. He bolted to the stairwell, tripping over a neighbor's stroller.

He took two, sometimes three, steps at a time, terrified that he'd stumble and fall down the sharp-right turns of the descending stairs, but also wanting it to happen, wanting something painful enough that it would eclipse everything else. And wouldn't Ethan feel terrible if Alek hurt himself now?

He flew past the doormen, ignoring the question he couldn't make out, through the innocents in the lobby, extras in a scene they'd never understand.

Alek exploded out of the front doors of the apartment building, gasping for air, as if he'd barely survived a supervillain's trap. The snow still fluttered gently outside, the weather suggesting a rom-com that couldn't be further from what Alek was feeling. The vendor's honey-glazed nuts, the gusts of cold wind, the honking cars stuck in traffic—all the sensations of New York in winter bombarded him.

He ran blindly, wildly, through stalled traffic and throngs of well-dressed New Yorkers, across Fifth Avenue, into Washington Square Park, past tourists and pedestrians, like he was late for a train only he could see.

He tripped over something—he didn't know what—and fell to the ground, into a puddle of slush mixed with New York pollution. He got up, panting, heaving, feeling tears he didn't know were there freezing on his face. The cold air stung his lungs.

He felt a hand on his shoulder and even through his jacket and sweater and undershirt, through all the layers, he immediately knew it was Ethan's.

Alek smacked it off and turned with a ferocity that surprised them both. "Don't. Ever. Touch me. Again." His voice sounded feral, even to his own ears.

Ethan snatched his hand back, as if he'd been bitten by a snake. "Alek, please. Please let me explain."

During his visits to New York, with Ethan or with his parents, Alek had witnessed countless scenes far too private for public: A strung-out party girl licking her equally strung-out party boyfriend's forehead on the subway. A man, almost entirely naked, sleeping peacefully under scaffolding, snoring gently with each exhale. Two guys kissing and groping each other in a building doorway one night, oblivious to (or aroused by?) the free, six-second peep show provided for anybody walking by.

The way passersby around Alek picked up their pace just the slightest, making a point of simultaneously averting their eyes and trying to catch a glimpse of the drama unfolding before them, told him he was performing in one of those scenes now. And just like all the performers in the scenes he himself had witnessed, he didn't give a damn.

"Alek, please—" Ethan started again.

Alek shoved Ethan back, full force, then turned and ran, sloshing through the puddles of melting snow.

He had no sense of how long he'd wandered through the city, stumbling through blocks he didn't know, neighborhoods he'd never visited, places he'd never remember. His adrenaline crashed, but he continued walking, until it was dark, then cold, then colder, then really really freezing too-cold. When he felt what could only be frostbite claiming the tip of his nose, he staggered in to the nearest subway station.

Luckily, he had grabbed his jacket. Luckily, his wallet had been inside his jacket. Luckily, he'd been coming into New York for months now, on trips chaperoned by his parents or

Ethan's dad. His six o'clock curfew was a thing of the past, he knew, obliterated, like roadkill. And he knew he should call his parents. But it hadn't occurred to him to grab his cell phone as he fled Lesley's apartment. And although he might've been able to locate a pay phone (did pay phones even exist anymore?), when he imagined what he might say to them, no words conjured themselves. So he didn't.

Half of the people waiting for the subway at the Canal Street stop were dressed like Alek: as if it were any other winter day. But the other half were costumed as Santa Clauses, drinking openly in a way that made it clear they'd been doing so all night. Something about the sight of all those Santas—men and women of all ages, clearly inebriated past the point where they could pretend they weren't—so happy, so rowdy, so innocent, so clearly not having just learned that their boyfriend had cheated on them—pissed Alek off. And the more drunken holiday cheer they seemed to possess, the more they pissed him off.

Nothing could've made Alek more miserable. Or at least, that's what he thought until a knot of carolers, emerging from the platform below in a mess of green and red, launched into holiday classics in three-part harmony.

He filed onto the first subway train that arrived, shooting very un-Christian eyes of hate, first at the carolers who followed him on and then at the girl with purple hair who ran in just as the doors started closing, jamming her foot between them so that her slower friends could catch up. If looks could kill, Alek would've committed first-degree murder. Purple Hair and the Tardies cackled continuously between Canal and Penn

Station, giggling at jokes unclear to everyone on the train car, and maybe even themselves.

Penn Station, that architectural abomination, was packed with travelers arriving to and departing from New York City for the holidays. Alek looked for the big sign in the main waiting area only to discover it had been replaced by two large video monitors on either side of the room. Apparently, nothing could be counted on. He hovered under the monitor on the west side, impatiently waiting for the next train on the Northeast Corridor to reveal its gate number.

His eyes darted left and right, knowing that Ethan couldn't possibly be in that cavernous room but still on the lookout for him. A few times, he was sure he spotted a flip of hair or a puffy coat that belonged to his Ethan. But on closer examination, the hair revealed itself as not nearly blond enough, or the jacket not the right cut. Besides, Ethan wasn't his Ethan anymore.

"There you are!" A hand planted itself on Alek's shoulder familiarly.

Alek turned around quickly, flinging Ethan's hand off.

But it wasn't Ethan. It was a stranger who'd clearly mistaken Alek for someone else. A stranger who looked nothing like Ethan.

"Sorry, man." The pimply twentysomething didn't even sound like Ethan. "You look just like my man Mahmud."

Alek told his quickened heart to slow down. He turned away.

The gate number finally flipped into existence. Alek waded through the crowd, ducking and dodging and even using an occasional well-placed elbow to guarantee his progress and seat.

He didn't know how he was going to explain to his parents why he was so shockingly, wildly, inexcusably late. Nor could he especially find it in him to care.

He plopped himself in one of the two-seaters at the back of the car, one of the banks that didn't even have a window, to ensure he'd be as far away from everyone as possible. A few drunk Santas stumbled on just before the doors closed, surrounding Alek with their foul stench and syntax.

As Alek contemplated moving to another seat, the Santa from across the aisle leaned over and asked, "Do you know where the bathroom is?" His fake beard was askew, the stuffing from his belly poked out from all sides, and his breath reeked of cheap, stale beer. "I think I'm going to . . ."

The vomit didn't land on Alek's clothes, per se. But looking down, he knew he'd never wear these shoes again.

Alek's mother was at the front door before he could turn the key in the lock. "Oh, honey, thank God you're okay." She wrapped him in a bear hug that surprised Alek with its strength, dragging him into the house. "We were worried sick. Why didn't you call? Why didn't you pick up when we called?"

He wasn't sure if he was supposed to answer these questions or if they were just rhetorical, so Alek chose to believe the latter.

As his mother wrestled with her cell phone, Alek kicked off his vomit-stained shoes.

"Boghos, you can come home." Alek's mom's voice quivered on the phone, as if she might start crying. "He's home."

He knew he should answer his mother, say something,

apologize, explain. But he was just so tired. Tired of his life, his house, his parents. Tired of it all.

His mother put the phone away. "We called you, then Ethan, then his dad, then the police. I tried to get them to issue an AMBER alert, but they said I had to be able to prove that an abduction had occurred. I explained to the officer that you've never even been missing for two hours, and by the time I could prove that you had been abducted, countless horrible things could've happened to you, like drowning in the Hudson River or being kidnapped by a cult and subjected to brainwashing, but he wouldn't listen, so I asked to speak to his superior officer, and she said . . ."

Alek shed his jacket on the stairs as he climbed them to go to his bedroom.

"Where are you going? Honey?"

He closed his bedroom door behind him and climbed into bed, still wearing his clothes. Mercifully, sleep came quickly.

"Alek? Are you in there?" The sound of his father's voice jostled Alek out of unconsciousness. "You've got twenty minutes before we leave for church."

He cheated his eyes open, cursing the brightness of day. The robot clock on his nightstand told him it was almost eight. But then again, nothing, literally nothing, sounded worse than going to church.

He closed his eyes and went back to sleep.

* * *

"Alek? Honey? Everything all right?" The closed door was Alek's only salvation, the only thing protecting him from the rest of the world. And this time, his mom.

Robot clock: 12:57 p.m.

"It was a wonderful sermon; I think you would've loved it. All about faith and facing the future."

He closed his eyes again. He wasn't tired anymore. But he begged that sleep reclaim him. Like a friend who did what you wanted even if it wasn't necessarily good for you, sleep complied.

"We absolutely cannot condone this kind of behavior." The door, against all odds, remained closed, but his father's voice on the other side was clear.

"Let him rest," his mother responded. "Something must've happened."

If they only knew the half of it, Alek thought, floating between reality and the nightmares that pursued him.

His robot clock, a bar mitzvah party favor, came to life, marching around the perimeter of the room before launching into a fully orchestrated *"Hello, my baby, hello, my darling, hello, my ragtime gal,"* with top hat, cane, and choreography.

And then, blessed sleep, again.

Almost two hours later, Alek's body reached its physical limit of unconsciousness. He thought about taking a shower, but just the amount of exertion required seemed un-musterable. Plus, he ran the risk of having to see or be seen by one of his family members and the interrogation that would inevitably follow. Staying here, by contrast, under the cover of the warmth of his bed, felt infinitely more attractive. There was a reason they called it a comforter.

But, as he was finding out, you can't always get what you want.

"Alek, honey, Ethan's downstairs." Alek's mother was trying to sound conversational. But even with the door between them, Alek could hear the concern straining her voice like a guitar string stretched too tight, about to snap.

The robot clock gazed at Alek unflinchingly. Almost three p.m. Too late to pretend that he was still asleep. Too late for many things.

"Tell him to go away," Alek croaked, his voice rusty from disuse.

"What's that, honey?"

Alek pulled back his down comforter. He forced himself out of bed, throwing himself on the floor so that the impact would force him into consciousness. He unlocked the door and opened it the most minute crack.

"Tell him to go away."

Alek didn't know what he looked like, but judging from his mother's reaction, it wasn't good.

"Are you sure, honey? I said *Ethan's* downstairs."

"I heard you the first time. And I'd like you to tell him to go away. Is there something about that you don't understand?" Alek didn't wait for his mother to respond. He closed the door immediately, the satisfying *click* giving him a moment of solace. The sound of his mother's retreating footsteps provided another. Being able to witness the scene below, between her and Ethan, would've made a perfect three, but he'd have to settle for his imagination of his mother's awkwardness and Ethan's hurt.

He stood in his room for a moment, disoriented. It was certainly his room, his furniture, his robot clock, his Andre Agassi tennis poster, his desk, his bed, his closet, his bureau. But it all felt wrong, somehow, like during his sleep, everything had been rearranged in its mirror opposite.

Now that he was up, there was plenty for him to do: change out of yesterday's clothes. Shower. Eat. He must be hungry, mustn't he? But none of those options felt nearly as appealing as getting back into his bed and under that inviting down comforter, calling to him more seductively than Odysseus's sirens.

He was already safely ensconced back in the cocoon of cotton and down when he heard another *knock knock knock* on his door.

"Honey, Ethan brought your cell phone. And your egg." It was his mother again.

Alek had no response to that information, so he didn't say anything.

"Honey, did you hear me?"

Silence.

"Do you . . . do want to talk?"

Did he want to talk?

No, he didn't.

"No, Mom."

A long pause followed.

"Honey, would you open the door?"

Would he open the door?

He didn't think he would open the door.

"Okay. I'm going to leave your stuff outside your room. You know we're here if you need anything, okay? Or if you want to talk, or . . . anything."

Alek wanted to thank his mom. But he didn't have it in him. All he could do was stay in bed, under his comforter, away from the world of cheating liars.

11

ALEK'S LIFE HAD BEEN BUILT ON A SERIES OF assumptions, ranging from the microscopic to the cosmic: Dark chocolate is better than milk. Tennis is the best sport. Older brothers are a pain. Eating eliminates hunger. Gravity prevent objects from floating off the ground. Ethan will always be my boyfriend.

True, Ethan had only been Alek's boyfriend for the last six months, while gravity had been anchoring objects and dark chocolate trumping milk for all of eternity. But that didn't make it any less of a defining tenet of his understanding of how the universe functioned. And although he could remember the time before he met Ethan, also known as the first fourteen and a half years of his life, those sepia-toned memories dissolved in the technicolor of post-Ethan. Now, post-post-Ethan, there was nothing.

Intellectually, Alek understood that people rarely end up

marrying their high school sweethearts, as he and Ethan had talked about on the *Intrepid* (was it possible that was only two days ago?). His parents had both dated plenty before they met in grad school. Becky's mother had already been divorced when she met Becky's dad. And he hadn't considered himself naïve about the obstacles he and Ethan would face when Ethan graduated in May.

But still, in his heart, he couldn't imagine a force powerful enough to wrest them asunder. In his known universe, they had no kryptonite.

Until, of course, they did.

Alek spent the rest of that Sunday indulging in the act of ignoring: ignoring his mother's plaintive knocks on his door, his father's more assertive ones, the buzzing of his cell phone, the alerts from his computer every time a new e-mail arrived. Previously, Alek had loved the beginning of winter break: that nebulous period leading up to New Year's, when nothing was expected of you. From now on, though, he was sure he'd remember it as the time he'd have to come to terms with the shame and pain of having been cheated on.

With the exception of two trips to the bathroom and one journey downstairs that consisted of walking past his parents to the well-stocked fridge and realizing that not even homemade cheese kadaif did anything to whet his appetite, Alek spent the rest of his day not just in his room but in his bed, like an invalid.

That day was lost, as if he'd been in a trance, like one of those days spent buried in a book or video game. Except that this time, he had nothing to show for it: no hundreds of pages read, no leveling up, no weapons unlocked. And then, thankfully, it was night and dark and he could surrender himself to sleep again.

The next morning, the first Monday of break, he waited until all the activity in his house died before venturing out of his bedroom. His mother would be at work, he knew, but the whereabouts of his father and brother were unknown. Alek imagined they'd probably gone off to do something together—a celebration of the first weekday of winter break and the freedom it afforded. He might've felt jealousy or anger at being left behind. But he didn't. He didn't feel much. He just knew the house was now empty, except for him, and that's all that mattered.

He tried to eat, more out of the knowledge that sustenance was important than actual hunger, wondering why the usually delicious homemade hummus and dolma tasted so much like cardboard, before giving up. He brushed his teeth afterward, just like he was supposed to, although the idea of a shower still felt like a Herculean labor, impossible for a mere mortal like himself to accomplish.

He managed to put on his jacket and boots, but only by outwilling he had the evil wizard controlling his mind, making everyday tasks seem impossible. Something as complicated as walking to Becky's seemed out of the question, obviously.

But he could open the front door. And then he could take one step in the direction of Orchard Street. And then one more. And another. And another, through the snow-turned-slush, until he finally stood outside the orange house with the white trim.

Alek rang the doorbell to his best friend's house, more grateful than ever that he had a best friend. Especially one within walking distance.

"Where the hell have you been? I've been texting you and e-mailing you and PMing you nonstop! I was about to release the homing pigeons!" Becky was tugging on the leggings under her burgundy-and-gray-striped skirt. "Also, you look horrible. Have you become a drug addict in the seventy-two hours that have elapsed since last I saw you? Or maybe you look more like a zombie. Maybe a drug-addict zombie? Do zombies take drugs?"

"Happy holidays to you, too, Becky." Alek tried to smile.

"Don't just stand there—you're letting all the cold air in!" Becky yanked him inside and closed the door.

"Hello, Alek . . ."

". . . and happy holidays!"

Mr. and Mrs. Boyce sat snuggling on their Dutch sofa with no back. Artifacts from their world travels decorated the living room: the most recent addition was a kakemono, a Japanese scroll, which had been hung just next to the tansu.

"Happy holidays!" Alek recited. He tried to sound normal, but he could hear the tinniness in his own voice.

Mrs. Boyce got up to adjust the thermostat. "Are you enjoying . . ."

". . . your winter break so far?" her husband finished for her.

It was a simple enough question. But for reasons entirely unclear to him, Alek was incapable of answering. He just stood, frozen, dumbfounded by both the question and his inability to answer it.

Luckily, Becky came to his rescue. "We've only been on

break like three days, Mom. One, if you don't count the week-end. So I'm sure he's enjoying it fine." She tugged on Alek's arm. "Now hurry up—I don't have a lot of time, so can we skip the part where you talk to my parents because you were raised with good immigrant manners?" Becky practically yanked Alek down the hallway to the basement stairs. "And I have been dying to tell you all about the marching band party Mahira and John *made* me go to, which I only did because the only thing that I could imagine that would be lamer was spending Saturday night at home with my parents."

"We heard that . . ."

". . . you know," her mother called down to them.

But Becky was already closing the door behind them, covering their escape. When they were safely downstairs, shielded from Becky's parents, she switched to the topic of true interest. "I've been calling you nonstop. I was going to do a skate-by tonight if you didn't pick up. What the hell is going on?"

"Ethan cheated on me," Alek blurted.

"Oh my God. Is that why you Houdini'ed on him Satur-day night?"

"How do you know that?"

"Ethan called Dustin."

"He did what?"

"Ethan called *everyone*. He even called me. He was freak-ing out."

"Don't you hate that thing when someone does something horrible and then they use the excuse of being worried about you to cause even bigger drama?" Alek plopped down on Becky's basement sofa, trying to disappear in its folds.

"Are you sure he cheated?" Becky climbed on the sofa next to him. "Maybe it was just, like, a stupid, dumb, meaningless kiss."

"Nope." Alek put his legs on her lap, something he'd never dared under ordinary circumstances. "He went all the way."

"You're sure?"

"One hundred percent. Because he told me right before we were going to—you know."

Becky removed Alek's legs from her lap. "No. I do not know."

Alek was tired of pitas and kebabs euphemisms.

"What it?"

"You know. *It.*"

"Oh."

"Yeah."

Becky leaned forward, putting her weight on her knees so that she could get right in Alek's face. "Tell me everything. And if you leave out even a single detail, Alek Khederian, you will live to regret it."

The story poured out of Alek like paint out of a tipped can. He spoke as the events came to him, out of chronological order, nonsensically, painfully, embarrassedly. If she hadn't been his best friend, if she hadn't known how his brain worked and how to follow its most convoluted meanderings, she probably wouldn't have even been able to make sense of it.

When he finished, Becky wrapped him up in a hug warmer than the down comforter he'd been hiding under the last two days.

"I love you, you know?" she said.

"I love you, too, Becky."

"And besides, I think you're overlooking something very important here," she said slowly.

"Please don't tell me you're going to stick up for Ethan."

"No—I'm going to tell you that clearly this happened the way it was supposed to."

Alek put his hands on his head. "How can you say that?"

"Because if you had sex for the first time without telling me beforehand, without giving me every pro and con going on in your mind, without deliberating the details with the kind of minutiae traditionally reserved for close readings in AP English, I would've killed you. And then where would we be? You'd be dead, for one. And I'd have killed my best friend, which would be a terrible thing to have to tell people for the rest of my life. 'What ever happened to that Armenian guy?' 'Alek?' 'Yeah, him.' 'Oh, I killed him.' 'Bummer.' 'Totally.'"

And then the impossible happened. Alek smiled.

"If you killed me, my ghost would come and haunt you, for—like—ever. And I'd do it at the worst times, too, like when you and Dustin were making out or during your driver's license test. I would be, like, the most annoying ghost ever."

"I don't doubt it. Because you're just about the most annoying friend ever."

"You better get used to seeing the most annoying friend ever because now that I'm single, I'm going to be here basically 24/7."

"You're not single."

"Of course I am!" Alek said. "He cheated on me."

"I'm not disputing that. What I'm disputing is that you think you two have broken up."

"If I say we're broken up, then we're broken up!"

"That's not how it works, Alek. You have to say it *to him*."

"Don't you think that's what 'don't ever touch me again' means?"

Becky contemplated Alek's words as she removed an Honest Tea from the basement mini-fridge. "No. I think you need to say some variation of the words, 'We're breaking up' or 'We just broke up' or 'You cheated on me and I can never forgive you because you betrayed everything holy about the world' for an actual breakup to occur. Like, if I were Ethan right now, I wouldn't know that we were broken up. I could think that we were just in some horrible fight."

"This is different. We've survived a horrible fight—remember homecoming?" Alek asked.

"I still don't understand how you managed to lose all those alpacas."

"And I still don't understand how you don't understand what 'I don't ever want to talk about those alpacas again' means."

"Okay, but you still have to break up with him." Becky planted her hands on her hips.

"So that's what you think I should do?"

"I didn't say that."

"So you think I should forgive him?" Alek demanded.

"I didn't say that, either—I'm just saying, you don't actually know what happened. You didn't give him a chance to talk. Maybe there are some—I don't know—extenuating circumstances."

The boiler in Becky's basement rattled to life, like an animal emerging from hibernation.

"Cheating is wrong. Period. And nothing can make it less wrong. So what else do I need to know?"

"Come on, Alek. That's such a dumb way to look at it." Becky finished her Honest Tea, burped, and then tossed it in a recycling bin like a basketball player shooting a free throw. "Like, stealing is wrong, but if your family were starving, would stealing bread to feed them be wrong? I don't think so."

"Okay—can you think of a situation in which it would be okay to cheat?" Alek came over and picked out the pieces of grapefruit from the bag of Haribo Fruit Salad candy Becky had produced from a cushion in the sofa. It was the first thing he'd eaten in two days, and he savored the bitterness and sweetness of the grapefruit candy, made all the more delicious by the knowledge that his parents would never let him eat this kind of food at home. Nor would they even call it food.

Becky handed Alek the bag of candy and produced a second one. "Okay, maybe not, but that's not the point."

"What's the point, then?"

"The point is that you have to talk to Ethan."

For once, Alek said nothing. He just chewed on it.

12

ALEK PRAYED THAT HE'D BE ABLE TO AVOID HIS
parents until he figured out what he was going to do about
Ethan. But when he returned from Becky's, they were waiting
for him, like predators for their prey.

"Hey, guys." Alek dragged his feet into the kitchen, grateful, at least, that Nik wasn't around.

"Alek!" The relief fairly poured out of his mother's eyes when
she saw her younger son awake, walking and talking.

"We're ordering dinner." His father had been tight-lipped
ever since Alek had returned from New York.

Alek sat down. He knew this might take a while.

"Hello, can I speak to Mr. Lee?" After years of criticizing
"these Americans" for ordering in instead of cooking their own
food, Alek's mom had recently surrendered to the ritual. But
naturally, she had developed her own methodology.

The first part involved getting the proprietor of the establishment on the phone. "Hello, Mr. Lee!" Mrs. Khederian raised her voice when speaking to the owner of Hunan House, as if volume was necessary to compensate for her imagination of his limited comprehension of English. In reality, however, when the Boyces took Alek to the same restaurant, he'd witnessed Mr. Lee effortlessly engage numerous customers in extended conversations.

"I'd like to put in an order for dinner," Mrs. Khederian instructed. She laughed at Mr. Lee's response, then put her hand over the receiver to relay it. "He said, 'Why not try Jade House this time?' Isn't he such a kidder?" She removed her hand and continued speaking into the phone. "Yes, I'd like to start with the wonton soup, but could you go a little light on the salt in the broth? And would you mind making the wontons with chicken, not pork? I find the pork a little stringy." Mrs. Khederian laughed again at Mr. Lee's response.

If Alek were Mr. Lee, he would've instructed his employees to never pick up the phone when they saw the Khederians' number appear on the caller ID.

"Next, we'd like some egg rolls, but they should be made right after the oil in the deep fryer has been changed. And what kind of oil are you using today?" She paused for his response. "Yes, but you do know that avocado oil has an even higher burn point than canola's? And it's healthier for you, too. There's a Mexican brand I particularly adore—Avoro. Why don't I e-mail you the information on where to get it?" Another pause. "Of course I'd be happy to pay extra. Maybe I can reach out to some of your customers and see if they'd be willing to join me? But do please make sure that each of our dishes is cooked at the same time today, so that none of it shows up cold. That wouldn't make for a good Yelp review, would it?" Mrs. Khederian giggled at Mr. Lee's response. "What a charmer you are, Mr. Lee."

Alek marveled at his mother's ability to goad, instruct, threaten, and flirt all within the same conversation. And now that she had discovered the power of leaving reviews online for businesses whose service she had found disappointing, she was even more empowered. Alek swore he could spot his mother's handiwork on all of the local review sites that he trolled. He would've bet his college tuition fund that she had authored "Chicken Breast Drier Than Sahara Desert" and "Better to Starve Than Eat Here."

"Don't forget to tell him about the vegetables," Mr. Khederian piped in.

"Mr. Lee, my husband has reminded me to talk to you about the order in which the vegetables are sautéed in your chicken and mixed vegetables dish." Alek had asked one time if they could order that same dish with shrimp, and his mother had looked at him as if he'd sprouted a third eye. Seafood was always a dangerous gamble, even in the finest restaurants, she had told him, and in takeout, the risk was too great. "As I'm sure you know, vegetables have to be sautéed in inverse order of toughness, and we felt like the carrots had been added *after* the peppers, making the peppers a bit soggy and leaving the carrots too tough. And are you sure that all the vegetables are fresh? I hope you'll pardon me for saying so, but some of the broccoli crowns teetered on yellow last time. How do they look today?" Mrs. Khederian listened intently, as if the voice on the other line were divulging state secrets. "Would you mind taking a picture and sending it to me? Of course I'll wait."

Alek's mom put her hand over the receiver and confided to her audience. "Isn't technology amazing?"

"You know, there's a mute button, Mom." Alek put his head in his hands.

She searched her smartphone until she found and pressed said button. "What will they think of next?" She spoke back into the phone. "Now, would you mind telling me about what goes into the white sauce? Can you hear me, Mr. Lee? Mr. Lee?"

"You have to unmute it now," Alek said.

"And how do I do that?" she asked.

Alek took a deep breath. And then another one. "You just hit the same button you hit the first time. The one that now says 'unmute.'"

"Of course." In attempting this Daredevil feat of agility, however, Mrs. Khederian accidentally hung up on Mr. Lee.

If it were Alek on the other end of the line, there's no way he would've picked up when his mother called again. But Mr. Lee, it appeared, was a glutton for punishment.

"There you are, Mr. Lee! I think you accidentally hung up on me. Now I wanted to talk to you about the white sauce. Last time, it felt—what's the word . . ."

". . . gloopy?" Alek offered, hating himself for acting as his mother's accomplice.

"Yes, gloopy. It felt gloopy last time. Are you using flour or cornstarch as your thickening agent? Maybe you should just include all of the sauces, on the side of course, so we can see which one best complements each dish."

Alek watched the minute hand continue its predictable arc on the kitchen clock, designed to look like a brass pan hanging from its handle. It took his mother longer to place the order than it would take the restaurant to prepare the dishes. "And can you make sure we're the first route on the delivery? I'd hate to have to reheat the food when it arrives."

"That's a good idea, honey." Mr. Khederian didn't even look up from the newspaper he was reading.

When all the details and instructions were issued, Mrs. Khederian hung up the phone.

"Now, honey, we wanted to talk to you." Mrs. Khederian settled next to her husband at the kitchen table, across from Alek, in their traditional "we need to talk" position. "But is there something you want to tell us first?" Mrs. Khederian poured a bag of pistachios into a bowl, and the three of them dove in, as if a multicourse dinner wasn't being delivered to them shortly.

"Not really." Alek prayed, against all odds, that that would be that. But, as he had learned, most prayers went unanswered.

"So we need to remind you of all the rules you broke last weekend?" Mr. Khederian shook his head. "On your first unchaperoned trip to NYC, you broke your curfew by hours. Do you know how worried we were?" His father barreled forward without giving Alek a chance to respond to the rest of the offenses: departing from the itinerary, failing to call every hour. The list went on and on. "Then you skipped church, spending the whole day in your room, which you barely left today. Even people as clueless as your parents can see there's something going on."

Mrs. Khederian laid her hand on her husband's. "We are trying to be understanding about this, but we're worried."

"Don't worry, guys, I promise this won't affect my grades, so you don't have anything to actually be nervous about." The sarcasm dripped off Alek's voice like sweet-and-sour sauce.

"I'm not going to rise to your bait, Aleksander." In spite of what she claimed, Alek could hear the ire in his mother's voice as she invoked his full name. "If you choose not to tell us what's happening, we'll have no option but to punish you."

"Oh, I see, so you're going to coerce me into confiding in you?"

"If that's how you choose to interpret it, we can't stop you," his father responded.

"So if I tell you what happened, you won't punish me?"

"We're not saying that, either, Alek. We just wish you'd tell us what's going on."

"And I just wish you'd leave me alone, okay? So can I go now?"

"Not yet. We still need to talk to you about something else." His mom fidgeted with her pile of pistachio shells. "Father Reverend spoke to us after church yesterday . . ."

"Yes?" Alek prompted.

"Was it absolutely necessary for you to come out to him?" his father blurted.

Alek put his hands on the table. "I was wondering when my parents' liberalness would finally spend itself."

"Now, now, Alek, don't be so dramatic." His mother began setting the table for the Chinese food. "Sometimes, you'll learn, it's just easier not to rock the boat. You know we have no problem with your sexuality . . ."

". . . except in church." Alek conjured his best-but-not-too-offensive impersonation of his mother. "Where it embarrasses us."

Footsteps thumped down the staircase. For once, Alek was grateful for his brother's presence, as well as his rudeness and total lack of concern for interrupting a preexisting conversation. "Can I take the car?" Nik yelled from the front door.

Anxiety and concern, rivals for Mrs. Khederian's default emotion, flashed across her face. "I don't know, honey. It may snow, in which case the roads will be icy tonight."

"I'll drive slowly the whole time." Alek heard the strain in his brother's voice as he tried his best to sound reasonable. "I swear."

"And where are you going?" their father asked warily.

"To hang out with some friends."

"Which friends?" his mother persisted.

"God—do you want me to send over their transcripts so you can make sure their GPAs are above 3.5?"

"Weighted or unweighted?" Mr. Khederian asked, with no irony.

Nik stomped into the kitchen and threw the car keys that he wouldn't be using tonight down on the table. "Never mind. I'll just have someone come and pick me up. Again. Because I have the only parents in the entirety of Central New Jersey who don't trust their son, whose GPA is 4.3 and who was accepted to Cornell early decision and who passed his driver's license exam three months ago with flying colors and hasn't gotten into a single accident since, to drive ten minutes to his friend's house!" Nik took his winter hat out of his jacket pocket and yanked it down on his head. "And I bet you by the time dumbass over here gets his license, you're going to let him drive wherever he wants. Maybe even buy him his own car. The way you always do whatever he freakin' wants."

"Nik, language, please." Alek feigned delicacy.

"You're such a dingleberry." Nik stomped back to the front door and stuck his feet into his boots, which had been removed by the front door to the house, the way all shoes had to be in the Khederian house during winter. And fall. And spring. And summer. "I'm going to the diner."

A dramatic exit was more difficult in winter, when you needed to bundle up. Confronting his parents about driving was one thing, but Nik knew better than to leave the Khederian house without a scarf, hat, and gloves lest he truly invoke their wrath. A few awkward moments later, Nik left, closing the door behind him with more force than he usually would, but enough to qualify for an actual slam, which would've clearly violated one of the many Khederian house rules.

"Are there any other places you'd prefer for me to stay closeted?" Now that his brother had left, Alek could get back to confronting his parents.

"Alek, I wish you didn't overreact to everything," his mother said.

"And I wish you guys weren't so embarrassingly heteronormative!" Alek shot back. Fighting about church, he was discovering, was infinitely easier than talking about Ethan.

"That's right. We're your terrible heteronormative, heterosexual parents who have repeatedly welcomed your boyfriend into our house and tried to show you and him every courtesy we can. And now we're even worse because we're worried sick because we believe you've had a breakup." Mr. Khederian pushed his glasses back on his nose.

"You don't *have* a breakup—jeesh—you just break up!" Alek corrected him.

"Is that what happened?" His mother masked her desperate hunger for the information as best she could.

"I don't know, okay? And why don't you guys believe me when I tell you that I don't want to talk about it? Is it confusing? Is it unclear? I don't want to talk about it, okay?"

"We just want you to know that we support you, honey, okay—"

"—as long as it doesn't cause any actual conflict," Alek finished. "Don't you hear yourselves, expressing concern over whether or not I broke up with my boyfriend but asking me to stay closeted at church in the same conversation? Don't you see how crazy that is? And why haven't you asked yourselves why you're going to a church that doesn't support women's rights, or gay rights, or any of the other values you have?"

"Just because we go to the Armenian Church doesn't mean we condone all of its positions, Alek," his father said. "It's not that black and white."

"Okay, but have you asked yourself where the money that you put in that collection plate goes? What if some of it goes to fight abortion rights? Or what if some of it goes to support laws that stop people from using whatever bathroom they want?"

His parents didn't respond.

"Okay. Whatever." Alek turned and left, calling over his shoulder, "Don't bother calling me when the food arrives. I've lost my appetite."

13

"YOU SAID THAT TO THEM?" ARNO'S EYES BULGED IN disbelief. "If I spoke to my parents that way, they'd pack me up this afternoon and send me to live with my cousins in Armenia, and I'm not sure they have indoor plumbing!"

"It wasn't that big of a deal." Alek played it cool, although he was pretty sure the only reason he hadn't been grounded for the rest of his preadult life was because his parents were taking pity on him. "Besides, can you believe that Reverend Father talked to them about me? Like he doesn't have anything else to worry about. Like, what about trying to find out who wrote *gyot* in your book?"

"Let that go, Alek. You already got the reverend father to come to class and talk about it."

"But that was total bullshit! And now my parents are freaking out because I came out to him."

"I haven't even come out to my parents yet. Or anyone else,

other than you. You are such a . . . badass." Arno stumbled over the profanity.

Alek and Arno both hushed up as they heard a swarm of people moving past the little alcove where they hid after smuggling two cups of coffee and a plate of frosted ma'amoul stuffed with pistachios from the main hall.

They should've been with their families, sampling the treats and shopping for gifts at the annual Christmas bazaar that took over the church. Coincidentally, the day was December 25— the same day that Western Christian religions celebrated Christmas, unlike the Eastern Orthodox churches, which celebrated it twelve days later. But the Armenian craftspeople, artists, and bakers from the congregation and the surrounding community seemed oblivious to this fact in St. Stephen's Church. Stands featuring a wide display of possible Christmas gifts alternated with the full array of edible delicacies, both savory (kibbi, hummus, bourmah, tourshi, and all six varieties of buregs), and sweet, like the stand from which Alek and Arno had got their ma'amoul, which also offered baklava, apricot squares, vanilla cookies, and nutmeg cake with rose, honey, and pistachios.

Technically, the two of them weren't doing anything wrong, hiding out here in the alcove. Technically, should someone have stumbled upon them, they wouldn't have had anything to hide. But it still felt clandestine, sneaking off together when they should've been with everyone else in the bazaar, buying tickets for the 50/50 raffle, watching children tell Santa what they wanted, or playing any of the lame carnival games.

"If we were, like, real badasses, we'd totally be smoking right now." Arno lifted his chin and looked away into the distance, fantasizing.

"You smoke?" Alek didn't disguise the surprise or disgust in his voice.

"Of course not!" Arno snapped back to reality. "Smoking is terrible for you!"

"I know," Alek agreed. "And the smell . . ."

"Right!" Arno took a small sip of his black coffee. The way he grimaced led Alek to suspect that black wasn't how he usually drank it. "It's like, if you're going to spend money killing yourself, can you at least do it in some way that's not so stinky?"

"And what's up with vaping?"

"I guess it's better for you."

"I guess. Until they find out it gives you lip cancer or whatever."

"It's all so gross." Arno grimaced through another sip of coffee. "Do you think people who do that think they're cool?"

Alek laughed. He dropped his voice, imitating his idea of a smoker's inner thoughts. "'Oh, look at me, I'm such a badass I'm willing to risk cancer to show you how much of a badass I really am.'" When Arno laughed, Alek continued. "'Everyone tremble at the sight of my badassery.'"

This time they both cracked up, leaning against each other, almost spilling their cups of steaming black coffee.

"I really appreciate what you did, Alek—all of it." Arno wiped away some crumbs of the ma'amoul that had been clinging to his lower lip.

"I'm only getting started," Alek confided.

"What?" Arno exclaimed. "I don't want you doing anything else that might get you in trouble."

"I'm tired of all this bullshit. Can you imagine if someone had written *boz* on Shushan's script? Or *vochkhar* on Nik's? Nobody would've stood for someone calling her a whore or him an idiot. But instead, because we're gay, we're supposed to just shut up and be thankful that we're not being excommunicated." For the first time since Alek had deduced Ethan's infidelity, he felt excited, like something in the world actually mattered. "If we let ourselves be treated this way, we're saying we don't deserve any better."

"But what can you possibly do about it?"

"In light of recent events, it feels like what it means to be Armenian has really changed for me . . ."

Arno slowly put down his coffee. "Alek, I don't like where this is going."

". . . and it would be dishonest if my award-winning paper didn't somehow reflect that, you know? And what more perfect opportunity for me than to share with the whole congregation exactly what I'm feeling? Don't try to talk me out of it, okay?"

"Okay." Arno put his coffee down so that he could wring his hands nervously. "Just say something to the reverend father before, okay? I have a feeling this isn't the kind of surprise he'd like."

Alek left his conversation with Arno feeling inspired, feeling like he had direction. But before he could work on the changes to his paper, before he could do anything, he had to do the one thing he'd been putting off.

* * *

Ethan's eyes were bloodshot, underlined with dark half circles, like a football player's. His hair jutted out of the deflated winter hat that usually sat jauntily on his head. Alek would be lying if he pretended that Ethan's misery didn't give him satisfaction. He didn't want to be the only one suffering.

"It's good to see you." Ethan went in for the hug, but Alek pulled away.

If Alek hadn't steeled himself for the abandoned-puppy look on Ethan's face, he might've caved right there. The temptation to succumb to the comfort and familiarity of Ethan's embrace was great. But that wasn't why he'd agreed to see Ethan, when he'd finally returned all those ignored calls and texts. Five days had passed since their six-month anniversary, and even though he hadn't felt the same conviction he had when he'd first talked about it to Becky, Alek was here to break up with Ethan, for good.

Alek stepped outside of his house, quickly pulling the door behind him shut. His parents were upstairs, he knew, but especially after their last conversation, he couldn't deal with them or their questions. Besides, he had nothing to tell them. At least, not yet.

Since they'd started dating, Ethan had come knocking for Alek many times. Every time Alek had opened the door to find Ethan, he felt surprised all over again that someone like Ethan could be interested in someone like him.

But Alek regarded the Ethan standing in the doorway now,

in rumpled clothes that looked as if he'd slept in them. This Ethan fidgeted, unsure of where to look. This Ethan slouched. If this Ethan inspired any emotion, it was pity. But it didn't really matter, since this was the last time Alek was going to answer the door to any of the Ethans.

"Should we hit the diner?" Ethan looked down when he talked, his hands stuffed in his jacket.

"Let's just walk." Alek hadn't meant to bark the words, but that's how they came out. He felt like a piano with only two keys, both painfully out of tune.

They walked in silence down Mercer Street, meandering without direction. An overnight snowfall had reblanketed the houses, whiting them out, making them even more indistinguishable.

"It's too bad it's so cold," Ethan observed. "Otherwise, we'd get your bike out and I could jump on my board. Or we could hit the courts."

Alek just continued walking.

They wound their way to the tunnel that had connected the two sides of the train station until the overpass had been built.

"Remember when," Ethan started, "this was before we even met, like officially—remember when you came over to the other side of the tunnel and Jack almost beat the shit out of you? And I was like, 'Pick on someone your own size'? And he let you go. Remember that?" Ethan kicked a rock that skittered down through the opening.

"Yeah, I remember that, Ethan. I remember what a sad, pitiful loser I was and how I dressed horribly and how I still hadn't come out and that I couldn't stand up for myself. And how you came to my rescue. Well, don't worry. You won't ever have to do that again."

Ethan turned, the smile on his face collapsing. "Come on, you know that's not what I mean."

"It was Remi, wasn't it?" The words surprised Alek. Only now did it occur to him that he had blocked out any imagination of the details of the cheating. But now that he was with Ethan, with the one person who had the information he'd denied himself wanting, he couldn't help himself.

Ethan nodded, his head hanging in shame.

"The night of my birthday." Alek wasn't accusing him. Nor was he asking. He was just stating facts.

Ethan nodded again. "Please, do we have to talk about it? Can't we just talk about what I can do to make it better? Or even what you've done the last few days. I haven't seen you. I haven't heard from you. I'm not used to not knowing what's up with you. Is your brother still pouting about the essay? How're your parents? And Becky and Dustin—do you think they have a shot?"

"You don't get to—" Alek felt like he'd bitten into a rotten grapefruit and was spitting out its bitterness. "You don't get to ask about things like everything's okay. You don't get to do that."

"Do you want to know what I've been doing?" Ethan asked pitifully.

"No. I don't. I want you to tell me what happened."

"You mean—that night?"

Alek nodded yes.

"Please don't do this," Ethan begged. "Let's just figure out how to put it behind us, and move on, and become Alek and Ethan again. That's all I want."

"I don't care what you want." Alek spoke slowly, intentionally, unsentimentally. He didn't have to look for the words. They were waiting for him, like ready weapons, itching to be used. "You gave up the right to have what you want when you cheated on me, then lied to me about it, remember?"

"I didn't lie—"

"Not saying anything is just like lying, Ethan, so don't pretend it's not."

Ethan nodded mutely.

"So now we're going to do what I want," Alek insisted. "I want you to tell me about it. All about it. Start at the beginning."

"Can't we at least go inside somewhere?" Ethan pleaded.

"No. Here. Now."

Ethan leaned against the tunnel. "Alek, honestly, there isn't much to say. We went to Greenpoint. The party was dope. A guy with this, like, crazy lumberjack beard was spinning some house trance beats. They were fine, you know, but after a while it got a little annoying because you could tell he thought he was being, like, mad edgy."

"I don't care about the music, Ethan. I care about how and why my boyfriend cheated on me!" Alek hadn't meant to use that word. He had been training himself to think of Ethan as his ex.

"Okay, sorry." But Ethan had spotted it, too, this "boy-friend." And his eyes flickered with newfound hope. "We had a few beers—"

"So you were drunk?"

Ethan paused. "I wish I could stand here and tell you, 'Yeah—I was blitzed, I didn't know what I was doing.' But before I came to meet you today, I made my New Year's resolution. And I'll say it now, five days early—that I would never lie to you again, never be dishonest in any way. And so, yeah, I had a few beers. But no, I wasn't, like, wasted. I wasn't, like, so judgment-impaired that I didn't realize what I was doing or any bullshit like that. And then we were alone, in one of the bedrooms, and he reached for me, and . . ."

"Why, Ethan? Why did you cheat on me?" Alek looked away. "Was it because, you know—I didn't want to . . ."

"No no no no. Please don't say that, please don't think that," Ethan begged. He took a step toward Alek, who stepped away quickly. "I've been thinking so hard about what to say, how to try and make you understand . . . But you have to believe me, it has nothing to do with that. It's just, you don't know what it's like having an ex, Alek. Especially one like Remi."

"Because he's like model-hot, is that what you mean?"

"No, because he's always had this, like, power over me. He's someone who it's just impossible to say no to. Have you ever had someone like that in your life, someone who could get you to do things that you never thought you would?"

Alek regarded Ethan. "I did. And then he cheated on me. And now I don't."

Panic erupted on Ethan's face. "What does that mean?"

Alek had thought that perhaps hearing about it, about the who, what, where, and how, would make the pain go away. Would make forgiveness possible. But it didn't.

"Becky told me that I had to tell you we were breaking up, and I wasn't going to ghost you because I think that's like the worst thing that one person could ever do. Except maybe cheating on them with their ex and then condescending and being like, 'You don't know what it's like to have an ex.'"

"You made me talk about it, Alek. That's what you wanted. Is there anything I could've said that would've made it okay?"

"How about 'I'm sorry'? How about, 'This the worst thing that I've ever done in my life and I'll spend the rest of my life regretting it and I wish you could forgive me'? Did it occur to you to say any of those things?"

Ethan closed his eyes and seemed to force tears back. "Alek, I'm sorry." He met Alek's gaze full-on, unflinching. "This is the worst thing that I've done in my life." But the tears proved stronger than him, and out they came. "I'll spend the rest of my life regretting it." Then he started ugly-crying violently. "I wish you could forgive me."

Alek looked at Ethan. He saw the guy, almost two years older than him, whom he'd looked up to in just about everything. He saw the guy who helped him come out, who helped him discover New York, who, really, helped him discover himself.

And still, it wasn't enough. "I do, too, Ethan. I wish I could, too."

The wind whipped against the tunnel's boarded-up opening, as if it were trying to beat it down.

"So what—you're going to turn around and just walk away from me? From us?" Ethan left the meager shelter that the mouth of the tunnel was affording him, stepping closer to Alek.

"What else can I do, Ethan? How'm I ever going to be able to trust you again?"

"I'm going to earn it back. Your trust. Your faith. You might not owe me anything else, but you owe me the chance to try." Ethan leaned forward. "We have been together for the best six months of my life. I know you're hurting, and I know I'm the person who hurt you. But you have to give me the chance to be the person to make it go away. You have to let me try."

"I don't know, Ethan," Alek said. "I just don't know."

"I do. And if you leave now, like this, I won't be the only one who regrets this day for the rest of his life."

14

"HE ACTUALLY SAID THAT? THAT'S THE MOST romantic thing I've ever heard!" Becky squealed. "Did music swell? Did Ethan jump on a white horse and swoop you up and carry you off into the sunset?"

"It was, like, three p.m., so the sun wasn't really setting." Alek sat on Becky's bed, wiggled his toes in their thick, woolen socks against the dark-blue carpeting of her bedroom.

"That is terrible planning on both your parts. There was a horse, though?" Becky asked hopefully.

"Sure, Becky, there was a horse." Alek was feeling generous.

"And it was white?"

"Totally."

"I knew it!"

Becky uncorked and sniffed a bottle on her vanity while they spoke, making eye contact with Alek in the mirror in front of her.

"Okay—tell me which one you like more." She dabbed one of Alek's wrists with a clear, oblong, silver-capped bottle. "I got this one for Christmas. Because we celebrate it on the normal date. Not like you Armenians."

He sniffed. "Smells like French toast."

"How about this one?" She sprayed his other wrist with a circular yellow bottle.

"This one smells like I'm being attacked by a rabid florist."

"You're useless!"

"Do you have any options other than 'Eau du Brunch' or 'Little Shop of Horrors'?"

Becky ignored Alek and lightly sprayed herself with a third, light-green bottle. A bottle she didn't let Alek sample first. "But seriously—are you guys back together now? Did you even break up in the first place? Because now that Mahira dumped John when she spotted him at Panera with a trombonist, you guys have the record for longest consecutive couple at South Windsor High."

"That can't be true."

"It is!"

"What about Nathan and Shoko?"

"They broke up during midterms week."

"Suzanne and Dev?"

"Irreconcilable artistic differences."

"Wow, I guess Ethan and I are really have been together the longest."

"I told you! People need you to stay together. You give us hope."

Alek stared at Becky's turquoise comforter, quilted with

pink, green, and brown squares in an asymmetrical design. "I thought I was going to break up with him—I had every intention of doing it."

"But?"

Alek wasn't sure if he'd done the right thing in letting himself be convinced to give Ethan a second chance. Before he'd been in Ethan's presence, he was sure breaking up with him was the right thing to do. In the actual moment, however, he'd doubted himself. In the past, Alek had had no difficulty identifying the "right" thing to do—actually doing it was the hard part. But now the needle on his moral compass was spinning, having lost its magnetic north.

"Ethan convinced me to give him another chance."

"So you guys are still together?"

"I guess."

"You sound about as excited as I do about my first appointment with the gynecologist. Which, by the way, is next week, my mother just informed me."

"You heard of TMI, Becky?"

"Are you going to be one of those gays who gets like super uncomfortable any time I talk about my lady parts? Because, I have to say, that is embarrassingly stereotypical." Becky quickly ran a lip gloss along her upper lip, then lower.

Alek opened the lid of the tea box that accompanied him everywhere. "Don't listen to her, Señor Huevo. She doesn't even carry her egg around with her."

"That's right, I don't. Because I'm not some weirdo like you."

"The assignment is to see how well we would take care of a child."

"Well then, I guess I'm the Medea of South Windsor High."
Becky pressed her lips together, smoothing out the lip gloss.

"I don't think it's normal that you talk about anything, especially this stuff like sex and periods, without being even the least bit squeamish. I don't subject you to reports about where hair is popping up all over my body or the intimate details of what Ethan and I did when . . ."

Becky began ritualistically brushing her hair out. "I wish you would divulge the secrets of your sex life!"

"You wouldn't be grossed out?" Alek asked.

"My parents are scientists, remember? Band practice, work, NASA's New Horizons images of Pluto, and my menstruation cycle are all acceptable breakfast table conversation topics. And since you and Ethan are still together, you'll *have* to tell me everything."

"What do you think, Becky? Do you think I should've just dumped him?"

Becky got up from her vanity and jumped on her bed, next to Alek. The perfume she had chosen was citrusy. And nice. Not that Alek would admit it. "I'm pretty sure I would've. Because when I think about Dustin doing something like that to me, I'd just want to claw his heart out and eat it raw while he watched."

"I think that would be difficult," Alek observed.

"Not if I already hooked him up to artificial life support." Becky sat up on the bed. "See—I've already planned for this possibility."

"And that's how you'd react to some guy you barely knew cheating on you."

"I'm not sure if I'd describe Dustin as some guy I barely knew. We've been dating for almost three weeks. Twenty days, to be exact, making tomorrow our three-week-versary."

"We both know that's not a thing."

"You continue talking like that, soon you're not going to be a thing."

Alek kicked his shoes off and rolled over, onto his back. "All I'm saying is that you think you would kill Dustin if he cheated on you, and Dustin's no Ethan."

"I don't know what you have against him." Becky semi-playfully swatted Alek with a pillow. "Can you please give him a chance at least before you get all judgy?"

"Fine." Alek caught the pillow before Becky could swat him again.

"And this isn't about comparing Dustin to Ethan or whatever. It's not about what I'd do in the situation. You're the one living it."

"So what does matter?"

Becky hopped off the bed and went to her closet. "When you think about it, what's the first thing that pops into your head?"

"How stupid I feel."

"Really? For what?"

"For not knowing. My birthday was a whole week before our six-month. That means for seven days, I was hanging out with Ethan, I was holding Ethan's hand, I was kissing Ethan."

Becky held up a pair of chunky black boots for Alek's approval.

"Trying too hard."

Becky tossed the boots back in the closet. "It sounds like you were doing more than just kissing him."

Alek shook his head no. "It's a euphemism."

"You're a euphemism." Becky dragged out a pair of slightly less chunky black boots.

"I thought I knew him so well, you know?" Alek stared back down at his toes. "That I could tell when something was upsetting him without him having to say anything. Like I could read his mind. But clearly, telepathy and not reality manipulation should be the power that I want. Or maybe not, because if I could manipulate reality, then I could just undo all this and we'd go back to being the way we were. Instead, I have to wonder if staying with him says, 'It's okay to treat me like this because I don't deserve any better.' When people find out, they're going to think I'm more of a loser than they already do."

Becky finished lacing her boots up and hopped back on the bed. "Look—the only thing I know is that the last thing you should be doing is worrying about your imagined reaction of the populace of South Windsor High. They're all idiots." She hugged Alek. "And besides, it's impossible for their opinions of you to sink any lower!"

Alek hugged her back. "You always know just what to say."

"I know."

"And what else is Ethan hiding from me?" Alek and Becky leaned back, against her bed's headboard. "And why did he wait for me to figure it out rather than just tell me himself? It must've been there, every moment we talked or touched or whatevered."

"Maybe it wasn't." Becky disentangled from Alek, got up from her bed, and continued brushing her hair.

"Wasn't what?"

"Maybe every living breathing moment he was with you wasn't about, 'Should I tell Alek that I cheated on him?'"

"How could it not have it been? If I had cheated on Ethan—"

"Sure, if it had been you, that's all you would've thought about." She gesticulated with the brush in her hand. "But maybe Ethan's not like that. Maybe he just buried it away so far and deep that he'd never have to think about it. Denial's not just a river in Egypt, you know."

"And that's another thing—if he had brought it up himself, sooner, in a less . . ." Alek coughed. ". . . charged situation, it might've been easier to get over it. But what if we hadn't—you know—been about to do it that night? Would I still not know?"

"Oh my God. It's called 'sex.' How can you have come so close to losing your virginity and still be afraid of saying that word? You're not going to summon Voldemort."

"Volde-who?"

Becky slammed the brush down in exasperation. "Sometimes, seriously, I can't even with you."

"I'm just kidding—I know he's from those books. Those books without a single gay character."

"Dumbledore was gay!" Becky protested. "She said it in an interview."

"Okay—if he was really gay, then where was his boyfriend? Or his husband? And more importantly, why wasn't there a single gay student in the entirety of that school for wizards? It is A SCHOOL FOR WIZARDS FOR GOD'S SAKE. Shouldn't, like, *at least* half of the population be queer? If not more? But that's not the point!" Alek jumped off Becky's bed. "The point is, what if we weren't going to try sex that night?" He managed to say the word without stumbling too much before or after. "Or what if I hadn't surmised with my Sherlock-esque deductive skills what the already-opened box of condoms meant? How long would we have gone, our relationship built on a lie?"

"I don't know."

"Me neither—that's why—"

"Becky . . ." Her dad called up the stairs.

". . . your gentleman caller has arrived." Becky's mom finished her husband's sentence, as they always did for each other. But usually they did it without giggling. The way they were now.

Becky rolled her eyes. "I am never letting my parents go to a community theater production of Tennessee Williams again." She turned to the door and sucked in air to holler to her parents below. "We'll be right there!"

Alek leaped from the bed. "Dustin's here?"

"What, you think I'm putting on perfume and lipstick for your benefit?"

"But we're hanging out now. We've had these plans for days. I still have around four more hours of talking to do, which I could conceivably compress into three."

Becky stood up and put all of her cosmetics away. "I invited Dustin along because it might be nice for the three of us to hang out together. We can watch a movie downstairs, or make my folks drive us to the movies, or . . ." Becky trailed off. "I guess the movies is actually the only thing to do around here."

"I would rather get called into the reverend father's office with my parents, which, by the way, is happening this weekend, than have to endure you and Dustin's stolen glances and 'accidental' finger-brushing in the popcorn bucket."

"You're the worst."

"I'm not the one who invited someone to crash our date."

"'Sup?" Dustin appeared in the doorway of Becky's room, a messenger bag slung over his shoulder, holding his bright green skateboard even though it was snowing outside and Alek knew for a fact there was no way he was going to use it.

"Dustin!" Becky leaped from her vanity and greeted her boyfriend with a peck on his cheek. "I was just telling Alek how much I was looking forward to the two of you spending some time together, and lo and behold, there's my mom calling me."

Dustin and Alek exchanged a quizzical glance. "I don't hear . . ." Alek started, but Becky cut him off.

"What's that, Mom?" Becky called out, loud, as if she were responding to her mother's voice from downstairs. "You want me to come down and help you with something so that my best friend and my boyfriend can spend some time together? What a swell idea. I'll be right down." She tidied up her room, putting away the rejected outfit options and an errant pair of slippers. "I have no idea how long this will take, as my mom might need a lot of help with that unnamed activity, but I'm going to guess around thirty minutes. I'm sure you two will be fine until then." She walked out of the room, closing the door behind her.

Dustin sat on the chair at Becky's vanity. If he were at all conscious of how incongruent he appeared there—a skater boy at a very girly vanity—he showed no trace of it.

"So . . ." Alek started.

"Yeah?" Dustin asked.

"Why don't I tell you about myself?" Alek launched into an unrehearsed monologue about his family, his Armenian-ness, his aspirations, his interests. "And now—what about you?"

"You know."

"No, I don't."

"Not much to tell."

Alek waited for Dustin to launch into his own monologue, but apparently "not much to tell" was all he had to say for himself.

Asking questions didn't help the conversation, either.

"What do you like?"

"Skateboarding. And rollerblading. And Magic: The Gathering."

"What do your parents do?"

"My dad works for the state. My mom runs her own business from home, I think."

"And what do you think you'll be doing when we're older?" Alek asked.

"I dunno—probably get a job. You?"

Alek put his hands up to his face to hide his mounting frustration. "I'll probably get a job, too, Dustin."

"Cool." Dustin nodded.

Alek stared at Dustin, trying to discern what his hidden superpower was. And more importantly, how Becky could possibly be with someone who didn't have any of her charm or wit or badassery. Was this the destiny of all cool girls, to end up with boring guys unworthy of them? Or were girls just designed to be more interesting than guys, so a degree of disparity was built into the equation?

The face of his ancient cell phone showed the time and date: Friday, December 27, 3:17 p.m. If he'd had an even slightly up-to-date model, he would've flipped the time display to show the seconds passing. But maybe it's better that he didn't, because then he'd be even more aware of how slowly time felt stuck in a room with a guy who he had nothing in common with, who didn't have the most basic idea of how to carry on a conversation. And who, more importantly, was in no way good enough for his best friend.

15

EVERY SILENCE HAS ITS OWN FLAVOR. THERE IS THE electric silence of expectation that charges the air around it, like a match point in tennis, or the moment before you receive a test back and see how you've done. There is the effortless silence of efficiency, which Alek saw in his parents: wordlessly working together in the kitchen, dicing, whisking, and passing each other ingredients as if they had been choreographed. There is the red silence of anger, the pulsing silence of accusation, the euphoric silence of unspeakable joy. And then there is the stilted silence of awkwardness, which changes the air around it to molasses: thick, oppressive, and, for reasons no one can quite articulate, impossible to overcome.

"So . . ." Ethan trailed off.

"So . . ." Alek repeated.

The day was so gloomy and cold and threatening to snow

that Alek had almost canceled. But the weather had held, and he'd met Ethan at the diner.

The ice cubes melted slowly in the amber-tinted, hard plastic glasses of water on the warped Formica table. The uneaten half of Ethan's grilled cheese sandwich lay next to the pile of room-temperature french fries, separated by a pool of crusting ketchup. The only evidence of the chicken club platter that had been on Alek's plate was the empty plastic thimble of coleslaw. Alek had considered getting an egg-salad club, but the presence of Señor Huevo, staring at him from his tea-box house, would've made him feel like a monster.

Before Alek had found out that Ethan had cheated on him, their relationship had never known the stilted silence of awkwardness. Their unlikely energies had always balanced each other out, like a seesaw. The conversation flowed naturally, twisting and turning and splitting as it might but always in motion. In the past, their silences had ease.

Now it felt like they were on opposite sides of a thick, dusty old curtain. Even if Alek had wanted to draw it open, he didn't know where to find the part.

"Did I tell you my dad's going away for a week after New Year's?" Ethan shuffled the french fries around on his plate aimlessly.

Alek shook his head.

"Yeah, he's got this retreat in San Francisco." Ethan stopped speaking, and Alek wondered if he was supposed to say something—maybe ask a question about Ethan's dad's trip? He was forming the words when Ethan filled the awkward silence. "So what's going on with you?"

"I'm almost done rewriting my 'What Being Armenian Means to Me' paper to reflect a more accepting, modern, pansexual and transgender perspective."

"And you think they're gonna be into your new version? It sounds—I don't know—a bit controversial. Especially for church."

"It's just a few paragraphs at the end."

"Tell me again why you guys celebrate Christmas later?"

Even when he was in the best of spirits, Alek hated having to explain this part of his cultural heritage. "Western Christians celebrate Christmas on the twenty-fifth, the alleged date of Jesus's birth. But the Armenians celebrate the baptism, which just as allegedly happened twelve days later. You know, twelve days of Christmas and all that jazz."

Alek thought about telling Ethan about the *gyot* in Arno's textbook. But for reasons he couldn't entirely articulate, he decided not to. "I can't believe it's taken me this long to see the church for what it really is. Its positions on homosexuality, abortion, gender rights—they're positively medieval. I mean, the Orthodox Church makes the Catholics look Protestant. I'm looking at this thing that I've had all my life, that's been holy, like, actually holy, and seeing it for what it really is, and it's depressing, you know? I feel betrayed." A silent *again* hung between them.

There was so much more Alek wanted to say, accusations to hurl, details to gather, defenses to mount, reconciliations to attempt—all things Alek would've said if things between them weren't so weird. The thoughts formed themselves in his brain, traveled down to his heart, where they were tinted with emotions, then shot up to his mouth, becoming words along the way. But they got stuck there, in the space between throat and lips, like stalled traffic. "So what's your dad's retreat?"

"I don't know—something where you're not supposed to speak, I think?"

Ethan continued talking about his dad, his retreat, and Alek nodded or threw in an occasional "mm-hm" to show that he was following along.

Mostly, he watched Ethan, his boyfriend, those three cubic feet of bone and blood and muscles, wondering who and what he was. "What do you want to do with your life, Ethan?" Alek hadn't waited for a natural lull in the conversation—he just blurted the words out, as if Ethan hadn't just been midsentence.

"Huh?"

"Like, when you're all grown up—what do you want to do?" They paused as their waiter with tattoos running up his forearms cleared the plates, trading them for the check.

"I got this." Ethan leaned forward, slipping his wallet out of his jeans.

"Why don't we split it?" Alek slid a ten-dollar bill over the table to Ethan.

"Please?" Ethan begged.

"Dutch. It's better." Alek removed his hand from the ten-dollar bill, letting it sit on the table. Ethan reluctantly pocketed it. "So—your life. What do you want to do with it?"

"I dunno. Something fun."

Alek rolled his eyes. "Something fun? That's it?"

"Yeah—what's wrong with that?"

"Nothing's *wrong* with it. I just don't know what kind of answer that is."

"All right, Ms. Schmidt. I guess I didn't adequately prepare for this surprise guidance counselor session on the rest of my life."

Alek closed the lid on Señor Huevo's tea-box house, placed it in a gloved hand, and followed Ethan to the register. "I like images and visual things and stuff, so I thought I could be a web-page designer." Ethan paid the bill, then popped a mint from the bowl by the register, something Alek's mom ensured neither of her sons would ever do by forwarding them articles about the fecal matter found in a random sampling of said bowls. "Or maybe one of those guys who comes up with logos—you know, like the eagle for Antihero boards or the smiley face for Roger." Ethan nodded, sufficiently pleased with his answer. "What about you?"

"I want to do something that makes the world better."

"Uh, could you be more specific?"

"You know, like work for Doctors Without Borders. Or maybe be a lawyer, but not the kind that works for those evil corporations. The kind that represents poor people. Like Matt Murdoch."

"Who?"

"You know—Daredevil?"

"Uh-huh." Another silence descended on them, until Ethan broke it forcibly. "You think your answer is better than mine?"

"No," Alek responded, avoiding the fight. But of course, Ethan was right. Alek did believe in the superiority of his answer.

"You know I'm not, like, a good-grades guy like you. And I think it's great that you want to make the world a better place, but there are lots of ways to do that."

"Sure."

They walked out of the main part of the diner, into the lobby. Alek's hands ached for the beat-up *Street Fighter II* arcade game that lived next to the three ancient quarter-candy machines.

"You wanna, I don't know . . ." Ethan trailed off. "You wanna come over?"

"I think I'm going to feed the beast a few quarters, okay?" Alek gestured back to the arcade machine inside the diner.

"I could wait . . ."

"It's good."

"Oh, I just . . ."

"What?"

"I thought we were gonna hang all afternoon." A breeze blew across them, threatening to take Ethan's winter hat with it. He yanked it down, tighter, across his head. "It would be nice to spend some QT, you know?"

"Sorry, Ethan—I gotta finish my Christmas essay."

"Okay. Are you doing anything on New Year's Eve?"

Alek paused before answering, a pause he would've never taken before. "Not really."

"You wanna come over?" Ethan asked pitifully. "My dad's going to be at Lesley's, and we could just chill."

"Yeah." Alek shifted on his feet, wanting this conversation to be over.

"Great. Around seven?"

"We'll order in?"

Ethan's eyes twinkled with their former mischievousness. "Or better yet, I might have a surprise waiting for you."

"Really?" Against rational thought, Alek felt the tug of Ethan pulling him, titillating him, exciting him about the unknown.

"Really." Ethan leaned in and stole a quick kiss from Alek's cheek. "I'll see you on New Year's Eve."

Alek had never actually spent time in Reverend Father Stepanian's inner office before, the small room behind the larger one where he usually met with congregants. The only nod to modernity was the sleek computer in the corner, the Apple icon glowing ominously. An Armenian flag hung limply in the corner, the red and blue and apricot-orange stripes folding over themselves in some kind of defeat, and built-in wooden bookcases lined the room itself, stained that perfect color between mahogany and dark brown that made you feel smarter just by being near it.

The reverend father's framed diplomas were prominently displayed, hung behind his desk. And everything was exactly where it was supposed to be: the pencils and pens all neatly protruding from the leather cup on the desk, the encyclopedia set with matching binding lined up alphabetically on the bottommost shelves of the bookcase.

"I still don't see why I'm here," Nik complained.

"Maybe the reverend father is going to ask Alek to head up the Armenian Youth Group, like you did last year." Alek's father adjusted his striped tie. "Your perspective could be valuable."

Alek closed his eyes so that his father wouldn't see him roll them. Whatever reason Father Reverend Stepanian had for asking to see Alek and his family had nothing to do with the Armenian Youth. Of that, Alek was sure. In some ways, he envied Señor Huevo, safely ensconced in his silver tin tea box, perched on the armrest of Alek's chair.

"I'm so sorry to have kept you waiting." The reverend father entered the room unrushed, radiating the kind of quiet and calm that Alek always admired in him.

Alek's parents rose to shake the reverend's hand when he entered the room. Alek and Nik followed their parents' lead.

"What a beautiful sermon today, Reverend." Mrs. Khederian beamed. "I'd never considered those passages in Luke about our own culpability in original sin that way."

"Thank you, Kadarine." The reverend father sat behind his desk, shuffling and rearranging a few neatly stacked pages. "I'm sorry to have summoned you with such little notice, but there was an item that needed immediate attention." He smiled. "I believe that last night, Alek accidentally e-mailed my wife the wrong draft of the essay he was supposed to read at the Christmas Eve service, and I wanted to call you in here so that we could clear it up as soon as possible."

"What makes you think it was the wrong draft?" Alek's father asked.

Father Reverend Stepanian presented the Khederians with two essays. He held up the first. "This was the paper that my wife granted a perfect grade, the one that had been selected to be read at the service." Then he held up the second one. "And this is the one that Alek sent a few days ago, which is almost identical, with the exception of a different last page that is intentionally provocative and verges on, I hate to say it . . . obscenity."

" 'Obscenity'?" Mr. Khederian wrinkled his eyebrows. "That doesn't sound like Alek."

"I agree!" the reverend father exhaled in relief. "Alek's always been a model boy. That's why I'm sure there's some other explanation."

"Could you give us an example of . . . these obscenities?" his father asked.

Nik snickered just audibly enough for Alek to hear as the reverend father flipped through the second essay, landing on the final page. "Here we go." He started reading from the paper. " 'In conclusion, although being Armenian is integral to my own sense of identity, it's a pity that so many aspects of the church are so archaic. Take its position on abortion, for example. The idea that the church would want to take the choice away from someone who was the victim of rape or incest feels hopelessly outdated. Especially since twenty percent of the one million abortions in this country every year are had by teenagers.' I'm sure you'll agree with me that the Christmas Eve service hardly feels like the place to discuss abortion and rape and incest."

"It is disturbing," Alek's father said quickly.

"And I haven't reached the paragraph about the church's position on gender and sexuality." The reverend father leaned forward.

"I'm sure Alek would be willing to change those sections," his mother added.

"Or just agree to read the original paper," his father offered.

"You know, you don't have to talk about me in the third person since I'm right here!" Alek sat up straight in his chair, startling the adults into silence. "The truth is, what being Armenian means to me has changed since I wrote that original paper, and I don't feel like it accurately reflects the topic. I updated the paper's last few paragraphs to make it a more accurate representation."

"So sending this draft was not a mistake?" the reverend father asked.

"Nope," Alek confirmed.

The reverend father cleared his throat, flipped to the end of the paper, and started reading. "'And how are we supposed to reconcile the church's belief that women can't be ordained as priests?'" The reverend father continued reading. "'We would never work for a company that explicitly forbade women from achieving its highest rank, and we wouldn't belong to an organization that discriminated against women. And yet, because it's church, we're supposed to think it's okay.' What do you have to say about what I just read, Aleksander?"

"I wonder if a little rehearsal might improve your delivery," Alek responded.

"This is not the time to make jokes," the reverend father snapped back. "You and I talked about all of this, and we agreed to keep your personal life personal."

"If 'we agreed' means you told me to keep myself as closeted as possible, then yes, I suppose our recollection of that conversation is the same. But if we've learned nothing else from the #MeToo movement, it's that consent needs to be articulated, not just assumed."

Nik had been sitting silently for this entire exchange, his eyes bulging out a bit farther with each act of Alek's impudence.

"Okay now, Alek, I think we just need to calm down a bit." Mrs. Khederian's smile grew even tighter.

"Reverend Father is being incredibly considerate," Alek's dad chimed in. "All you have to do is read the original paper and everything will be fine, is that correct?"

The reverend father nodded curtly. All the eyes in the room turned to Alek.

"Since I would never bear false witness against my neighbor, Reverend Father, I don't think it makes any more sense to bear false witness against myself." Alek moved Señor Huevo's tea box off the armrest, to make sure he didn't accidentally knock it off with his increasingly expressive gesticulating. "I'm not going to lie to you, and I certainly don't intend to lie to the entire congregation. This new essay reflects, most accurately, what being Armenian means to me."

"How dare you try to turn the annual Christmas Eve service into propaganda?" The reverend father's face turned red. "Did you think we were just going to let this happen? Can you imagine what the members of this congregation would do if you read this essay to them?"

"I don't know. But I'd love to find out. I think you'd be surprised how many of them would appreciate something that addressed what being Armenian feels like to them right now."

"I guess we will never find out, because these words will never be uttered in this church." The reverend father gathered up both essays. "Your original essay was selected for this honor. If you choose not to read it, then I have no option but to rescind the honor." He handed the essays to Alek's parents. "In addition, I'm suspending his Saturday school privileges. I think it'll be best for both Alek and the other students."

"Reverend Father, please—" Mrs. Khederian protested.

"I'm sorry, Kadarine, but Alek's actions are intentionally antagonistic, and I'm afraid that this behavior would interfere with the other students' learning. If you'd still like Alek to attend services, he can do so with you. Maybe after a year of this probation, we can reconsider his role in the classroom. And as for the Christmas Eve service, Mrs. Stepanian will ask the student who received the next-highest grade to read his or her paper." He looked at Nic. "I'm sure *he* will be grateful for the opportunity."

"It's me." Nik, who hadn't spoken for the entire session, suddenly spoke up. "My essay got the next highest grade."

"Then you'll be reading it at the Christmas Eve service." The reverend father clasped Nik's hand heartily. "Congratulations, son."

16

"I MEAN, YOU'RE NOT ACTUALLY GOING TO DO IT, right?" Alek spoke to his brother from the back seat of the car as Nik drove their family home from church. For once, his parents hadn't criticized Nik behind the wheel. Even when he forgot to signal before changing lanes and almost rammed them into an eighteen-wheeler. "Guys," Alek said, addressing his parents, "you're not going to let him do it, right?"

"You turned it down, Alek," his father reasoned. "Why does it matter to you whether or not your brother accepts the honor?"

"It's going to be someone," his mother chimed in, from the passenger's seat. "Why not Nik?"

"Because Nik doing it is basically an endorsement of all of the church's worst positions! It would be like agreeing to perform at 45's inauguration!"

"That's enough, Alek," his father said from the back seat, next to him. "Aren't you being just a bit hysterical?"

Alek stared out the window, holding back tears of anger, wondering if he'd survive hurling himself out of the car at its current speed. The major reason he didn't pursue this line of action was that he didn't want to abandon Señor Huevo to this pack of hypocrites.

Nik remained suspiciously, annoyingly, smugly quiet.

To make it worse, Alek suspected that Nik was intentionally driving poorly, because now he could get away with it. He waited as long as possible to put on his blinker before making a turn, changed lanes so abruptly that the move was basically horizontal, and instead of coming to a full stop when faced with those octagonal signs, he just slowed down, daring their parents to criticize their new favorite son. But the Khederians said nothing.

Route 33 continued, unchanging, even more anonymous because of the snow covering the few landmarks that distinguished it from every other highway in every other suburb in every other state.

When they finally pulled into the driveway of their home, Alek didn't even wait for Nik to turn the car off before jumping out and slamming the door behind him.

"What're you wearing?" Alek asked Becky on the way to Ethan's house on New Year's Eve, on his birthday gift.

"You are such a perv," Becky responded. "What're you wearing?"

"Nothing fancy—jeans, button-down. It's not like we're doing anything special, you know." Alek had dreaded making plans with Ethan on New Year's Eve, but now that he was actually walking over to Ethan's house, he felt a few of those familiar old butterflies flapping in his stomach.

"I am rocking this skirt with a hemline that swoops down one side. But look, I have to go. Dustin's going to be here any second and my parents have insisted on spending some time with him today before they head out to whatever fancy schmancy party they're going to and Dustin and I go to Dev's party, where John will be with the trombonist and Mahira will be with her new boyfriend from choir. I don't even need to tell you how many things could possibly go wrong, and as I'm sure you can imagine, I'm hoping for all of them."

"Happy New Year, Becky."

"You too, weirdo."

Alek hung up by snapping his phone shut, grateful, at least, that he could accomplish the act without having to take off his gloves, the way he would've needed to if he'd had a smartphone. His parents had offered to drive him to Ethan's, but he didn't mind the walk. It was cold—he could see each exhale, and he could feel the tip of his nose was turning red. But it wasn't that kind of bone-chilling cold that a gusty wind produced. It was just cold, and he could live with just cold.

When Alek came home, he could tell if his parents had been cooking by the smells that greeted him, even before he opened the front door. The savory welcome of onions or garlic sautéed in olive oil were pretty much standard. Alek could usually make out additional ingredients (cumin's muskiness, allspice's nuttiness, thyme's fragrant bouquet, or cayenne's sinus-clearing heat). Sometimes, he could even guess the dish itself, all from the odors that met him.

Standing outside Ethan's door on New Year's Eve, Alek felt his nervousness evaporate, like the excess liquid of a sauce being reduced, when he inhaled the undeniable smell of cooking. Or, at least, something similar to it.

After a few unanswered knocks, Alek opened the door himself. "Hello?" he called into the cloud of smoke hovering ominously at the entrance to the house. "Hello?"

"In here!" Ethan hollered over the music blasting from the kitchen.

Alek cleared some space on the small table by the front door for Señor Huevo, safely ensconced in his tea-box house. After a moment of deliberation, Alek decided to remove the box lid so that Señor Huevo wouldn't feel claustrophobic. Then he began the ritual of shedding his winter layers: gloves, boots next, then jacket, and then finally his woolen scarf, which he stuffed into one of the jacket sleeves so that he wouldn't lose or forget it.

"Wish me luck, Señor Huevo."

Señor Huevo did not respond, but Alek felt like he received his blessing nonetheless.

He followed the trail of smoke into the Novick kitchen, undoubtedly the most underused room in the house. What he saw when he entered was just some yellow tape away from being a crime scene.

Ingredients were strewn haphazardly on the L-shaped

counter, the stovetop, the kitchen table, even inside the sink. Knives lay on cutting boards that were stacked on top of one another with the herbs or vegetables abandoned midchop, as if a deranged cook decided last-minute to change the recipe altogether. The refrigerator door was ajar. Three of the four ranges were lit, with pots and pans sizzling away. The oven itself was emitting smoke like a witch's cauldron.

"Everything okay in here?" Alek asked gently.

"Of course!" Ethan, apparently, wasn't going to let the impending culinary disaster bring him down. "I thought I'd make us a little dinner to celebrate New Year's Eve!"

Alek struggled to reconcile the tragedy he was witnessing with Ethan's chipper mood. "And how's it going?"

"Great, I think. The garlic bread is baking in the oven, the mousse is setting in the fridge, and I'm almost done with the coq au vin."

"You made coq au vin?" Alek said, correcting Ethan's pronunciation, which was more butchered than the chicken carcass on the counter. "That's—really complicated. Like, way more complicated than something I'd try. How'd the trial run go?"

"The what?" Ethan asked, struggling to peel a few garlic cloves.

"You know—the trial run you do when preparing a dish you've never made before. To work out all the kinks and stuff."

"That's a thing?" Ethan scoffed. "No way."

As if to corroborate Alek, a frying pan sizzling with bacon started hissing and splattering oil. A few drops landed on Ethan's arm (*who cooks in short sleeves?* Alek thought to himself. *And without an apron!*). He howled as the oil burned him but recovered quickly. "I just downloaded a few recipes online, mixed and matched until I thought it sounded good, and gave it a whirl."

"You compiled recipes you've never made before?"

"Sure! And when I didn't have the ingredients, I just substituted with whatever was in the house."

Alek hoped that he was able to keep his groan internal. "For example?" He gently slipped the serrated knife Ethan was using to hack an onion out of his grasp and deposited it in the sink, then fished out and rinsed the closest thing he could find to a proper chef's knife, and slipped it into Ethan's hand, hilt first, of course.

"I didn't have enough bacon, so I added some sausage. And we didn't have any red wine, so I used some beer."

"You used beer in coq au vin?"

"Sure, why not?"

"You know that coq au vin means 'chicken in wine.' That's sort of the whole point of the recipe."

"I'm sure it'll be . . ." The ringing of the fire alarm cut Ethan off. "Damn it!" He jumped up, unsuccessfully trying to swat the alarm into silence.

"Here—let me." Alek picked up a broom propped against the kitchen counter and guided the handle to the red button on the fire alarm, gently quieting the maddening *beep beep beep*.

"So let's see." Ethan consulted three different recipes he'd printed, each stained with different liquids. "Now I put the chicken back into the Dutch oven with the sausage and bacon and beer and onions, and then put all of that in the oven."

"Can I give you a hand?" Alek dubiously eyed the pot masquerading as a Dutch oven. His mother would never cook with such a shabby pot, let alone place it and its potentially meltable handles into the oven.

"No need." Ethan picked up a plate holding a pyramid of chicken parts and dumped them into the pot unceremoniously, splattering liquids everywhere. He grabbed a towel and, using it as a makeshift pot holder, opened the oven door with his knee. When he went to put the pot inside the oven, however, he discovered the two racks were too close to each other for the pot to fit.

"Are you sure you don't—"

"Nah, man, I'm good." Hugging the pot to his body with one hand, Ethan reached for the top rack. Since the garlic bread was already baking inside, however, the hot rack burned his flesh the second he made contact. He flinched and dropped the pot of something that not a single person would've guessed was coq au vin.

Bacon, sausage, beer, hacked vegetables, and raw chicken spilled all over the kitchen floor.

Ethan, who usually moved with a skateboarder's agility, just stood looking down at the mess he'd made.

"I screwed it all up, didn't I?" Ethan surveyed the scene with honest eyes. "I had this idea that you'd walk in and I would've made this beautiful meal for you, and it would've all been perfect, and you'd see how hard I worked and how much I cared, and everything would be great again. But I screwed it up, just like I mess everything up."

He crumpled on the tiled kitchen floor like a marionette whose strings had been snipped.

"Hey—it's okay. It's okay!" Alek put on a set of ancient moss-green oven mitts and picked up the pot before all its contents spilled out. "It's the thought that counts, right?" He began turning off the burners on the range before the fire alarm sounded again or, more likely, the house burned down. "And besides, I'm sure it would've been delish." He felt great relief, actually, since the accident allowed him to get out of sampling the contents of the pot and risking salmonella. Instead, he inhaled the aroma, which almost made him gag. But he put on a good face anyway. "Mmmm!"

Ethan looked up from the kitchen floor. "Alek Khederian, you have always been a hundred percent honest with me. Don't stop now. Admit it—this would've been a disaster."

Alek contemplated the culinary pandemonium before him. "At best," he agreed. "But don't worry. I know exactly what to do."

"You do?"

Alek nodded. He picked up the receiver to the Novicks' landline and dialed from memory. "Hi, Mr. Lee? It's Alek, Mrs. Khederian's son—please don't hang up! Are you still there? Okay, good. Happy New Year to you, too! How does the broccoli look today?"

"Four of these is never enough." Alek smeared the last remaining pancake with plum sauce and deposited a healthy serving of moo goo gai pan on top. "Do you think there's something we don't understand about this dish? Or that it's just a conspiracy to get us to pay more for an extra order of pancakes?"

"Definitely a conspiracy." Ethan slurped his hot-and-sour soup with relish. "What do you think people do in places where there isn't any Chinese food delivery?"

"You think such horrible places exist?" Alek asked between bites. "I've always wondered—why is it called an *egg* roll? Is there supposed to be egg inside? Or is the roll itself made with egg?"

"How about duck sauce?" Ethan said, riffing along. "Where's the duck?"

"This is most certainly not made with duck," Alek said, holding up one of the little orange-red plastic packets. "This is made with Red Number Four, sugar, and an extra dose of something carcinogenic, I'm sure."

"And who's General Tso?" Ethan gesticulated with his chopsticks. "Was he, like, a real general in Chinese history? Like their version of George Washington?"

"When I first heard about wonton soup, I thought it was called *wanton* soup, and I kept on imagining this, like, really dangerous, irresponsible soup that didn't have a care in the world."

Alek and Ethan enjoyed each other's laughter. They spent the remainder of the meal riffing like this, as they might've in the past.

"Sorry about a few days ago, at the diner." Alek fished the fortune cookies out of the takeout bag, choosing one for himself and handing Ethan the other.

"No prob—it sounds like you've been really busy lately."

"Yeah, getting kicked out of Saturday school has really taken up a lot of time." Alek caught Ethan up on everything that had happened with Arno, the reverend father, and his family in the last week.

"I'm proud of you." Ethan beamed. "You always do the thing you think is right. I've always dug that."

Alek smiled. Ethan was the only person he knew who would've listened to that story and arrived at that conclusion.

Ethan cracked his cookie open and read out loud from the little slip of paper inside. "'You like Chinese food.' Okay—(A) that's a pretty good guess since that's what I ordered."

"And number two," Alek picked up, "that's not a fortune. That's a description."

"Exactly!"

"'You will amass great wealth.'" Alek folded his paper and put in his pocket. "That's more like it."

"You will amass great wealth. In bed," Ethan joked.

"You like Chinese food. In bed. With sheep," Alek played along. "What about you—what've you been up to?"

"You know—burning vegetables, burning chicken, burning beer. The usual." Ethan laughed.

Ethan had shrugged off the trauma of his failed meal as effortlessly as he did everything. This ease, Alek knew, was what had made him like Ethan so much when they met. And it still did now. And it's what made it possible, over the course of their meal, to slowly find their groove again. A few bites later, after they'd eaten their fortune cookies and compared their fortunes, they embarked on the task of restoring the kitchen.

They cleaned up the remnants of the Chinese food first, placing leftovers in Tupperware, putting the Chinese food containers in the dishwasher (top shelf, Alek insisted, where there was less heat and the chances of plastics releasing dangerous chemicals was lower). They moved on to the grand project of cleaning up the aborted meal itself. Alek threw away everything that was unsalvageable, like the mostly raw chicken, and gave Ethan copious instructions for what he could do with the rest.

"The mousse actually came out pretty good, although it's a little watery. With some heavy whipped cream and a touch of confectioners' sugar, or a dollop of crème fraîche, I'm sure it'd be delish."

Even though Ethan nodded studiously, Alek felt like he was giving directions to someone in a foreign language, who barely understood what he was saying, let alone where to turn right.

They fell into an easy rhythm, Ethan holding the garbage open while Alek scraped the leftovers off the plates, or Alek grabbing the dustbin when he saw Ethan begin to sweep the floor as they neared the end of the work.

By the time they finished, the kitchen sparkled cleaner than Alek had ever seen it. They stood amid the shining surfaces, the low rumble of the dishwasher underscoring their silence.

"So," Ethan started, ". . . you wanna come up?"

"Up?"

"To my room." As if he could read Alek's mind, Ethan said, "I just want to play you a song."

Alek nodded yes and followed Ethan upstairs, his extra-thick winter socks bouncing up the carpeted floor to Ethan's room.

Where he was shocked to find the walls bare.

"Where'd they all go?" The collage of men, celebrities and models, half-naked or more, that had adorned every surface of Ethan's room were gone, as if they'd never been there.

"I needed a change." Ethan shrugged. "To put away the clutter. Help me think straight."

"But now it looks like everyone else's room. Before it was so . . ."

"So what?"

"So Ethan!"

The shock of Ethan's bare walls hit Alek so viscerally, he felt like he might start to cry.

"Hey, man—it's okay." Ethan sat Alek down on his bed. "They're just pictures. And besides, this will allow me to put up something else."

"Like what?"

"I don't know—I've got a few ideas. But for now it's nice to have an empty canvas."

"Tabula rasa."

"Is that Armenian?"

"Latin. It means 'blank slate.' The Romans used to take notes on wax tablets. Then they'd heat them up and smooth them out to erase them when they needed to be used again."

"Out with the old . . ."

"Exactly. Feels especially appropriate, you know, with it being New Year's Eve and all."

The pause between them lingered. But this was not the silence of awkwardness. This was the silence of something else.

Alek suddenly felt all of his senses heighten. He could smell the detergent on Ethan's recently laundered sheets, the traces of sandalwood incense that he'd probably burned that afternoon. He could feel the surprising roughness of the down comforter, the warm draft of hot air blowing into the room from the vent behind him.

And most of all, he became conscious of Ethan, of his energy, of his physical presence, sitting next to him on the bed, the closeness of their bodies, the closeness of their lips, how long it had been since they'd . . .

The one thing he knew for sure was that if he met Ethan now, the draw he felt, the tug, the chemistry between them would be as powerful as ever. Maybe even more.

"You wanted me to listen to something?" Alek managed to get the words out without his voice breaking too much.

"Yeah." Ethan turned up the volume on his computer. "This is Brandy Clark. Country."

Alek made a face. "Country music? Isn't that all hillbillies and ukuleles and coal miners?"

Ethan laughed. "Just give it a chance, would you?" He clicked his mouse. "This is her first album, *12 Stories*."

They sat in his room, listening to the music.

Sometimes, their silence was interrupted by Alek's laughter. "The songs are really funny!"

"I know, right?"

"Even when sometimes you think a song is funny, it's not like laugh-out-loud funny. It's like, 'I intellectually recognize that as funny, but it doesn't actually make you laugh.' But 'Crazy Women' is hilarious. Like really, really funny."

Sometimes, Alek would ask Ethan to replay a tune. "I can't believe she wrote an entire song about getting high."

"I know—that one is funny and sad, too."

"It's just nice to hear someone writing about this stuff without that kind of after-school-special judgment, you know." Alek dropped his voice into a deep, movie-of-the-week announcer. "'His life was perfect. Until he tried one beer. And then he died.'"

Ethan laughed, his eyes twinkling. Alek relished, as if he never had before, the joy he received from making Ethan laugh.

"And you know, she's a lesbian," Ethan added.

"No way!" Alek exclaimed. "That's so cool—I didn't even know there were gay country music stars."

"The world is full of surprises—like gay marriage being legalized all over the world now."

Alek leaned forward. "Don't get my mom started on that."

"Your mom isn't for gay marriage?" Ethan asked incredulously.

"Of course she is. But she says we need to be careful, especially now, otherwise the same thing that happened to abortion rights will happen to gay rights."

"And what's that?"

"The Supreme Court voted to make abortion legal in the early seventies, but since then individual states have been rolling back those rights, especially the red ones. She says there's no reason that couldn't happen to gay marriage, too."

"That's what happens when you're the descendants of the greatest unacknowledged genocide—you get paranoid about everything."

"Okay, but look at how black people are treated in this country—and that's a hundred and fifty years after the Emancipation Proclamation. And it still feels like every month there's another video of a cop—I mean, a *cop*—doing something so horrible, you're embarrassed to be American."

"I'm not embarrassed to be an American. I mean, yeah, horrible things happen, but do you think it's better anywhere else?"

Alek let the subject slide, but he couldn't help feeling like even though they were talking about the country, they were talking about their relationship, too. "Ethan, was there something you wanted me to listen to specifically?"

"Yeah." Ethan clicked on his computer's mouse. "Here we go."

They listened to it in silence, Alek painfully aware of how close his hand was to Ethan's.

Don't let this moment linger. Now would be the time. To reach out with your fingers and get 'em tangled up with mine. Ethan half sang, half whispered whenever the chorus came. *This'd be a real good time to hold my hand.*

"Why this one?" Alek asked after it had finished.

"When we were at the restaurant, with Remi, I pulled my hand away from yours."

"I remember."

"I don't know why I did it. But when I think about that night, when I think about how I could've done something so stupid, that's what I always think about first. How you've always held my hand everywhere. In New York, where no one cares. In suburban malls, where we got funny looks. In private, where our hands felt like they were made to fit in each other's. Somehow, I think, if I had just held your hand that day, none of it would've happened. That's why I wanted to play this one for you. When I heard the lyric 'This would be a real good time to hold my hand,' I thought, *Every time is a good time for me to be holding my boyfriend's hand*."

Ethan leaned in, and Alek stopped fighting the impulse, the instinct, the programming that had been wired into his body for the last six months. He kissed Ethan.

Kissing Ethan.

Kissing Ethan rocked.

"I'm so happy you're here." Ethan ran his fingers through Alek's hair, familiarly, happily, joyously. "Being with you is even better than . . . being in the city."

"Now that's a compliment." Alek's hands found Ethan's face, his chin, his neck.

"After you left me at the diner a few days ago, the only thing I could do was run away to the 212. It's the only place I wasn't going to feel suicidal."

"And what'd you do?" Alek asked a few moments later.

"When?"

"Then. When you went into the city?"

"Hit some party," Ethan shot off nonchalantly.

Too nonchalantly, Alek thought.

"Where?"

"Who cares where?"

Like Spiderman's spidey-sense, an inexplicable, intuitive instinct told Alek to pursue the line of questioning. "If who cares, then why don't you tell me?"

"It was in Bed-Stuy, okay?" Ethan adjusted.

"Who do you know in Bed-Stuy?"

"Some guys I met in Greenpoint," Ethan said.

"That same night?"

"Yeah."

"Oh." Alek pulled away.

"What 'oh'? No 'oh'! We were just making out. It was awesome. Let's do that more!"

Alek and Ethan kissed for a few more minutes. But the demon of distraction was already ripping down that magical bubble.

"So . . . how was the party?" Alek asked.

"Which party?"

"The one in Bed-Stuy."

"It was lame. I'd rather have been with you."

And then Alek asked the question he hadn't realized he was holding back until it came tumbling out of his mouth. "Was Remi there?"

"What?"

"I'm sorry—was I unintentionally speaking Latin or some other language you don't understand? I said, 'Was Remi there?'"

"No." Ethan paused. "I mean, not really . . ."

Alek's spidey-sense wasn't just tingling anymore. It was screaming, like a siren. He pulled away. "What do you mean, 'not really'? Either he was there or he wasn't. It's not a trick question, Ethan."

"He wasn't there when I got there. And the music was pretty cool, and so were the peeps."

"And . . ."

"And then he showed up."

"So he was there."

"I guess, technically, yes. Remi and I were both at the same party for the five minutes it took me to get my shit and go." Ethan adjusted again, doing his best to make eye contact.

"What 'technically'? He was there. He was physically there. I don't understand why this required such a complicated exchange." Alek got up and walked out of Ethan's room. "Thanks for the song. And tunes. And dinner."

Ethan scrambled to follow. "Where are you going?"

"Home."

"But why?"

Alek yanked on his winter clothes, taking his frustration at not being able to make a clean getaway out on them. "Gosh, Ethan, it is hard to think of something more fun than being lied to by you. Again. Let me see—maybe I can work really hard and force myself to come up with something." He tugged on his boots unceremoniously. "Okay: here's a list of things." He reached the front door. "Root canal, chores, self-amputation, stigmata in my eyes, another four years of 45."

Ethan ran his fingers through his sandy hair. "Come on, man—I just went to a party. I didn't know he'd be there, and I left the second he got there. It's not like anything happened, you know?" When Alek didn't say anything, Ethan continued. "Alek, it's New Year's Eve. We were getting along so well. Come back. Let's talk about this. Don't you think you're overreacting just a bit?"

"Let me get this straight." Alek spoke slowly, methodically, with the kind of emphasis reserved for escape plans in action movies. "You go to a party that you were invited to by some people you met with the guy you cheated on me with, then when I ask you if he was there you lie to me, and I'm the one who's overreacting?"

"I didn't lie to you."

He wrapped his scarf around his neck. "Yes, you did. You said he wasn't there. And he was. If that's not a lie, I don't know what is."

"I just didn't see what the big deal was."

"There was no big deal." One glove. "Until you lied to me." The other glove.

"Stop saying that."

"Stop saying what? That you're a liar? That Ethan Novick is a liar? Why would I stop when it's the truth? I mean, maybe there's more you're not telling me. Maybe you guys didn't just overlap for five minutes. Maybe you hung out the whole night. Maybe you even slept together. Again. Who knows? I certainly don't."

"Stop it, Alek! Please, stop it!"

"I know you won't understand this, Ethan, but when you're not a liar, you actually take great pride in telling the truth. And the truth is, you're a liar."

"I didn't mean—I never meant to lie to you. I just didn't want to get into a fight about it. And especially because things were so nice."

"I'll see you later, liar. And just so that I don't have to deal with Becky asking me about this, and just so there's no confusion: you and me—we're done. This is what it feels like to be dumped. Happy New Year." Alek grabbed the nearest thing to him and hurled it at Ethan, full force.

Señor Huevo went flying through the air, missing Ethan but hitting the wall next to him. He splattered into chunks of hard-boiled egg and shell, some of them ending up in Ethan's clothes, his hair, on his face.

returning from wherever they'd been celebrating. Once inside, Mrs. Boyce immediately slipped off her heels and removed her earrings, two loops of tiny diamonds surrounding a translucent pearl.

"Is Becky expecting you?"

Mr. and Mrs. Boyce had really dressed up for the occasion, Alek saw when they removed their coats: him in a jacket and tie and her in a maroon, floor-length gown. Alek knew that he should ask them about their evening, their resolutions, their holidays. But right now, he just couldn't be bothered.

"Not really." Alek tried to play it cool, as if dropping by unannounced at your best friend's house just before midnight on New Year's Eve was totally normal.

The three of them stood awkwardly in the Boyces' foyer, waiting for something to happen. Becky's mom broke the silence.

"Well, she's probably back from the band party . . ."

". . . and in the basement."

Surely Alek was imagining the nervous glances he saw the Boyces exchanging.

"You all have fun tonight, and . . ."

". . . happy New Year's!" Mr. Boyce opened the door to their basement and yelled down, "Becky, dear . . ."

". . . Alek is here!" his wife finished for him, a little louder than perhaps was necessary.

Alek clomped downstairs in all his winter layers, feeling like the abominable snowman. Every familiar detail was a balm: the zigzag carpeting on the steps, the creaking banister, the tiny landscape windows at ground level—even the inexplicably unfinished concrete floors and exposed drywall.

He was crashing now, spent, turning back to human form, emerging from the shock of having done the unimaginable: actually breaking up with Ethan. His racing heart, exhausted, slowed down, decelerating to its normal beats per minute.

The more the numbness faded, the more he hurt, like novocaine wearing off mid-drill. Telling Becky what had happened was the only thing that would make the surfacing pain go away. He just needed to get to Becky. Who was sitting in her usual place on the mammoth brown couch.

Right next to Dustin.

"Oh my God, what happened?" Becky jumped up, adjusting her tights, her cream blouse with ruffles, and her skirt with an asymmetrical hem.

"I dumped Ethan." All of Alek's emotions came bubbling out of him, like a mad scientist's experiment gone wrong.

Dustin let out a long exhale. "Damn, man. That is rough." The top few buttons of his slate-gray button-down were suspiciously undone, Alek noted, and he made no move to redo them.

"OMG, Alek, I can't believe it!" Becky got up and met him at the foot of the staircase. "What're you doing tomorrow? You wanna come over and tell me all about it?"

"Tomorrow?" Alek kicked his boots off. "What's wrong with now?"

"It's just that we were"—Becky fake-cough-coughed—"in the middle of things."

"No, look, I get it from the smudge of lipstick on Dustin's

face and the way you keep fidgeting with your tights." Neither one of them had the decency to blush, Alek noted. "But I really need you, Becky. Like, desperately."

"Becks, I'll catch you later." Dustin stood up. "And Alek, happy New Year, buddy. Sorry it's starting so whack." He snatched his stupid green skateboard that he apparently insisted on carrying around with him everywhere even though it was way too cold to actually use it since it was THE MIDDLE OF WINTER.

"Dustin." A low rumble that Alek didn't recognize erupted from Becky's mouth, full of reverberating bass. "Sit!" Slowly, sheepishly, Dustin sat back down. She turned to Alek. "I'm sorry you and Ethan broke up. Seriously, I am. But you're not kicking my boyfriend out because you chose to break up with your boyfriend tonight, not any more than you ever would have kicked Ethan out for me or anyone or anything!"

"You don't even know—" Alek began to protest.

But Becky cut him off. "Yes, I do. And I'm pretty sure I can tell you exactly how it happened, too. You showed up there, things were going nicely, then Ethan did something to piss you off and you lost your temper and dumped him and stormed out." Alek's silence was all the confirmation Becky needed. "That's what I thought. So you have to ask yourself, Aleksander Khederian, why are you choosing to end this year by being such an asshole?"

"Me? An asshole?"

"You heard me."

"If I were half the asshole you think I am, I'd tell you that no one understands what you're possibly doing with Dustin."

Alek referenced Becky's boyfriend as if he weren't in the room. "You're amazing—funny and smart and wicked. You're like a chocolate cheesecake. And he's so tapioca. You could do so much better."

"Get out." Becky was physically quaking with anger, and her voice trembled with the attempt to constrain it. "Get out of my damn house."

"Are you serious?" Alek asked.

Becky started speaking before he'd finished the question, raising her voice over his. "Are you deaf as well as—"

"Okay, guys, I think you both need to take a step back." Dustin hadn't raised his voice, but somehow his calm, clear tone cut through their hysteria.

"But he—" Becky protested.

"But she—" Alek sputtered.

"That's enough."

Both Becky and Alek shut up.

"Becks." Dustin rose from the sofa and stood between them. He placed his hand on her shoulder. "You know Alek doesn't mean any of the things he's saying tonight. He's all kinds of bent because of what he's going through. You gotta cut him some slack."

"I guess," Becky semi-conceded.

"And, Alek, my man." Dustin turned to face him. "I may not be fun and quirky and weird like you and Becks. But I treat her right and think she's the aces. And I know that you do, too. Isn't that enough common ground? So why don't you take a seat and tell us both what happened?"

Alek regarded Dustin anew. Was it possible that he'd

underestimated him this whole time, that what seemed like blandness was just pure chillness? How would Alek have responded if one of Ethan's friends had talked to him the way he'd talked to Dustin? And wasn't the most important thing about whomever was lucky enough to be with Becky that he thought the world of her and treated her well?

"When I showed up at Ethan's, I could smell from the front door that he'd been cooking." Alek plopped himself down on the sofa.

"Ethan, cooking?" Becky sat herself next to him, leaving just enough room for Dustin between them.

Dustin took the cue. "This doesn't sound good."

"*Cooking* is a strong word for what I discovered in the kitchen." Alek relaxed, letting the story flow out. Whenever he found himself editing something out for Dustin's benefit, he went back and included the detail, as he would have if he'd been alone with Becky.

Sometimes, it was Dustin who asked for specifics. "So were you guys just kissing or, like, really going at it?"

"We were definitely hitting it." Alek gave Dustin credit for not being one of those straight guys who freaked out when in the proximity of anything gay, as if it were a contagious condition or asking about it was tantamount to coming out.

When Becky was dissatisfied with the level of detail being provided, she let it be known. "Where was his father during all this? And what color flannel was he wearing?"

"Lesley's. Red and black, small pattern, you know? With a wifebeater underneath."

"Could we please use a different name for that?" Becky protested.

"Okay—A-shirts, or whatever they're called."

When he reached the end of the story, Alek felt like a poison had been purged from his system. "Pretty amazing, right? I actually did it."

Becky had one of those quizzical looks, the kind Alek had learned to recognize as being a precursor for her saying something totally unexpected. "Is it my duty, as your solemnly sworn best friend, to point out that you basically dumped Ethan for no reason?"

"What do you mean? He lied to me. Again!"

Alek could tell Dustin wanted to say something but didn't. So Becky did. "I mean, not really."

"He said Remi wasn't at the party when he was."

"Oh my God—are you seriously going to . . ." Becky looked up suddenly. "Hold on! It's almost midnight!" Becky unmuted the TV, giving voice to the flickering lights that had been playing in the background.

Alek joined in as Becky and Dustin counted down to zero with Ryan Seacrest and his suspiciously perfect teeth, then turned away so that they would have some privacy for their first kiss of the New Year.

"Get over here, Alek." Dustin yanked him between them, where Becky and Dustin kissed him on either cheek. Alek kissed Becky first, then Dustin, before all three of them launched into a loud and off-key version of "Auld Lang Syne."

It certainly wasn't how Alek had expected to spend his

New Year's Eve—living out the worst possible stereotype of the single gay sandwiched between his coupled, hetero friends. But between being alone and this, he'd choose the latter every time.

18

ALEK STUMBLED OUT OF BECKY'S AT CLOSE TO
one a.m., aware that he'd broken his curfew again, aware that
he'd probably be grounded, aware that he still hadn't been
grounded for the first infraction the night of the six-month
with Ethan, aware that the cumulative grounding would probably last until he left for college or later.

It was that funny time when it still felt like the night before
but was technically the next day. Alek wondered why the day
change didn't happen later—like at two a.m., or even four, to
prevent this confusion. But he didn't rule the world. If he
did, that would be one of the many things he'd change, like
why the United States still used inches and pounds when the
rest of the world was on the metric system.

It was colder still than when he'd stormed out of Ethan's.
Even though that had been just a few hours ago, it felt like it
had happened in a different decade. And although he wanted

to ignore them, Becky's words about breaking up with Ethan for no reason still tugged at him, at the corner of his consciousness, like a star you could see only if you didn't look directly at it.

Any other night, the entirety of his neighborhood would've been asleep at this time. In fact, once Becky bet Alek that she could lie down in the middle on her street at midnight and stay there until six a.m. unharmed. But on New Year's Eve, he passed the occasional lit window or parking car, its inhabitants returning from the night's festivities. He didn't take the most direct route home, weaving circuitously through blocks and parks and houses that all looked suspiciously alike, an homage to the uniformity of suburban planning.

He took his time returning home.

He opened the door to his house quietly, not really trying to sneak in, just not wanting to wake up anyone who might already be asleep. The light in the kitchen told him he needn't have bothered. Either an army of badgers was attacking the Khederian kitchen, or his brother was making a late-night snack.

Alek walked into the kitchen, not bothering to greet Nik, who was in the throes of assembling an impressive sandwich. A half-sliced tomato presented itself on the kitchen counter. The savory scent of a sizzling onion, sautéing on the stove, enticed him. How many of the greatest recipes in the world started with sautéing an onion? The kebab meat and pita warming up in the toaster oven, however, made Alek think of Ethan, and in spite of everything, a ripple of laughter erupted from him.

"What's so funny?" Nik asked.

"Nothing."

Alek didn't think he was hungry when he came home. But the sight and, more importantly, the smells of the kitchen reminded Alek how long it had been since he'd devoured the Chinese food. As if Nik could read his brother's mind, he slid the Tupperware containing the kebabs across the kitchen counter. Alek caught it, unsnapping the lid that ensured air-free storage.

"Do you sometimes," Alek said as he placed his kebab next to Nik's in the toaster oven, "wish we had a microwave? You know, like everybody else?"

"Mom says that microwaves destroy food's nutrients. And taste."

"Mom says lots of things."

Nik sliced another onion, throwing it into the skillet. Alek understood this was as close to an invitation as he'd receive to stay and talk.

Alek filled the electric kettle. "Mint?" he asked his brother.

His brother grunted his consent.

They had two sets of tea ware, of course: porcelain for every-day use, fine china for guests. Alek filled an empty tea filter with three teaspoons of loose mint tea (one per cup, plus one "for the pot"). Using loose tea was not just a flavor-palate deci-sion, his mother had explained to them. "Who knows what they use to make those tea bags? Adhesives? Bleach? It's the last stuff you want to be pouring boiling water over and then ingest-ing! Besides, the tea used in most prepackaged tea bags is usu-ally just the dustings and breakings from actual tea leaves, which means they release more tannins and don't taste as good. Really, loose tea is the only option."

"Can I ask you something?" Nik munched on some almonds.

Alek gave his head the barest of noncommittal nods as he got the ketchup (for himself) and mustard (for his brother) out of the fridge.

"What did you write in your essay? The one that beat mine?"

While they waited for their meat and pita to warm up, Alek threw together a small salad: greens from the fridge, the remainder of the sliced tomato that was already on the counter, and a carrot that he quickly rinsed (rinsing vegetables, his mother had repeatedly reminded them, should always take place before any incision was made, peeled, then transformed it into paper-thin ribbons using the peeler again.

"We had just finished making all that dolma for Thanksgiving, remember?"

Nik laughed. "There were, like, grapevine leaves everywhere."

"Exactly! And I thought about how this is a dish that Armenians have been making forever."

"I'd say between three and five thousand years." Nik tilted his head. "Grapes probably arrived in what is now Armenia around 5000 BC from Phoenician traders."

"Okay then—so like I said, forever. And Mom was using the food processor for the pie crusts, so we had to chop the peppers and onions and parsley by hand. And it got me thinking how, like, for the history of time, Armenians had been making this dish just about the way we were making it then. Families sitting at the table, making the filling, stuffing the leaves, rolling them out, and cooking them up. And how lucky we were to be part of that lineage. That is what being Armenian means to me."

"No wonder you beat me." Nik nodded appreciatively. "I just wrote what I thought I should write about: the indignity of being the victims of an unacknowledged genocide, the well-known story of how we were the first people to convert to Christianity, yadda yadda yadda."

"You know, *odars*"—Alek used the Armenian word used to describe non-Armenians—"don't know that story."

"Huh. Seriously?" Nik asked.

"Totally," Alek confirmed.

Nik removed the meat and pitas from the toaster oven and began assembling the sandwiches.

"What does being Armenian really mean to you?" Alek whipped up a little salad dressing: equal parts oil, lemon, and vinegar with a squirt of Dijon mustard, a dash of fresh chopped mint, and a healthy shake of salt and pepper.

They sat down at the kitchen table, not bothering to put place mats down but still folding napkins on their laps. Nik spoke between bites, something he'd never have done if their parents were present. "I would've written about anything *but* the genocide. Yes, it was horrible, and yes, the fact that it's unacknowledged makes it even worse. But the Armenian people were around for thousands of years before that and will be for thousands more, and wouldn't it be sad if we let our entire identity be defined by the worst thing that happened, versus the great stuff we've done?" Nik sprinkled a little vinegar on his sandwich. "Can I ask you something?"

"Shoot."

"What's the big deal about being out in church?"

Alek put his sandwich down. "God, you can be such a prick."

"Why? Because I'm asking about this?"

"Sure. And what about you throwing around that 'hetero-phobic' bullshit? It's like white people insisting that all lives matter."

"Don't act like you're such a freakin' angel, you know? Ever since you came out, Mom and Dad have been fawning over you, like just because you're gay, you're special."

"My being gay is only a small part of the inimitable spec-tacularness that is me."

"So what—because I'm straight, I'm not allowed to ask about the gay stuff? I want to know why it means so much to you, because I don't get it. And I'm trying to. So you can either make me feel like an asshole for not understanding, or you can just tell me already."

"Fair enough." Alek swallowed.

"Because, seriously, the last thing I'd want the reverend father knowing is anything about who I'm dating."

The gentle hiss of the boiling water provided Alek an excuse to leave the table. He prepared the pot, pouring a little hot water in and swirling it around first. Once it was sufficiently warm, he discarded the water, placed the packed filter inside, and slowly poured the boiling water over the loose tea. "Okay. It's like this. Let's say you were hanging out with a bunch of people, and one of them started talking about how the Armenian genocide didn't happen." Alek returned to the table with the teapot and two mugs.

214

"A denier?"

"Exactly. What would you do?" They both knew to wait three to five minutes for the tea to be properly brewed before pouring it.

"I would try to swallow my rage and fury, then, as calmly as I could, cite all the impressive historical facts to support my case."

"Great! Now, why would you do that? Why would you risk angering this person, making the people around you uncomfortable, why would you feel compelled to do all that, when you could just Elsa-let-it-go?"

Nik wrapped his hands around the warm teapot. "Because it would be dishonest not to. I don't want them believing a lie. And I'd want to try to change this denier's mind."

"Great. So why am I out at church? Because we lived in a world built on assumptions, and one of them is that everyone is straight."

"That's not—"

"It isn't?" Alek interrupted. "Come on—how many times am I asked at church if I've found a nice Armenian girl yet versus how often you're asked about your boyfriend, Nik? Huh?" Alek responded, plowing forward. "And even though gay marriage has been legal in this country for, like, how many years now, when you meet a woman who says she's married, what gender do you imagine her spouse to be? It's woven into our society, these assumptions, and every one of them is a microaggression to someone queer like me."

"Okay—point made," Nik conceded.

"So I have to make a decision: either let everyone assume

215

I'm straight, which is a lie, or come out. I don't get to not make the decision. And just as you want the people in the group to know the truth about the Armenian Genocide, I want people to know the truth about me. And just like you might want to try and change the denier's mind, I want all those old Armos at church to see that queer people are just like them. You know, it's infinitely harder to be homophobic when you actually know someone gay? Well, I could be that gay person to everyone in our church." Alek took a deep breath, looked up into the distance, and used his movie-trailer voice. "EveryGay, they'd call me, showing up in Armenian churches everywhere, changing perceived notions of homosexuality and queerness just by his sheer normalcy!"

Nik laughed. "Thank you." Deeming it had brewed sufficiently, he poured them both some tea. "I think I get it now."

"Anytime." Alek took another bite of his sandwich. It tasted good.

"And is that what you wrote about when you resubmitted your paper?"

"More or less. There was nothing really shocking about it. I just wanted to be honest about who I was. And how going to church makes someone like me feel."

Nik finished his sandwich and moved on to the salad. "I've been dreaming about reading my paper at the Christmas Eve service since—I can't even remember how long. And every year, it's gone to a senior. So yeah, I really thought it was going to be me this time. Losing out to any sophomore would've been hard. Losing out to you made it worse." Nik blew on his tea, then took a tentative sip.

"I didn't care about it, honestly. But once I got it, with every-thing that's been happening, I thought, *What a great chance to share with the people in the congregation who I really am*. I know it wouldn't change some of their minds—I'm not that naïve. But I think some of them, at least, would've thought about it. At that moment, or on their drive home, or maybe in the days or weeks to come. And wouldn't that have been a great way to spend Christmas Eve?"

"Yes, it would have." Nik nodded. "It would've been a great way to spend Christmas Eve."

Alek woke the next day knowing that the first thing he'd have to face in the New Year, before school and homework and Ethan and Becky and everything else that would populate the upcoming 365 days, was his parents.

"We have to leave for church in one hour if we want to be on time for the New Year's Day service, Alek," his mother called to him through the closed door that had been his salvation during the last two weeks.

Alek showered, brushed his teeth, and made himself pre-sentable before he went downstairs. He hated to disturb the portrait of suburban kitchen table bliss he found: his father eat-ing a bagel with cream cheese, reading the *New York Times*; his mother munching on a croissant, the *New Yorker* folded back in her other hand; two freshly brewed cups of coffee filling the room with their invigorating aroma. "I'm not going."

The breakfast carbs came down first, then the literature,

folded carefully next to the cups of coffee in the hope they could be resumed quickly.

"And why not?" His father spoke first.

"I've been banned, remember?"

"Just from Saturday school," his mother reminded him.

"It doesn't matter—why would I possibly want to go somewhere I'm not wanted?"

"This is important to us, Alek," his father said. "For our family. We have been exceedingly reasonable with you these last few weeks. Do I need to remind you how you weren't punished for when you broke curfew ten days ago with Ethan in the city? And we haven't even spoken about last night, when you broke your curfew again!" His father picked up a bowl of sunflower seeds.

"And . . . ?"

"What 'and'?" his father responded. "There doesn't need to be any 'and.'" His father and mother began eating the seeds: placing them between their front teeth, cracking them open in a swift diagonal motion, extracting the meat of the seed, spitting the shell out into a bowl on the table, and chewing and swallowing the seed, all in one swift nanosecond of a gesture.

Alek moved a small pile of sunflower seeds closer to him. "But nothing bad actually happened, right? I wasn't mugged or killed or kidnapped. I didn't spontaneously burst into flame, right? So what's the big deal?"

"The big deal is that it's easier for any of those to happen at night." His dad consumed two seeds in rapid succession.

"Not burst into flame," Alek pointed out. "That would only be possible in daylight."

"If you were a vampire." His mother joined in, pouring a pile of seeds out in front of her for easier access. "A phoenix, for example, could burst into flame at any time."

Alek nodded at his mom appreciatively.

"We're not talking about bursting into flame." His father rerouted the conversation. "We're talking about you respecting the rules we lay down. You don't need to understand them or even appreciate them. But you do need to follow them."

"Guys, do you have any idea what most fifteen-year-olds are like in this country? In this world? There are fifteen-year-olds who are pregnant. Fifteen-year-olds who drink and do drugs. There are even fifteen-year-olds, and get ready for this, who haven't started preparing for their PSATs."

This last item, apparently, was too shocking for his parents' sensibilities. Mrs. Khederian inhaled sharply, aghast, while his father covered his mouth, mute at the horror he was forced to confront.

"It's scary, I know, but it's true," Alek continued. "The worst thing I have ever done in my life was get home a few hours late the night my boyfriend told me he had cheated on me and then again the night I finally dumped him. Is that so horrible?"

"Oh, honey." Mrs. Khederian moved the bowl of sunflower seeds closer to Alek. "We weren't going to make you tell us what happened that night—obviously we knew something did."

"But it helps us to know that there were extenuating circumstances," his father added, more understanding than Alek would've guessed. "Does that have anything to do with how you've been acting at church?"

And there it was—the opening that Alek hadn't realize he'd been waiting for until it presented itself. "Dad, you and I may disagree about this, but I don't need an explanation for how I've been acting at church. The church is the one that needs an explanation." He felt his father go rigid, so Alek changed his tactic. "What do you think, Mom?"

Mrs. Khederian got up to empty the now-full bowl of sunflower seed shells. She spoke deliberately, weighing each word. "You know that your father and I are agreement when it comes to our children, Alek, so don't try to play us off of each other."

"God—I'm not a spy that's been sent in here to infiltrate and perform espionage. In three years, I'll be old enough to vote and join the army and die for this country in war, so can we assume that I'm mature enough to have a frank conversation about something? I just want to hear *your* opinion. Is that too much to ask?"

His parents exchanged one of their wordless communiques, engaging in the kind of quasi-telepathic exchange that Alek assumed was bestowed on all married couples on their wedding day.

"I have a different relationship to the church than your father." Alek's mom started slowly, speaking to Alek but maintaining eye contact with her husband. "My parents—they were intellectuals. So even though they went to church like all Armenians, they didn't take the religious part of it very seriously."

Alek looked over at his father, who didn't say anything.

"What other part of church is there?" He spat out an especially large sunflower-seed husk into the pile. They continued to work their way through the pile as they talked.

"The cultural part."

"But both Metzmama and Metzbaba had religious funerals." Alek spat out empty shells. "Service in the church, coffin dropped into consecrated ground under the supervision of the priest, the whole thing."

"It's true." His mom performed the insert-crack-extract-spit ritual. "But that didn't mean they considered themselves devout. Like my Catholic friends who are personally pro-life but politically pro-choice. Or my Jewish friends who keep mostly kosher but enjoy a good bacon cheeseburger every now and then." Insert-crack-extract-spit. "People are funny that way."

"My parents weren't like that." Alek's father spoke softly. "They met at church. They went every week. And when Dede passed away, the only way your nana made it through the grief was with the support of her reverend father. If anything, she's become more devout in the last few years."

"And yet, she had no problem with Ethan. She follows him on Instagram, for God's sake!"

"I guess you're her bacon cheeseburger!" Mrs. Khederian exclaimed.

"People, in my experience, will surprise you if you give them the chance." Alek licked the salt remnants from the sunflower seeds on his fingertips.

Mr. Khederian consumed two sunflower seeds in quick succession. "You have to remember, Alek, she believes it all.

Literally. That Jesus was the human incarnation of the son of God sent to Earth, and that he sacrificed himself for our sins. And that's what I believe."

"I don't have that many sins. I bet he would've been okay just giving up a finger. Or maybe a hand. But his whole body? That seems a bit excessive." Alek discarded a seed that proved uncrackable.

His dad didn't laugh. But his mother did. "That's enough, Alek. It's too easy to make fun of literalists. But that's what your father is. He believes that the reverend father is the liaison between us and God, and that by offending him, you offend God."

"I am offended that women can't be priests!" Alek wiped his fingers and lips clean with a napkin. "Is there any kind of profession or institution that could get away with that blatant sexism?"

"Of course I've thought about those things—especially as a feminist." Alek's mom poured out another pile of seeds. "But have you thought about all the pain you're causing your father and this family? About how easy it would be just to apologize to him, and to Reverend Father, and end all of this?"

"I have been thinking a lot about apologies and forgiveness lately, *mayrik*." Alek rarely spoke in any of the little Armenian he knew, but the word for *mother* was on his limited vocabulary list. And then he told his parents what had been going on the last few weeks. He didn't tell them everything, obviously—but just enough about Ethan and New Year's. "So it's not like I just decided, 'Hey—you know what I'm going to do today? Break my curfew—doesn't that sound fun?!' This was some real stuff going on, you know?" It felt good to unburden himself, like taking the heaviest textbook out of a stuffed backpack. "All of this is to say that I think the most important part of an apology, like penance in the church, is the belief that you'd behave differently given the chance. That if you could, you would turn back time, to quote the most fabulous of all Armenians—"

"I just wished Cher had dressed more decently in that video." Mrs. Khederian shuddered inadvertently. "Is it so much to ask?"

"—and do it differently. But I don't feel that way. I'm sorry that you and Dad don't see it that way, but I don't need to persuade you, because I know it's true. I have nothing to apologize to the reverend father for."

"Well, there it is," his mother said.

The three Khederians sat, without speaking, continuing to devour the sunflower seeds until only a pile of husks were left before them.

"Just out of curiosity, did you guys even read my new essay?"

His parents shook their heads with just a wisp of sheepishness.

Alek produced a printed-out copy and placed it on the table. "Give it a look, would you? I worked really hard on it. And while you're reading, think about what it must be like to have to go somewhere every week where you're told that there's something wrong with you. That you're less. That your very life is wrong. You know how much it sucks that I'm not going to be able to get married by an Armenian priest in an Armenian church? It's something that you and Dad and Nik just take for granted. So yes, I know that 'just apologizing' would make everything better. But it wouldn't be honest. And you didn't bring me up to be a liar."

They sat at the kitchen table, the silence punctuated by the sound of sunflower seeds being devoured.

"Thank you, Alek. For all this." Alek's dad took his essay.

Alek knew he'd made his points. Alek knew he'd "won," that his parents weren't going to make him go to church. So he was perhaps the most surprised of the three of them when he heard himself say, "If we're going to go to church, can we at least try to be on time?"

19

THE NEW YEAR'S DAY CHURCH EXPERIENCE WAS, IF anything, even more excruciating than usual. And since his family, in an uncharacteristic attempt to honor his wishes, arrived early, Alek had to spend the ten minutes before the service evading questions about why he wasn't attending Saturday school any longer and why his brother was now scheduled to speak at the Christmas Eve service instead of him.

He couldn't tell if it was just his imagination, but Alek felt like people were watching and treating him differently. It wasn't anything he could put his finger on—Mr. and Mrs. Papazian still smiled their toothy grins when they saw him, and Gregor from Neptune High asked which schools Alek was thinking of applying to as he always did. But every interaction was weighted in a way it hadn't been before, Alek felt. He knew how small communities gossiped. If he had to make a bet, he'd wager he had become the subject du jour.

As the reverend father spoke in the service, his rich baritone resonating through the sanctuary, Alek thought about the conversation he'd had with his parents that morning. He looked at all of the individuals sitting in the sanctuary, wondering how many people there, like his father, believed in the Bible literally—that the Virgin Mary conceived immaculately, that Jesus Christ was the embodiment of the Holy Father on Earth, who died for our sins. On the one hand, the mythological nature of it made perfect sense to Alek, who'd grown up on a diet of superheroes and fantasy and science fiction. But on the other hand, trying to engage all the stuff that he knew was made up in any kind of non-fictitious way seemed ludicrous. And if Christianity were literally true, that meant all the other religions were wrong. If Jesus were the Holy Savior, then he couldn't be a prophet, as the Muslims believed. Or, if the savior had already come, then how silly were the Jews, all waiting for something that had happened over two thousand years ago? Not to mention the impossibility of trying to reconcile the Abrahamic religions with any of the rest of the religions in the world.

As a philosophy, he got it: "treat others the way you'd like to be treated" was all fine and good, although treating them the way you thought they actually wanted to be treated felt a bit more on point. Nonetheless, philosophically, it seemed like a pretty good way to engage the world. The idea that we're all born with original sin, on the other hand, felt cynical as hell. Although when Alek looked at climate change, the arms race, racism, sexism, and the genocides in the history of humankind, it was difficult to believe that a species born inherently good or even neutral could commit so many atrocities.

When the service ended and the congregation finally filed out to enjoy a potluck downstairs, Alek and Arno snuck back into the sanctuary, each holding a napkin full of flaky nazook. They didn't have much time: Alek knew his parents would want to embark on the ninety-minute trip back home shortly, since it was already five p.m. and the sun would be setting soon. But until then, he'd infinitely rather be here with Arno than downstairs with everyone else.

"Did you do anything special for New Year's?" Arno asked.

Alek barked out a dry laugh, launching into a description of the evening's events.

"You dumped Ethan?" Arno shook his head. "That is un-freakin'-believable." He added just a moment later, "Excuse my language."

Alek didn't know if Arno was necessarily talking to him or to the image of the Virgin Mary and Jesus inlaid in gold above them in the sanctuary of St. Stephen's.

Even though no one else was in the cavernous room, the two of them still whispered, as if the stained-glass saints lining the walls could eavesdrop on their conversation.

"And do you regret it?" Arno licked a flake of the pastry off his finger.

"Hell no!" Alek replied, with perhaps more conviction than he felt. He didn't apologize for his language, like Arno had, but he couldn't help but glance up and see if the Virgin Mary or the baby Jesus had any response to his cursing. They appeared nonplussed.

"And I didn't even tell you about Becky almost kicking me out of her house, or actually having a halfway decent conversation with my brother. And then my parents!"

"You have had a very eventful twenty-four hours," Arno observed.

"Riiiiiight?" Alek took a nibble of his nazook. "You know, since I found out about Ethan and Remi, I've been wondering what an Ethan-less world would be like. And when I finally broke up with him, I thought it would be exhilarating and liberating, like all the pain of having been cheated on would finally go away."

"Has it?"

"Not yet."

"It's only been a day. Just give it time, Alek. Think of everything you've been through. Not to mention getting kicked out of Saturday school."

"And how is good ol' Saturday school?" Alek changed the subject eagerly.

"Boring as usual. I . . ." Arno stumbled. "I feel horrible, Alek."

"Why?"

"It's because of me you got kicked out. I should've—I don't know—gotten up in class and made some big speech about what happened. And how messed up it was, and totally unfair."

"That's crazy."

"I wanted to. Honest, I did. And I tried. But I couldn't. I'm not brave like you."

"More like stupid." Alek finished his pastry and used his napkin to wipe the confectioners' sugar off his face.

"Everyone knows something is messed up." Arno scooted even closer to Alek, conspiring. "Even Shushan."

"Who cares?"

"I care!"

"Arno, do me a favor."

"Anything."

"Do nothing, okay? It's just not worth it." Alek's insistence echoed off the vaulted ceiling. "You're too good for this place."

A draft swept through the sanctuary, blowing out a few of the candles, shifting the shadows, giving the ornate columns and baroque detail an even heavier feel.

A smile crept onto Arno's face. "It's nice, Alek. That you think that."

"Of course I do! You and me—we have to stick together. Now, promise me—don't do anything, okay?" Alek solemnly held out his right pinkie, which Arno hooked with his own. Alek was about to say something about the church and acceptance and Jesus and love, but before he could—

Arno kissed him.

Arno's kiss was warm and soft and tentative, a question mark more than an exclamation point, an invitation extended expecting a polite decline. Alek didn't know which one of them was more surprised when Alek put his hand on Arno's face and leaned into the kiss.

RSVP: yes.

Arno's eyes popped open, like without visual proof, he wouldn't have believed Alek was actually kissing him back.

Under the gaze of the Virgin Mary and baby Jesus, of the

stained-glass saints and Christ's stations of the cross, the two Armenian boys kissed.

"Where did that come from?" Alek asked finally.

Arno blushed. "I've been wanting to do that since that day you found me in the classroom. Since before, actually."

"Seriously?" The warmth of the kiss filled Alek like a sip of communion wine. "I had no idea."

"Oh my God, you can be so clueless!" Arno said. "But let me finish, okay?" Arno took a deep breath. "I'm going to tell you something that's going to make you not like me very much."

"Seriously?"

"Seriously."

"Come on, Arno, what could you possibly say?"

Arno looked away. The words came out haltingly, tinged with shame. "I'm the one who wrote *gyot*."

"What?" Alek's hand dropped off Arno's face.

"I was alone in that classroom, just messing around, writing whatever, and it just came out. I don't know why. I know it's wrong. And then you were there, and you were so angry about it, and I was embarrassed to tell you since I felt so stupid, you know? But then it gave us something to talk about. And after years of coming to church every week and sitting in these pews and hating it and feeling horrible about myself for who I was, things changed. Because I had a friend. Who was like me. And instead of feeling so far away from the church and the love of Jesus, I started feeling how powerful it could be. Because of you. And I'm sorry I didn't tell you, Alek." Tears started rolling down Arno's face. "So you see, I'm the one who's

230

responsible for everything that happened to you—all because I'm too much of a coward to speak up. I'm so so sorry."

Alek stood, intending to leave, to turn his back on another liar, another person who had let him down. He'd already done it with the person who'd meant most to him in the world. This, if anything, should've been easier.

But something about Arno, in all his wretched misery, something about being in the sanctuary with Jesus and the Virgin Mary looking down gave him pause.

Yes, if Arno had been honest with him from the start, Alek's life would be infinitely easier. He wouldn't have been kicked out of Saturday school. He wouldn't have fought with the reverend father or his parents. He'd still be reading his paper at Christmas Eve service. He wouldn't feel like he had the plague every time he came to church. That was all true.

And as messed up as he found so much of the church, its homophobia, its sexism, its corruption, its patriarchy, its hegemony, its insistence that all other gods were false, there was one part of Christianity that always struck him as inherently, profoundly, true—as true as his knowledge that he was gay. The part about forgiveness. Although Alek hadn't always succeeded in living by that precept, that didn't mean he couldn't try now.

"It's all right, Arno." Alek forced the words out, feeling them just enough for it to be sincere. He embraced Arno, letting him cry against his chest. "It's okay."

Alek couldn't make out what grateful words Arno said as he wept in Alek's embrace, drenching his shirt in tears and snot. But it really didn't matter.

The Virgin Mary, Jesus, and all the saints etched in stained glass glowed in jewel tones above them. Alek knew it just meant that some January clouds had parted, freeing the sun. But that didn't stop it from feeling any less miraculous.

It was only two days: a Thursday and a Friday. It didn't seem unreasonable to ask for them. Those two days, with the weekend that followed, of course, would have made for a truly epic break. But the gods of the South Windsor School District were stingy. And the next day, January 2, Alek had to return to school. The unforgiving fluorescents shattered any illusions: winter break was over.

Everyone else had already celebrated Christmas, or Hanukkah, or Kwanzaa. So everyone else was sporting new coats, new jeans, new shirts. But not Alek. Armenian Christmas Eve was still three days away. Alek took some comfort in the weather, which was as miserable as his mood for having to come back to school: a snow/slush dropped from the skies, the kind of precipitation designed to soak and ruin any December-gift shoes. It fell just heavily enough to fuel fantasies of a snow day, but not actually enough to warrant that miracle.

He could've waited for class, but he wanted to get it over with. So he got to school a few minutes early and went to Mrs. Sturgeon's office. The door was open. He knocked on it anyway, poking his head in. "Hello?"

"Come in." Mrs. Sturgeon sat in her cramped closet of an office, so small that he could smell the coffee in her Styrofoam cup. "How can I help you, Alek?"

Alek sat down across from his Health teacher and her severe bangs. Somehow, in spite of the room's size and lack of windows, Mrs. Sturgeon had made it homey, keeping the horrendous fluorescent lights turned off and using an iridescent halogen torch lamp to light the room. Personal touches like framed pictures of her family dotted the crannies of the hutch on her desk. He rubbed his suddenly clammy hands against his jeans.

"It's about your child, isn't it?" Mrs. Sturgeon spoke without irony.

"Yes, it is. You see, Mrs. Sturgeon, Señor Huevo had an accident over winter break."

"I was afraid of that." She started flipping through her folder. "Can I see him?"

"Unfortunately, no."

"Did you lose him?" she asked solemnly. "That would be very irresponsible parenting."

"No, I didn't lose him. I . . ." Alek took a deep breath. "I hurled him at my now ex-boyfriend and splattered him into a broken mess of shell and white and yolk."

Mrs. Sturgeon stopped flipping through the sheets in the folder she'd procured. "You killed Señor Huevo?"

Alek nodded, feeling intensely both solemn and foolish.

"Infanticide is a very serious offense, Alek." His teacher adjusted her cat's-eye glasses.

"I know, Mrs. Sturgeon."

"Do you know why I assign the egg-cersise?" Mrs. Sturgeon giggled at her own joke.

"To show us how difficult the responsibility of parenting is?"

"To put their needs before your own. And in all of my

years of teaching this must be the most violent story I've ever heard. You realize, I will have to fail you on this assignment."

"I know, Mrs. Sturgeon."

"But also, you know"—she smiled as if she were telling him a secret—"it's only a grade in Health class."

Alek smiled back. "I know that, too, Mrs. Sturgeon."

20

DOORBELLS RARELY RING UNEXPECTEDLY IN THE suburbs. Most unexpected bell-ringers turn out to be Jehovah's Witnesses or Mormons: strangers hiding hopes of conversion behind smiles and pamphlets. On a late Friday afternoon in early January with its decidedly unneighborly weather, an unexpected doorbell is even more of an anomaly. But just a few minutes after Alek had gone upstairs to his room and resigned himself to working on his *Madame Bovary* essay, he heard the bitonal chime, followed by his father hollering from downstairs, "You have a visitor, Alek."

Since Becky had plans with Dustin, there was only one person it could be. Part of him leaped at the knowledge that he'd get to see Ethan. They'd passed each other twice in the hallway in the two days back at school, both times between periods seven and eight, Alek going from Honors History to Honors Bio, and Ethan between Standard Trig and his elective in

Media Technologies. As hard as he tried to just keep on walking and look straight ahead, Alek couldn't help but cheat a glance at his ex-boyfriend, surrounded by his skater friends. A part of him yearned to reach out and touch Ethan. But he scolded that part, like a puppy that had destroyed a piece of furniture.

That was the same part he had to tamp down now. He'd make small talk with Ethan, Alek decided, before telling him that it was too early for them to see each other. Maybe in a few weeks, or months, or years, when the part of him that yearned to touch Ethan and be touched by him had finally been reprogrammed, they'd be able to hang out again, as friends.

He took a moment to make sure his hair looked good and tousled, but not like he'd worked to make it look that way, and change out of the sweatshirt he'd just put on and into a crisp button-down with pearl buttons and sawtooth pockets. If Ethan was going to stop by unannounced, he'd have to get used to waiting for Alek to get ready. And there was no way that Alek was going to look anything other than fabulous every time he ever saw Ethan again. Alek came downstairs, slowly, calmly, like he had all the time in the world.

But it wasn't Ethan who was sitting at the kitchen table, eating sunflower seeds with his parents as if he were their long-lost son. It was the person who Alek least expected, and least wanted to see, in the world.

"Remi?" Alek felt the taste of bile in his mouth.

"Ah, finally, the young prince descends!" Remi plucked a seed from the pile in front of him, popped it in his mouth, extracted the meat, and spat out the shell without missing a beat. "Don't tell me you forgot about our plans tonight!"

As sure as Alek was that Ben Affleck playing Batman was a sin for which the superhero gods would never forgive humanity, he was equally, 100 percent, indefatigably positive that he and Remi did not and had not ever made plans to spend the first Friday of the New Year together.

"Remi, the only thing I'd rather do less than spend time with you tonight is rot in hell."

"Alek!" His mother stood up immediately.

"May we have a word with you in the living room?" Mr. Khederian's smile was all steel.

Remi continued popping sunflower seeds, left alone, as Alek's parents guided him into the living room.

"Now, Alek, we don't know what could possibly have transpired that would lead you to talk that way to that wonderful young man." Mr. Khederian kept his voice hushed, but that only served to increase its intensity.

"But you know how important hospitality is. Remi is a guest in our house," Alek's mother said. "So if you'd like to tell us what has happened, we'd be happy to hear it. Otherwise, we insist that you show him basic hospitality."

Alek considered his parents' offer. He was positive that if he'd told them that the reason he and Ethan had broken up was because Ethan had cheated with Remi, that his parents would've had his back. And in spite of how important hospitality was to Armenians, he was sure that his folks would've politely but firmly asked Remi to leave.

But when he worked the equation out, he arrived at the same conclusion that he imagined Remi did when he decided to come visit Alek at home in the first place: that it was easier to keep his parents in the dark. Partially for their sake, partially for his. He knew that he could tell his parents almost anything—one of the great things about having come out to them was that knowledge. But that didn't mean he had to. Or wanted to. Even if it meant having to endure the company of the guy who ruined his relationship.

"You're right, guys."

Mr. and Mrs. Khederian exchanged looks of surprise, then suspicion, at Alek's capitulation. But ultimately, they were happy enough to get what they wanted. "Very well, then."

Alek braced himself for another encounter with the Menace from Down Under. But maybe, Alek thought to himself as he went back into the kitchen, he could find some satisfaction from beating Remi at his own game.

"Please forgive my previous outburst, Remi." Alek scooped the pile of sunflower seed shells into a napkin and tossed it into the garbage. "It's so nice to see you. Can I get you a glass of water? Flat or sparkling? Chilled or at room temperature? With or without ice? And tell me, please, what have you been up to?"

Remi sat up straight in the chair, sensing his opponent's new tactic. But he played along. "You know, the usual."

"And what classes are you taking this semester?" Mrs. Khederian joined them at the kitchen table.

"I don't think we even know your major!" Mr. Khederian exclaimed, sitting next to his wife, across from Remi.

"Please, tell us everything," Alek chimed in. He sat right

next to Remi, in spite of how being this close to him made Alek feel like he might catch a very contagious and lethal disease.

"I was actually hoping to spend a little time with you alone, Alek." Remi, in the act of the perfectly deferential young man, looked to the Khederians for permission. "If that's possible, of course."

"As much as I'd love that, Remi, I've got a very important test on Monday that I have to study for, unfortunately." Alek gave Remi as large a smile as he could muster. "I'm sorry you made the trip all the way down here for nothing."

"That's okay," Remi said, getting up. "I guess my empty stomach and I will just head back to the city all by ourselves!"

Alek saw the tactic a moment too late to prevent it.

"I know!" Mrs. Khederian piped in. "Why don't you stay for dinner?"

"What a great idea, honey!" Mr. Khederian exclaimed. "That way, Remi's trip won't be for naught."

"I'd be delighted!" Remi plopped back down.

"Let's see—I've got some buregs that I can warm up in a jiff." Mr. Khederian riffled through his mental inventory of the house's food. "And we've got that roast chicken from yesterday, right? What about the string beans?"

"Do you think they're still good?" Mrs. Khederian worried.

"Of course, honey. And I'll whip up that new kale pesto recipe I've been wanting to try."

"The four of us, sitting, chatting, we'll just have the loveliest of times, don't you agree, Alek?" Remi continued before Alek had a chance to respond. "And did I tell you how lovely you look in lavender, Mrs. K? What a beautiful color on you. It really brings out your eyes."

"Do you think so?" Mrs. Khederian asked, blushing.

"Of course. I'm sure of it—just like I'm sure that Mr. K hits the gym a few times a week, am I right?"

Now it was Mr. Khederian's turn to blush. "I try to do push-ups and sit-ups when I'm home, you know."

"Oh, you don't have to be modest. Not around me!" Remi made a show of squeezing Mr. Khederian's bicep. "Thank goodness for this country's Second Amendment—no way you could carry guns like those around otherwise!"

Alek performed a quick mental calculation, weighing the horror of spending one-on-one time with Remi versus watching his parents blush at Remi's heinous flirtation all night. The sharpening taste of vomit in his mouth told him that he could survive the former, while the latter would most probably end in homicide. "You know what, Remi, why don't we go out?" As the one person who could see through Remi's charm, Alek felt he had a moral obligation to protect his parents. "There's a local establishment that I think you'd just love."

"Sounds great," Remi said, accepting the compromise.

Sensing his parents' disappointment, Alek moved fast, gathering his stuff and getting himself and Remi outside before they could invite themselves along. "See you guys soon. Good-bye!"

And they were out the door, where a silver-blue Tesla had materialized in the Khederians' driveway. Remi produced a fob from a pocket in the jeans that looked so tight it was hard to believe there was enough space for said fob, and clicked it. The

Tesla's door handles actually popped up, like it was from the future.

"After you." Remi bowed with faux deference.

"Faceplant." Remi's voice activated the stereo, and music Alek didn't recognize, with a soulful, hypnotic beat, pulsed through the car's surround-sound speakers.

Alek was unaccustomed to how low the seat was and, to be real, how freakin' awesome it felt to be in the front seat of a sports car, let alone one of the fabled electric-powered Teslas. Remi slid a pair of reflective sunglasses on and tapped the smartscreen that glowed where a normal car's radio would be. The car turned on without a sound.

"This is everything," Alek whispered.

The Tesla zipped them out of the driveway.

"Where are we going?" Remi asked.

"You'll love it. Very hip. Very cool. Very much like you." Alek let around 15 percent of the sarcasm he felt drip into his voice.

"Lead the way."

Alek typed the address into the smartscreen.

The Tesla, a car that relied on electricity rather than fuel to run, drove without sound, without gears, without transmission, gliding on the earth like a silent assassin, moving in for the kill.

"Remi, forgive me for stating the obvious, but I can't help but wonder: Why did you show up on my doorstep, unannounced, in a car that we both know you have no right driving, to take me out? I mean, it really does beg an answer."

Remi smiled into the rearview mirror, but with those damn reflective glasses, Alek couldn't tell if the smile was in response to what he'd just said or something else entirely that had amused Remi in that moment. "Isn't it obvious?"

Alek exhaled slowly. "No, Remi. It's not. In fact, it's anything but."

"I'm going to convince you to get back together with Ethan, of course." The car accelerated faster than any vehicle should be able to. "Now buckle up."

21

"SO REALLY, YOU CAN DROP ME OFF BACK HOME whenever." Alek took a sip of his now-lukewarm tea across a warped yellow Formica tabletop from Remi at the Prestige Diner. It was difficult for Alek to imagine any time that Remi would've fit in at the diner. But the early bird crowd that came on a Friday night at six p.m., for two dollars off entrees and a free extra side, was probably his least likely cohort.

Alek had spent the last thirty minutes watching Remi devour his turkey club with bacon, steak fries, and coleslaw, while he simply sipped his cup of Earl Grey tea.

At first, Alek had just wanted it to be over with—to get Remi out of his house, away from his parents, and back to New York City as soon as possible. He couldn't imagine that he'd want to endure spending time with the guy Ethan had cheated on him with. But as time progressed, he found that being with

Remi wasn't as painful as he'd thought. If anything, it was fascinating. All the pain and hurt and feeling of betrayal—all of that was reserved for Ethan. Being around Remi was more curious than anything else, like getting to spy on your mortal enemy.

Alek had just finished explaining to Remi why the chances of him getting back together with Ethan were equal to him sprouting a horn and discovering he was actually a unicorn in human form. The points had come easily and effortlessly, like a defense lawyer in any of those TV courtroom dramas, presenting his argument to the jury with the confidence of certain acquittal. And whenever Alek heard a hollowness in his own words, he just plowed forward, manufacturing conviction as needed. Just like a real lawyer, Alek imagined. "You see, it's not just that he cheated on me with you. He lied to me about it. He lied to me after. I mean, how can I ever trust anyone like that again? Why would I even want to try?

"So as noble as your intentions are, you see why this whole facade is a waste of time. You don't want to start your New Year with a Sisyphean task, do you?"

"A what?"

"You know—Sisyphus. He angered the gods with his craftiness, so they punished him by giving him an impossible task to perform in his afterlife. He had to roll this boulder up a hill. But the moment before he got to the top, it would slip out of his grasp and roll back down, and he'd have to start all over again. For all we know, he's still doing it now. A truly existential, futile waste of his time. Like you trying to convince me to forgive Ethan."

Remi devoured his last steak fry, taking the entire thing in his mouth in a single bite. "Why do you talk like that?"

"Like what?"

"Using words like *Sisyphean*." Remi's question didn't carry any judgment. Rather, he just sounded objectively curious, as if he were conducting a sociological experiment and Alek was just another subject.

"There's a reason those stories have survived all these centuries. There's a spark of truth in them, some profound kernel. It's comforting, isn't it, to think that we've been dealing with the same stuff for thousands of years?"

Remi nodded, apparently satisfied with Alek's answer.

"So, should we ask for the check and get out of here?"

"All in good time." A small smile curled Remi's lips.

"What else could you possibly want from me? I mean, you are the reason that Ethan and I broke up. Have you no shame?"

"Shame?" Remi asked, as if it were a foreign dish he'd heard of but never sampled. "I guess I just don't have any use for it."

"Obviously. Or you wouldn't have slept with my boyfriend. On my birthday!" Alek's hushed tones contrasted Remi's everyday volume.

"I admit the timing wasn't especially grand. And I admit I wouldn't have done it if I knew you guys were monogamous."

"Did it occur to you to ask?"

"Of course not! I had assumed you had too much imagination to imitate the most boring, heteronormative standard possible." Remi didn't even bother to stop speaking when the grandmotherly waitress returned to fill their water cups. "Especially in this wonderful age of polyamorous pansexuality."

Alek squirmed in his seat.

"Of course, the reason I probably wouldn't have touched Ethan has nothing to do with it being 'wrong.' I wouldn't have done it because it would inflict pain on someone I cared about, which is not something I like to do . . ."

"Why, Remi, that might be the first halfway decent thing I've heard you say."

". . . as much as I like to inflict pleasure on myself."

This time, Alek couldn't help himself. "You know how cheesy you sound when you talk like that, right?"

"Most people really like it." Remi grinned.

Alek forced himself to look past Remi, past his perfectly symmetrical teeth, his perfect tan, his perfect body, past all those exterior trappings. "I'm not most people."

"I am starting to understand that. Which makes the fact that you're doing this all the more unfortunate."

"Doing what?"

"Torturing yourself and Ethan."

"What did he tell you?"

"Nothing. He hasn't spoken to me since that night. But his dad called me today. Rupert's worried—like, really worried. Which is why I decided to spend my very valuable time driving into the suburbs of New Jersey to try and make things right. You know"—Remi smiled—"like a superhero."

Alek shook his head in disbelief.

"He said Ethan was a real wreck—even worse, if you can believe it, than after I'd left him."

"It's a real gift you have, to make everything be about you."

"Thank you." Remi sounded genuinely moved.

"Why do you care so much about what happens to me and Ethan?" Alek asked, taking a sip of his now-tepid tea.

"I supposed it's possible that in one interpretation I am somewhat responsible for what happened between you two. But mostly, I love Ethan. Always have. He's a great mate, always has been." Remi wiped his lips with his napkin. "So waddaya say? Why don't we pay up and I'll drop you off at his place? You two can make up, then make out, and we can all go on our merry ways."

"I don't think so." Alek made eye contact with their waitress, and made the universal sign of "check, please": miming a pad with his left hand and a scribbling pen with his right. "I'm going to say something, and I know it's going to be very difficult for you to understand, Remi. And it's not that I don't appreciate everything you've done and the time that you've taken out of your day, and God knows how you were able to get that Tesla in the first place, but here it is." Alek took a sip of his tea, which was as lukewarm as his desire to be in this diner with Remi any longer. "I make my own decisions. And if I change my mind, it's not going to because some impossibly hot Aussie asks me to. Okay?"

Remi swallowed the last drops of his carrot juice. "You think I'm impossibly hot?"

Alek shook his head, contemplating his own Sisyphean endeavors. "I think you're impossible—how's that?"

"Fair enough."

The waitress arrived, made a few notations with her tobacco-stained fingers on her small green pad, and left the slip of paper on their table.

"But let me ask you something, Mr. Khederian. You say you broke up with Ethan because you can never trust him again. But how do you *know* you can never trust him again? Without actually trying, that is?"

"I did! I did try again! And he lied to me! Again! About you! Again!"

"Were you really giving him another shot? Or were you just punishing him for hurting you?"

Alek acknowledged that Remi may have had a point, but he made sure not to do or say anything that might reveal it.

"Cause I'll tell you—Ethan's never looked at me the way he looks at you."

"Really?"

"Would I lie to you?" Remi smiled broadly.

Alek said nothing, trying to take in the series of deeply improbable events that had begun when he invited his ex-boyfriend's ex-boyfriend out to a diner for a meal.

"One last thing. And this one's important, Alek." Remi flashed one of his trademark smiles. "Would you mind picking up the check? I'm a bit short on funds these days."

Alek allowed himself a proper, unapologetic, complete eye roll.

22

"I DON'T THINK I WAS SURPRISED THAT YOU CHEATED on me." Alek didn't bother with chitchat when Ethan opened his front door. "I think part of me was waiting for it to happen, because deep down inside, I never believed that someone as everything as you would ever really be with someone as whatever as me."

In the moment after he'd knocked on Ethan's door, a million things had run through Alek's mind. He had wanted to run, he had wanted to scream, to pound the door with his fist, to curse Remi for making Ethan's case, to curse himself for listening to that unbearably persuasive Australian, to curse Arno for making him consider forgiveness, to curse fate for returning him to the place he had just (melo)dramatically fled only five days ago, vowing never to return.

"So when I found out about Remi, it all made sense."

But before he could do any of those things, the door had swung open, revealing Ethan in an oversize flannel shirt and sweatpants with dragons embroidered on the sides, looking more puzzled to see Alek than anything else.

"I think I thought I deserved it."

"That's so messed up," Ethan finally said.

"I know."

They stood on opposite sides of the open door while the heat leaked out of the house. When Alek had stormed out of this house, he thought he was closing the Ethan chapter forever. But in those days, so much had happened. When Alek looked back, what struck him most was not the surprisingly civilized conversation with his brother, or Remi's visit, or even kissing Arno. What struck him was how profoundly he felt the absence of Ethan.

Ethan stepped out of his house, barefoot, as if it were spring, closing the door gently behind him. "I wish—honestly, I'd give anything to take it back. To undo it. To make it go away, to make it be like it never happened."

"I know." They sat down on the stoop at the same time, as if rehearsed.

"But I can't."

"I know."

Silence.

"So what do we do now?" Ethan looked at his bare feet as if he were surprised to see them.

"I don't know," Alek admitted.

"So why'd you come here?" Ethan asked simply.

"I don't know that, either."

They sat, in silence, longer.

"How's your New Year going?" Ethan's attempt at small talk was intentionally comical.

Alek played along. "Fine, thanks. Yours?"

They talked about the last five days. It wasn't like before, when the conversation just flowed like a river after rainfall. It stuttered now, like a faucet doing its best in spite of a running shower. Ethan talked about his dad and Lesley and a new art project he was starting. Alek talked about Mrs. Sturgeon and Becky and Dustin and school. He did not talk about Arno. Or Remi.

"And tomorrow," Alek continued, "I get to go to church and sit in a room full of people who hate me, while my brother gives the speech that I should've."

"Merry Armenian Christmas." Ethan flashed one of his half smiles, which somehow achieved sincerity and sarcasm at the same time.

"Yeah, it'll be hell on Earth, which I suppose is especially ironic for church. But my parents didn't ground me. So it's the least I can do, I figure." Alek stood up.

Ethan followed. "It's really good to see you." He leaned in slightly, and Alek felt his aura, his essence, his Ethan-ness. He almost let himself crumble into the familiarity of it all. Almost.

"You too."

"Can we see each other again? Soon?"

Alek nodded. "That would be nice."

* * *

"If we don't leave soon, we're going to be late."

Was it Sisyphean, Alek mused, or Herculean, Nik's labor to get the Khederians to church on time?

"And since I'm giving my paper tonight, I *really* don't want to be late, okay?"

Oh, that's right, Alek thought to himself. *It's just selfish, like most things Nik does.*

"Oh, honey, you have nothing to be nervous about." Mrs. Khederian adjusted the silver brooch on her burgundy jacket in the hallway closet mirror downstairs, immune to her son's anxiety.

Even a few days ago, his family talking about church and Nik's speech would've upset Alek. But with everything that had happened, he'd gotten to the place where he could just let it go. "That's right, honey," he whispered to his brother. Letting it go and not getting a good jab in when the opportunity presented itself were two very different things.

Since Christmas Eve fell on a Sunday, the church had decided to consolidate what would've been the morning mass and the Christmas Eve mass into one ginormous evening megaevent.

"You wanna drive, Nik?" Mr. Khederian asked, handing the keys to his elder son. Then Alek's dad put his arm around his wife and carefully ushered her in the direction of the interior garage door.

"But it's nighttime," his wife protested.

"I think he's ready," her husband said gently.

His wife silently nodded.

If this is the only miracle I witness this whole year, Alek thought to himself, *I will already have surpassed quota.*

"Let's go, boys."

Nik was the model of a perfect driver, signaling thirty seconds before changing lanes and remaining at least ten miles below the speed limit at all times. In spite of how she started the trip clutching her seat belt with whitened knuckles and praying under her breath in Armenian, Nik engaged his mother from what she was sure was the precipice of death by asking for her advice regularly throughout the trip.

"Do you think I should pass this driver, *mayrik*, or stay in the lane?"

"Do you think I'll make the light?"

"Is it warm enough in the car?"

Alek wordlessly watched Nik convert their mom from terrified passenger to engaged copilot. And, perhaps even more impressively, Nik got his family to church at six forty-five, early enough that they were even able to park in the parking lot proper for once.

"I can drop you guys off and find parking," Nik offered, gliding the car up to the curb.

Alek wondered what Nik could possibly be angling for, with his newfound generosity, as he and his parents got out of the car and walked up the sidewalk to the church's main entrance.

In spite of the cold, a sea of Armenians lingered outside, greeting one another, exchanging "Merry Christmases" and "Happy New Years." And impossibly, in the middle of them all, his blond hair sticking out against a sea of dark, was Ethan.

"Ethan!" Alek's mom was perhaps even more surprised than Alek himself. "How . . . lovely to see you here?"

"Are you planning on staying for the service?" Alek's dad asked, fidgeting nervously.

"Hello, Mr. and Mrs. Khederian, nice to see you guys." Ethan shook their hands warmly. "And merry Christmas."

"Merry Christmas," they mumbled back in unison.

"Don't you guys have to get inside and do that thing?" Alek asked, the thinnest mask veiling his words.

"What thing?" Mr. Khederian responded.

But at least his mom picked up on the clue. "You know, honey." She shook her head apologetically at Alek before addressing her husband again. "That thing."

Mr. Khederian's delight at finally understanding what was happening delayed the exit that everyone else was desperate for. "Oh, yes, that thing. We got here early especially to do it, and now that we're here, I guess we should. Go. Do. That thing."

Alek's parents entered the church, leaving Alek and Ethan outside.

"You're here," Alek said evenly.

"That I am," Ethan confirmed. He adjusted the knot in the dusty rose tie that, against all odds, matched the dusty rose coat he had donned for the evening.

"How come?"

Ethan leaned against the wide column that framed the church's Byzantine entrance. "It sounded like tonight might be a rough one for you. And I thought maybe being here would make it a little easier, so I had my dad drop me off."

Alek said nothing, processing.

"I can leave if you want." There was no bitterness in Ethan's voice. Just a plain, simple, honest offer.

"Stay." The word escaped from Alek's mouth before he could contain it, a wish released like a djinni from a bottle.

"Okay."

"Aleksander Khederian!" Mr. Papazian's piercing tenor shattered Alek and Ethan's fragile moment. "I didn't expect to see you here."

His wife hung on his arm, competing with her husband for who could look more desperate to extract a bit of gossip from Alek.

"Hello, Mr. and Mrs. Papazian." Alek attempted to be as natural as possible, but he was painfully aware of how out of place he and Ethan were.

"I thought you'd be reading your essay tonight." Mrs. Papazian wasn't even making the pretense of fishing for the information she sought—she just went in for the kill. "What happened?"

"I decided to include a section on my homosexuality in the discussion of what being Armenian meant to me, in addition to a critique of which parts of the church feel hopelessly outdated. It was decided that the content wasn't exactly appropriate, so rather than change my essay, the powers that be decided to confer the honor to my brother." Alek reported the incident as calmly as he could, like he was reciting statistics with the rankings of the top-seeded tennis players in the world. "Merry Christmas, Mr. and Mrs. Papazian, and happy New Year!"

The flabbergasted Papazians responded with a shocked "Merry Christmas" of their own before staggering inside.

"That. Was. Amazing," Ethan whispered.

Alek and Ethan reached the church entrance without much more incident. The imposing wood doors, braced and studded with wrought iron, dared Alek to open them.

"I can't believe I'm going in there."

The thought of an entire evening of interactions like the one he'd just had with the Papazians—it all felt so exhausting. It would be so much easier to wait in the vestibule for the evening to be over and then go home and cuddle up with his favorite book, or even write that *Madame Bovary* paper.

"Only if you want to."

"Hold my hand," Alek asked.

"What?" Ethan turned, as if he couldn't possibly have heard Alek correctly.

"*This would be a real good time . . .*" Alek half spoke, half sang the words.

Ethan didn't finish the quote. He just slid his hand into Alek's, which was waiting for him, like a perfectly tailored glove.

When they'd been together, Alek and Ethan had understood, intuitively, that if they stopped holding hands when they earned looks or sideway glances or outright sneers, they'd lose. So whenever that happened, they just tightened their hold the slightest of bits, finding resolve in each other, their held hands an unspoken pact.

Holding hands now made something perfectly clear to Alek: that what he wished he could make the reverend father, his own parents, and all those well-meaning straight people understand was that he and Ethan would never really have the privilege of holding hands as a neutral gesture. The act, taken for granted by people all over the world, would never be just that for him and Ethan. Part of him mourned that possibility— of never knowing what it would mean to perform that act unitalicized.

But, at the same time, Alek wondered if the rest of the world would ever know the pride and strength that he felt in that moment, when he and Ethan decided to hold hands at church. He may not have a choice. But that didn't mean he would have it any other way.

Alek's fingers intertwined with Ethan's, and he felt a new force field blossom around them. He opened the large, creaking door.

"Let's do this thing," Alek said.

They stepped into the church.

"Yeah—the service is going to start any minute."

"Don't worry," Alek confided. "If it's like everything else Armenian, it'll be at least half an hour late."

23

"HELLO, ALEK, IT'S GOOD TO SEE YOU." IF THE reverend father was at all surprised by Alek's presence at the Christmas Eve service, or that Ethan was accompanying him, he didn't show it.

"Thanks, Reverend Father. This is Ethan, my . . ." Alek stumbled for the right word. He dismissed *boyfriend* immediately, even though it was the one that had popped up to his lips first. *Ex-boyfriend*, while accurate, felt aggressive. He settled on the best, most ambiguous word he could conjure. ". . . friend. My friend Ethan."

Ethan nodded, accepting the description. "Good evening, Reverend Father." Ethan's extraordinary ability to stay absolutely himself, regardless of his surroundings, made him as comfortable in an Armenian Orthodox Church as he was hanging out with a bunch of skater kids by the tracks.

And the reverend father, to his credit, made a point of being equally at ease. "I'm glad you could make it, Ethan." He shook Ethan's hand, guiding them to the pews as he spoke. "We welcome all friends of congregation members tonight."

Alek fantasized about what it would be like if he and Ethan were back together, so he could've introduced him as his boyfriend and witnessed the reverend's response.

"You know what, I think we'll be good here." Alek stopped them a few rows from the back, optimal for the clean getaway Alek wanted to make the moment the service ended and a comfortable six rows back from where his parents sat with Nik.

The hundreds of candles lit at the front of the altar didn't provide the only lighting in the sanctuary, but the glow made everything look otherworldly, even mystical, as the flames danced to their own silent music.

"This place—it's so intense." Ethan arched his neck up to admire the arcane detail of the vaulted ceilings above them. Having someone who'd never had been there before allowed Alek to see the church anew. The Armenians had gone all out this season, decorating the sanctuary with Christmas trees (bedazzled with twinkling lights, tinsel, a rainbow of ornaments, and sparkling stars on top), wreaths crowned with big red bows, and a sea of poinsettias spilling out from the altar.

"My mom once said that the Orthodox Church makes the Catholics look Protestant." Alek nodded.

"And did you check out Reverend Father's cowl?" Ethan asked.

"I know—very Doctor Strange."

Across the aisle, even farther up than his parents, Alek spotted Arno, sitting with his parents and five younger siblings.

The memory of their kiss, in this very room, flooded Alek's senses. And even though he and Ethan hadn't been together then and weren't together now, he still felt a shade of guilt, as if he'd cheated.

Ethan, attuned, followed Alek's gaze. "Who's that?"

"Arno."

"The kid from Saturday school?" Ethan asked.

"Yup."

Ethan nodded, watching, listening, clocking.

The last audience members took their seats in the pews, which were almost entirely full by now, as the reverend father started speaking. He stood on the floor, between the pews and the stage, amid the sea of red.

It was nice to see the reverend father speaking to the congregation from the floor, rather than from the altar, where he usually spoke. In spite of the black cowl, he spoke with a casualness about the history of the church and the traditions of Christmas that was absent from all of his more formal Sunday services.

"For a long time, many Armenians would fast for up to three days before Christmas!" the reverend father told the congregation.

"The only time Armenians have ever abstained from food," Alek deadpanned under his breath, forcing Ethan to struggle to keep a straight face.

"But really," the reverend father continued, "it's important to remember that the birth and baptism of Jesus Christ is a time to remember forgiveness. Forgiveness is Christianity's major philosophical contribution to the dialogue of the world. We take it for granted now, but the notion that you should love your enemy was a new thought at the time of Jesus's teachings. And it's all based in God's love for us—for he did not send his son into the world to condemn it, but rather to save it. In love." He paused, like he was going to say something else, but then changed his mind. "But you'll get enough of that during my sermon next Sunday!"

All the little kids, under the supervision of Mrs. Stepanian, marched out onstage and began singing a medley of Christmas carols, interspersed with a few Armenian classics.

"This is so surreal." Ethan looked on, fascinated, as if he were observing an alien species.

"What—you've never heard of that holiday classic, 'Kef Kef'?" Alek asked, as the children segued out of the Armenian song and into "Deck the Halls."

"I can say, with full confidence, that I have never heard of 'Kef Kef.'" Ethan slouched in his pew, summoning the spirit of disaffected skater bad boy, even in his button-down shirt, tie, and jacket. "What're they singing now?"

"'Gaghant Baba'—another standard." Alek bopped along. "It's about Santa Claus."

"He knows when you've been bad or good?" Ethan asked.

"Something like that."

The choir finally sat down and the rest of the service continued, the reverend father speaking in Armenian that the congregation pretended it could understand perfectly, broken up with the adult choir singing songs equally antiquated and Armenian.

After the last choir song, the reverend father introduced Nik. "Every Christmas Eve service, it is my pride to introduce a young member of the congregation, who shares his or her essay, 'What Being Armenian Means to Me.' This year, Andranik Khederian was chosen."

Nik, flush with false humility and true pride, walked up to the lectern and launched into his beautifully written, totally predictable essay about the wrongs committed against the Armenian people, the unacknowledged genocide in Turkey during World War I, the diaspora that followed, and the recently observed hundred-year anniversary of those events.

"Read it to me sometime," Ethan whispered.

"What?" Alek whispered back.

"Tonight—or whenever—I want you to read your paper to me," Ethan said. "I'd like to hear it."

Alek gently placed his hand on Ethan's and gave it the slightest of squeezes.

Nik continued his pontification as Alek's mind wandered. He couldn't have predicted that he'd be sitting here in church, with Ethan. Being next to Ethan made everything feel okay. Even now. Even here, with the stained-glass windows that during the day would be glowing, the baroque columns, the candles, the poinsettias.

His thoughts had drifted so far from Nik's speech that he needed Ethan's gentle smack on his arm to bring him back to reality, just in time to hear his brother say, "And yet, for all we talk about acceptance and a God who loves us unconditionally, when I think of being Armenian, I can't help but think of everyone who the church excludes. And by attending church, do we condone this exclusion?"

Ethan leaned in, allowing Alek to inhale that sandalwood-sweat fragrance that was profoundly him. "Did you have anything to do with this?"

Alek shook his head vigorously and honestly. He was as startled as everyone else when he heard those words coming out of Nik's mouth. But unlike everyone else, he knew what was going to be said next. Because he had written it.

"And why do we allow this from the church when we'd never get on a segregated bus or work for a company that explicitly and unapologetically prevented women from having the same jobs as men?" It was funny to hear his words coming out of Nik's mouth. "When I think of being Armenian, and how proud it makes me, I can't help but think how much prouder I'd be if the church were more inclusive."

The congregation shifted uneasily. In previous years, the most controversial topic that had been discussed in the "What Being Armenian Means to Me" speech had been whether the words *dolma* and *sarma* were interchangeable when discussing stuffed vegetables.

"What if rather than staying behind, waiting for change to happen, the church led the way? We are a people who have been defined by the discrimination that has been committed against us." Nik had found his voice, and the microphone carried it strongly through the chapel. "How do we justify, then, our own discrimination?"

The reverend father rose and strode down the center aisle, apparently having decided this had gone on long enough. "Okay, thank you, Nik, very much, and merry Christmas." He gestured for Nik to resume his seat, a strained smile stretched across his face.

Nik's courage faltered, but he didn't step down. "But I'm not done yet."

"I think you've run a few minutes over time; besides, I'm not sure that the congregation is entirely interested in hearing the rest of your speech."

In spite of the reverend father's broad smile, it became clear to everyone in the chapel that they were witnessing an altercation. The room hung in delicate balance, like a car seesawing on a cliff, figuring out whether it would level itself to safety or plummet to certain death.

"I'm interested." A small voice rang through the sanctuary, determining the room's fate. Arno seemed more surprised than his parents, Alek, and even the reverend father when he stood up and spoke. "I'd like to hear the rest. And I'm a member of this congregation, aren't I?"

"We'd like to, also." Alek couldn't believe it when his father stood up next.

"We've been coming here for twenty years." Alek's mother was in her professional mode: cool, collected, and confident. "We've always been incredibly proud of both our sons, Reverend Father, and we'd love to hear the rest. And I bet we're not the only ones here who feel that way."

Nik's voice boomed through the microphone at the podium. "Alek, do you want to come up here and finish this? They're your words, after all."

"Go!" Ethan whispered, nearly shoving him out of the pew and into the aisle.

Alek tried to gather whatever dignity he could as he scrambled down the large center aisle, through the mostly confused congregation. Standing next to his brother, he spoke into the microphone, spoke the words that had got him kicked out of Saturday school, the words he never thought he'd be able to say to this congregation in this house of worship.

"When I think of what inspires me most about the teachings of Jesus Christ, it is the message of love and forgiveness that he shared. He was born into a cruel world—a world with dictators and profound economic inequality. And whether or not you believe in heaven or hell, he believed that our basic responsibility was to love, to reach out, to treat everyone the same. It was radical in its time. But really, when you think about it, it's pretty radical right now. That's all I wanted to say. Love thy neighbor and thy enemy. And merry Christmas, everyone. Merry, merry Christmas."

24

ALEK WISHED THAT, LIKE AT THE END OF A MOVIE, the entire congregation had leaped to its feet and applauded for him thunderously. He wished that the reverend father had come over, heartily shaken his hand, and told him that what happened here tonight had forced him to reexamine his perspective.

But those aren't the kinds of things that happen in life.

Some clapping greeted the end of Alek's speech from a few members of the congregation. Mostly the younger ones, Alek noted, but some from other generations, including Mr. and Mrs. Papazian, unlikely enough. Arno's parents notedly did not clap, glowering at their son, who sat, back straight, ignoring everyone but Alek.

The rest of the congregation just sat, awkward and uncomfortable, until Mrs. Atamian finally launched into the opening chords of "Away in a Manger" on the booming organ.

Everybody sang, not just the children, using the music to recover.

The reverend father, to his credit, didn't kick anyone out of the church. He sang along with his wife, the children, the congregation, and even Ethan, as Alek and Nik made their way back to the pews.

The song ended and it was time to go. There was nothing left for Alek at the church. And as he gathered his stuff and turned to leave, he knew it would be the last time he'd ever be in this building, the place he'd been coming every week for as long as he could remember.

As a kid, going to church had felt like a chore, and he'd fantasized about being old enough to sleep in on the weekend. But knowing he'd never step back in here didn't fill Alek with elation. Instead, he just felt sadness, like he was saying goodbye to a friend he'd outgrown.

Before he left, however, there was one last thing that he needed to do.

"I'll meet you outside, okay?" he whispered to Ethan.

Most of the congregation was already milling around. It would be an interesting night, Alek speculated, as parents and their children tried to make sense of what had happened. At least, Alek thought, they'd be talking. Hopefully, dialogue would happen, and that in itself would be a good thing, he thought.

"You were amazing, Arno." Although his parents hovered by the Sanctuary exit with the other five children, Arno had lingered.

"I didn't do anything—you and Nik—that was amazing!"

"That moment—when everything hung in the balance—that was all you, man. You did that!" Alek said.

Arno fairly beamed, in spite of the stone-cold, stoic faces of his parents, who were trying to get Arno's attention. Arno pointedly ignored them. "Did you and Nik plan that?"

"One hundred percent no," Alek admitted. "I don't even know how he got my paper!"

"When I stood up and said I wanted to hear the rest of Nik's speech? I did it for you, you know." Arno pulled Alek into the alcove off the main room, where they'd spent so much time alone and together. "For you."

"I know, Arno." Alek didn't lean in. But he didn't move back, either. "I need to tell you . . ."

Alek stumbled for a second. He hadn't seen Arno since they'd kissed four days ago, on New Year's Day, in this very room. The way Arno was looking at him, with his open face, so full of yearning, was so much like the way he imagined he looked at Ethan when they'd first met all those months ago. As much as he wanted to believe that the kiss with Arno had meant the same thing for both of them—a dalliance, a delight, a wonderful unexpected thing without any strings—Alek knew that wasn't the case.

He was about to say all those things when he felt Arno's gaze shift from Alek to behind him. And the look on Arno's crestfallen face told him exactly whose presence that was.

"Hey—the parking lot is stupid bottlenecked. Your folks told me to tell you that they'll pick us up in the back." Ethan tried to sound as nonchalant as possible.

"Thanks." Then Alek took a step back from Arno. He hadn't been doing anything wrong. And yet still, Ethan's presence changed things.

"You're Arno, right?" Ethan said.

Arno, to his credit, didn't look away or even flinch. "Yes, I am. It's a pleasure to meet you, Ethan." Arno held out his hand and shook Ethan's, like a good young Armenian who'd been brought up right.

Ethan regarded him for a moment. "You rocked, standing up back there." Ethan tried to finger-snap him, but Arno, unused to the gesture, couldn't quite pull it off.

"I'll see you back at the car, Alek, okay?" Ethan slipped away, but his presence had changed things.

Arno's gaze followed Ethan's departing figure; then he turned back to Alek, questioning.

"It's not . . ." Alek tried, but didn't know how to finish.

"It's okay," Arno said simply, cutting him off. He did his best to smile, looking from Alek to departing Ethan and back to Alek. "Not everyone gets the happy ending."

Alek pulled Arno into an embrace and held him for a few precious minutes, pulling away at just the right time. Or maybe a moment later.

"Mom, Dad, seriously, you guys are the best." Alek sat sandwiched between his brother and Ethan in the back seat of their car. Even though he'd been invited to drive, Nik had declined the offer. Apparently, he had had enough excitement for one night.

"Did you see the look on the reverend father's face when we stood up?" Alek's mom was giddier than Alek or Ethan or Nik had been.

"And then when people clapped?" his father piped in, driving five miles above the speed limit.

"What I want to know is, how did you get a copy of my essay?" Alek asked Nik.

"The way you talked about it on New Year's Eve made me curious. So I just picked up the copy you gave Mom and Dad when they were done with it."

"Nik, Mr. and Mrs. K—I'll never wonder where Alek gets his stuff from. It must run in the family."

The five spent the rest of the ride home recounting their favorite moments of the night.

"You know I'm not going back to church, right?" Alek said.

"Neither are we." Alek could hear the sadness in his father's voice.

"Really?"

"We're going to have religion in our lives," his father said. "I'm still a proud Christian. So we're just going to find another place to go. A place—how did you say it—more inclusive."

Alek hoped against hope. "And maybe a little closer, too?"

"Don't hold your breath," his mother told him.

"I've heard about an Armenian Episcopalian church in North Jersey that sounds promising," his father said.

"Promising in what way?"

"Women can be deacons in the church; they're incredibly progressive about gay rights and abortion."

"And how far away?"

"Two hours. Each way."

Alek groaned. Apparently, it was impossible to have your baklava and eat it, too.

When they exited Route 33, back on the local roads of South Windsor, Ethan spoke up.

"Alek, do you want to come over?"

"On a school night?" his mother asked.

"I finished all my homework, and I won't be long, okay?" Alek leaned forward, into the front of the car, so his parents could see him. "Besides, it's been a hell of a month."

His parents considered. "Okay," his father said. "We trust you know what you're doing."

"As long as you're home in an hour, of course," his mother finished.

"Of course."

Ethan's room surprised him yet again.

"When did you . . ." Instead of the blank walls Alek had been expecting, he was greeted by photos of him and Ethan, woven into a collage of all the memorabilia of their relationship: the pin from their first trip to New York, to the Metropolitan Museum of Art. Brochures from the Intrepid, receipts from their Citi Bikes, menus from the restaurants where they'd eaten. The lyrics from Rufus Wainwright songs, juxtaposed with lyrics from Brandy Clark. The skyline of New York painted—or was it drawn?—on an entire wall. The collage spread over all the walls in Ethan's room, even the ceiling, enveloping them. Ethan had transformed his room into a three-dimensional living monument to their relationship.

"When you asked me what I wanted to do in my life, it got me thinking. This is what I want to do. I want to make things like this. I want to make big weird things that bring people joy. And you, most of all."

"Thanks for coming tonight." Alek sat down on Ethan's bed, hoping Ethan would sit next to him.

"Thanks for letting me."

"Can we—I don't know—can we talk—about what happened? That night."

Ethan considered. "I'm not sure. I don't know if I want to. I don't know if it will help."

"I think it will help me."

"Why?"

"Because I can't imagine doing something like that. I'm not trying to make you feel bad or be all judgy. But when you grow up on comic books, the way I did, you can imagine just about anything: being bitten by a radioactive spider and getting superpowers, or being exposed to some freaky gamma rays and getting superpowers, or being born with a mutant gene that gives you superpowers—"

"Is the point here that you can imagine lots of ways to get superpowers?"

"The point is that for everything I can imagine, cheating's not one of them. So I think helping me understand what you were thinking, or how it happened, will help me."

"Okay." Ethan took a deep breath. "Something started happening to me, a few months ago."

"What kind of thing?"

"Our relationship was going so well, you know."

"Except for that alpaca debacle around homecoming," Alek reminded him.

"That was horrible," Ethan agreed. "How did you manage to lose—"

"I said I DON'T WANT TO TALK ABOUT IT."

"Okay, okay." Ethan got back on track. "But we were so in a groove, you know, so synced up. It just seemed too good. Like, better than anything I'd ever had. And I started becoming obsessed with making sure that I didn't mess it up."

"Why'd you think you were going to mess it up?"

"Because that's what I do, Alek. I mess things up. Or I stop myself from caring about them so that I don't care if they get messed up or not. How do you think I've managed to fail three classes in my high school career? You don't get it, because you're not like that. But I am. And I became obsessed with it—every time it looked like we might get into a fight about something, or whatever—I thought, *Is this the thing that's finally going to break us up?*"

"I wish I'd known."

"I wish I'd told you. But I'm not sure I was even aware of it. But this is what weeks of soul-searching can teach you. And time with a shrink."

"You're seeing a therapist?" Alek didn't know why this moved him so much.

"When I said I'd do anything to make this work, Alek, I meant it." Ethan shifted. "So that night, when I was with Remi and he came on to me, it just felt like—finally—the thing I'd been obsessed about was finally presenting itself to me. The ultimate self-fulfilling prophecy, giving me the chance that I needed to destroy the thing that I care about most. I know now that I'll never do that again. When I cheated on you, on us, I destroyed the most important thing in the world to me. And if we don't get back together, at least I'll have learned that. It's painful as fuck, but hey—it's something that I can take from the worst decision I ever made in my life."

"One more thing, Ethan, okay?"

"Okay."

Alek took a deep breath, trying to speak with as little judgment or hurt in his voice as possible when discussing the most painful event of his life. "Why didn't you tell me, when it happened?"

Ethan looked away. "I know this is going to sound so stupid and that it's not going to make any sense."

"That's okay."

"I didn't want to hurt you. To disappoint you. I knew I messed up, obvi. But I thought if I didn't tell you, I could just bury it and it would go away and we'd have never to deal with it. That we could stay in our Garden of Eden."

"That's not how it works, you know."

"Of course I know that, like, in my head I know. But it felt so much easier to keep it inside rather than actually have to deal with the hurt on your face. That's what I was scared of the most, and then when it happened, that's the thing I can't get out of my mind. The way you looked when you found out. That's what I'm going to have to carry around for the rest of my life."

"You're so dramatic," Alek teased.

"Yeah, well, you disappoint the person you care about most in the world and see how you feel. But I guess you're incapable of that, right? I mean, that's what makes you, you. You're too honest to hurt someone."

"I don't know if that's true."

"I do."

"I mean, I'm not sure that being honest means you don't hurt the people you care about. When I look at that time, after I found out, I was 'honest' with you that whole time, at least to the best of my abilities, about what I was feeling, what I was going through. But that doesn't mean I wasn't hurting you also."

"But I had that coming, Alek! I cheated on you. On us!"

"But honesty without kindness is suspiciously similar to cruelty." Alek shifted. "Speaking of which . . . Arno, who you met today?"

"Yeah?

"I kissed him."

"I know." Ethan kept his voice neutral.

"How could you possibly know?"

"You think I couldn't see it, dude? The two of you hovering around each other with a magnetic field of attraction? Anyone with eyes could see it."

"It was after you and I broke up."

"I figured."

Alek threw his hands up in the air. "How did you know that, too?"

"Because you'd never cheat on me, Alek. Or on anyone. You're not wired that way."

Alek tried to think of something to say—something funny or witty or defusing. But nothing came to him. So he said nothing.

"So what?" Ethan sat down on the chair at his desk, the tension in his shoulders and neck betraying the nonchalance he was projecting. "Do you think you and Arno are going to start, like, dating?"

"I don't think so."

"How come?"

"The thing is, Ethan, when I kissed him, I realized something very important."

"And what was that?" Ethan tried, and failed, to keep the hurt out of his voice.

"It wasn't like kissing you."

"It wasn't?" Ethan's eyes twinkled, the way they did when he was suggesting something that he knew he shouldn't do but could probably get away with.

"Nothing is."

Alek leaned in and slid his hand into Ethan's.

Kissing Ethan.

Kissing Ethan rocked.

ACKNOWLEDGMENTS

Mayson Maxwell Badders, whom I've never met, who messaged me on Facebook and told me to write a sequel to *One Man Guy* with the following plot: "Personally i hope to see alek and ethan break up and get back together."

Kyle Khandarian, who continues to inspire me with his activism.

Barry Kleinbort, who gave me a great piece of dramaturgical advice about how to approach this book.

Topher Payne, who is a great guy to call and ask questions about story.

Dr. Jessica Casey, who took me on a ride in her Tesla.

Ivy Aukin, who reminded me of the importance of food in this story.

Sarah Braunstein, who read a draft of this book (as she did with *One Man Guy*), and told me what was good and what was not and how to make the latter into the former and really what kinder thing could any writer friend do for a friend?

Joy Peskin, my editor, who is so good at her job, it makes me want to be better at mine.

All the readers of *OMG*. Your feedback, responses, posts, messages, reviews, and tweets gave me the courage and faith to write this book, and more importantly, they gave me hope for the world.

• • • • •